Something Human

A.J. Demas

Part I

Adares

CHAPTER I

THE LETTER PROBABLY still lay on the desk in his study, half finished. That is, if the archon's palace had not been burned to the ground by this time. It did not matter very much, since the news that the letter would have conveyed was old now. But at this rate, if it had been sent, it would have been the last communication his parents ever received from their eldest son.

Dear Mother and Father, the letter had said,

I hope this finds you well, and Chares and Leta too. I am well myself, though my new duties are of course keeping me very busy still. I hope you are having fine weather in Pheme. Here the autumn rains have not yet set in, but are expected any day.

It may be some time before I am able to write again. We are once again threatened with war by one of the local tribes. The Luth have begun moving south, and they will soon reach the coast. There can be little doubt that they will attack Tios. As I write this, our troops are preparing to defend the city in the event of an attack, and we are readying ships to evacuate as much of the civilian population as we can. We are still hoping that it will not come to that, but it is as well to be prepared.

In your last letter …

That was where he had stopped writing, because he had realized that he did not remember a thing his mother had written in her last letter. There had been too much to think about since he read it for the details of Leta's engagement party and Chares's progress in school to stick in his mind. Then he had gone looking for the letter to reread it, but an urgent message from the First Spear of the legion had interrupted him before he ever found it.

Now he wished that he had not bothered trying to explain the situation, had not made light of the threat, had not delayed finishing the letter in order to reply to whatever his mother had written before. He wished he had just scribbled a few lines of uncomplicated love for his parents and his younger siblings, and sent them off before the Luth began pouring down out of the wooded hills around Tios, blowing their shrill war-horns and trailing their blue snake pennants from upraised spears.

Dear Mother and Father, the letter should have said,

Be well, now and always, and Chares and Leta with you. Long before you receive this letter, I will have breathed my last, in a muddy ditch in a field outside Tios, joining scores of my comrades who fell alongside me. Forgive me for breaking your hearts, but know that I loved you.

Your son,

Adares

That would have been accurate enough, and then they could have pictured him prone like a hero in a vase-painting, a barbarian spear through his chest, his armour gleaming in the sun. They did not need to know that he was going to die of thirst, or possibly of asphyxiation, trapped under a Luth siege-cart along with a dead horse that was beginning to attract flies. They would be better off not having to picture that.

The horse had been his own, and it had been killed by the impact with the cart, so it was really his fault it was dead. He had not been thrown clear when it fell, and one of his legs was still trapped under its body—if it weren't for the mud, he would certainly have broken bones. As it was, he was largely unhurt. By this time, that hardly mattered. A dent in his breastplate made it painful to breathe, but he could not move either arm to reach the buckles at his shoulders. His muscles burned with cramp. He was sick with the stench of mud and dead horse and half mad with thirst.

Though he had missed the conclusion of the battle, he knew how it had ended. He had heard the Phemian officers sounding the retreat, and the battle-cries of the Luth chasing them, soon after he went down. It had been a rout. He just hoped some remnant of the legion had made it back into the city to defend it, because the Luth had come prepared for a siege.

The Phemians had known what they were in for, but it hadn't helped. They had one infantry legion and one-and-a-half hastily-drilled cavalry units, but the Luth were horse-breeding people from the northern steppes, and they had brought the cream of their mounted warrior class. Armed with spears and heavy swords, impressively fearsome with their flying fair hair and their tattoos, they had hurtled down the hill toward the Phemian lines like they had been born on horseback.

They had brought superior numbers, they had brought siege equipment—big hide-covered carts in which warriors could approach the city walls under cover—and they had brought wild bulls, huge as monsters from some ancient legend, charging at the head of their attack. The Phemians stood firm in their orderly lines, in their burnished greaves and freshly bleached military tunics, but they hadn't stood a chance.

Adares had tried, as soon as he regained his senses, to heave the weight of the cart off himself, but from where he was lying it was impossible even to make it budge. He had no idea how long he had been there by this time; he barely even remembered the details of how he had got there. He lay and wept with exhaustion and with grief for the pointlessness of it all.

It was the crying that saved him. Sounds in the world above the collapsed cart had long ago ceased, and the darkness of Adares's shallow grave was beginning to deepen. He heard, but did not quite understand, a soft noise of something moving on the boards above him. Then there were more noises: a slow dragging, and then a soft scratching and scrabbling. It was not until he felt loose dirt falling in a shower across his forearm that he realized someone outside was digging to try to reach the place where he was trapped.

Hope gave him new strength, and the location of the sound gave him a new place to focus his efforts. Everything depended upon straining towards the source of that sound, wriggling painful inches through the mud, trying to move his trapped arm to clear away the dirt that was falling down inside.

After what seemed a very long period of this, the boards above him creaked and shifted, and he froze, terrified again, certain that the full weight of the cart was going to settle and crush him at last. But it didn't, and in a moment he realized that the cart was not falling, but had been lifted. His rescuer had heaved up one edge of it and propped it on something, and between that and the hole that had been dug, Adares could see a distinct sliver of light. Better still, he discovered that his arm was no longer trapped, and he could move.

He dragged himself free of the dead horse at last, tugging his numb leg out from under the saddle, and pushed and clawed and wriggled his way up towards the light. The mud slithered under him, and he slipped back, whimpering with frustration.

The cart's boards creaked again, and the opening between it and the ground widened a little more. As he pushed himself forward one last time, a pair of hands reached in, grasping his arms above the elbows, and hauled him upwards, his dented breastplate scraping agonizingly between the wood and the earth, until he lay half out of the hole, his face on the cold grass, his eyes screwed tight shut against the low, slanting light of early evening.

Opening them finally, he saw clearly for the first time the hands that had drawn him back into the world. They were long, pale hands, marked with curling blue lines of tattooing. Adares managed to push himself up onto one elbow and raise his head, and he and his rescuer stared tensely at one another.

The Luth warrior was very young—certainly a few years younger than Adares—and smaller than Adares, lightly built but all taut muscle, like an athlete. He wore a short blue kilt of subtly chequered wool, a gold torque around his neck, and soft leather boots. His hair was a mass of long, fair curls, falling down his back, and his bare skin was patterned all over with the same intricate, alien blue lines that marked his hands. There were even twists of blue on his cheekbones, almost the same colour as the eyes that stared out of his pale face at Adares, the olive-skinned, black-haired Phemian he had just pulled out of the earth.

The Luth was the first to move. Still kneeling in the grass where he had bent down to haul Adares out of his grave, he gestured with one pale hand toward the Phemian's sword and pointed to the ground.

Adares, understanding, reached down and fumbled to undo the clasp of his sword belt, then let the sword, scabbard, belt and all fall down into the hole behind him. His rescuer put a hand on a long, light Luth spear that lay on the ground beside him, and with a decisive motion, pushed it from him, so that it rolled away across the grass. He gestured again to Adares: go!

Adares scrambled unsteadily to his feet, staggering because of the numbness in the leg that had been trapped under the horse. Words of gratitude failed to come to his clouded mind. The Luth warrior's mercy was too unexpected, too sudden, after all the ugliness of the battle and the misery of the muddy hole and the dead horse and the immoveable cart, for him even to react. He tried to wipe the tears from his face with a grimy hand.

The Luth had not risen from where he knelt in the grass. Something about this struck Adares, even through the fog in his mind, as strange, and it was this that caused him to hesitate, to look back down at his rescuer instead of hastening away across the battlefield. That was when he finally noticed the crossbow bolt.

It was half hidden by the folds of his kilt, and it had obviously been in him for some time; there was a trail of dried blood down his leg. It was a small, slim atropa-wood bolt, more of a dart really, a style recently imported from the east. Adares's mind spun off on a trail of irrelevancies. A couple of officers had been disciplined recently for allowing their troops to use atropa bolts, and Adares recognized the bolt from examples he had seen at the trial. The defender had made an ugly argument that amounted to claiming that barbarians were not quite human. The prosecution had demolished it.

The bolt had gone in from the front, just above the young man's knee, and pierced upward through his thigh, the point just emerging on the other side. He'd had the sense not to try to pull it out himself.

With an effort, Adares marshalled his thoughts. Atropa was a slow poison, and it had a reliable antidote. But the young Luth was shaking with exhaustion from the effort of lifting the cart; if he could have made it across the field to the Luth camp before, he couldn't do it now. And even if he could, it wasn't likely that anyone there would even know that the bolt in his thigh was poisonous, much less have any of the antidote on hand to treat him.

In his present state, Adares could not even begin to explain all this in any of the Karganian languages that he knew—and the Luth language was not one of them, anyway.

"You saved my life," he said simply, picking a language at random. "Let me help you."

The Luth looked up at him. There was fresh blood soaking into the hem of his kilt where the strain of lifting the cart had caused the wound to bleed again.

"The Luth have won," he said, in the same language that Adares had used. He did not speak it any better than Adares. "You should go. I do not need help."

"Yes, you do." He pointed to the bloody flights of the bolt. "It is very bad. I can fix it."

The Luth shook his head, tight-lipped. "No. It's Phemian wood. It's poison. I know."

Adares gestured hopelessly, the words eluding him. "Yes, but—I can fix it for you." In theory, anyway. Right at that moment, he was not at all sure that he could fix anything.

The look on his rescuer's face reminded Adares of how he had felt a few minutes before, when he first realized that someone was trying to save him. This young man had believed he was doomed as surely as Adares had believed it when he lay in the mud under the cart. He had done all that work to pull Adares out from under the cart, and shown him mercy when he saw what he was, believing it was probably the last thing he'd do.

"I will help you," Adares repeated firmly.

For the first time, he looked around at their surroundings, trying to make sense of where he was. The valley was a carpet of churned-up earth and wreckage: dented bronze helmets and leather shields with spears through them, dead Phemians prone between the hooves of dead horses with dead Luth still tangled in their reins, lying where they had fallen. Neither side had gathered up its slain, but here and there in the distance anonymous figures moved, stooping, from body to body, casting long shadows, either looking for survivors or looting corpses. Adares looked towards Tios, perched on a steep angle of land which thrust out over the battlefield. He could see that the bulk of the Luth forces had already regrouped around the base of the city walls. He shivered and looked away.

To his left, the forest that covered most of the region crept down into the valley, dark with pine trees. Looking in that direction, Adares found what he had been seeking: the warm colours of tiled roofs and stone columns, standing out against the background of trees on the lower slope of the nearest hill. It was an old temple complex, one of the first that the Phemian colonists had built after Tios was founded. It was still in use, but it would be empty now, as all the population outside the city walls had been brought in to shelter in Tios at the first sign of the Luth attack. It was some distance away, though not as far as the walls of Tios. And Adares remembered being taken on a tour of the complex, and the priests proudly showing off their pharmacy. He thought he even remembered where it was.

He pointed. "Can you walk that far?"

The Luth looked, considered, and nodded. His hand

reached out toward the spear that he had rolled away. He paused, looking up at Adares.

"To lean on?" he said.

Adares nodded. It was just as well. He did not feel sure of his ability to support anyone just then without falling over himself.

Still, by the time they were halfway across the valley, Adares found he had taken the younger man's arm. The walk was agonizingly slow. They leaned on each other, dragging themselves along by what felt like pure will. One foot in front of the other, on and on. Adares tried not to look at the faces of the men lying still on the ground, for fear of seeing someone he knew. He thought from the way his companion stared fixedly at his feet that he was doing the same thing. Now and then they crouched down to avoid attracting the attention of the scavengers. Neither of them had spoken since they left the scene of the rescue.

Finally, after Adares had settled into a kind of dreaming numbness in which it seemed they were always dragging themselves forward and never getting closer to the temple complex, abruptly it loomed up in front of them.

They hauled themselves up the broad stone steps and through the gate under the colonnade into the tranquil, paved courtyard beyond. It was, as Adares had expected, deserted of all human occupants. Mourning doves cooing under the temple eaves made the only sound.

Or not quite the *only* sound—from somewhere Adares could also hear the faint, enticing trill of running water. He recalled a petition that the priests had made, back when Hesteios was still archon, for pipes to be laid to connect the temple complex to the main water supply of Tios. Of course—they had a fountain here. Turning a corner, they found the little tiled shelter housing the fountain, which was pouring sweet, fresh water out of a limestone lion's head into an ornamental basin below.

As desperately thirsty as Adares was, his manners hadn't quite deserted him, and he gestured towards the fountain, offering to let the Luth drink first. And Adares's rescuer, who must have felt that the poor soul he had dragged out from under the siege-cart was in a worse state than he, was making the same gesture, the same offer, at the same time. They stared at each other for a moment. Then, quite suddenly, they both burst out laughing.

They staggered to the fountain together, weak with laughter, the Luth clinging to Adares's tunic, Adares gripping the Luth's tattooed shoulder. They fell down together at the basin and drank greedily from the stream of water at the same time, like a pair of lambs suckling from their mother side by side. When they drew back to catch their breath and caught each other's eye, they began laughing again.

"Oh Water! Divine beverage!" Adares apostrophized the stream. "I will never drink wine again!"

The Luth, who had drunk his fill already, was leaning against the edge of the basin, laughing. Adares gulped down more water and kissed the nose of the stone lion, calling it a thrice-blessed fountain, of all fountains on earth the sweetest and purest, deserving to be praised forever by poets for its heavenly wetness. The Luth cupped his hand expertly and swatted a big spray of water from the basin up into Adares's face. Adares swiped his forearm through the water and sent back an even bigger spray.

"Ah, that's lovely," said the Luth, and leant over to scoop up more water and splash it on his face.

Adares sat back and tugged at the buckles of his breast-plate, which he had not had the sense to remove until now. He pulled the wretched thing off at last and threw it clattering onto the pavement. He washed his muddy face and hands in the basin, and then sat back, leaning against its stone rim.

He pressed his hand to his bruised chest. "It hurts to laugh," he remarked.

"Ah, but it is good to share something human with one of you people at last!" said the Luth.

"Isn't it just?" He looked at the Luth. "You speak my language," he observed with surprise.

The Luth nodded. "So it would seem. I didn't know it was your language. At home we call it Firhat Kosoth—the language of Kos. Possibly Kos is near Pheme?"

"Not far off. We all speak the same language in that part of the world—Pheme, Kos, Ariata, Boukos, all the city-states of the Pseuchaian League have the same language."

The Luth looked impressed. "I did not know. That is very different from the Karhan. Every tribe has its own language here, almost." He shivered.

"Here," said Adares. His cloak had come unpinned when he took off his breastplate, and he pulled it out from under him now and draped it around the Luth's bare shoulders. Most of the mud on it had dried by this time, and it was a good, warm cloak. The Luth drew it about himself gratefully.

Adares laid a hand on his shoulder. "I'll be right back," he said. "You just wait here."

CHAPTER II

HE GOT TO his feet and walked back out the way they had come, into the outer courtyard of the temple complex. He found he was thinking much more clearly now. This was not entirely a good thing. He had undertaken to save his rescuer's life, but he was not at all sure that he really knew how to do that. He might know more about foreign poisons than a Luth warrior, but vague things that he had heard in a prosecutor's speech were not exactly a sound basis for practical medicine. He stopped in the middle of the courtyard to draw a deep, slow breath, then he set about looking for the temple pharmacy.

When he returned to the fountain a short time later, a cup of wine in one hand and the clay bottle in the other, the Luth was sitting where he had left him, eyes shut, head leaning back against the fountain's rim. His fair skin had turned an alarming greyish white, and he was breathing fast and shallowly.

He opened his eyes when Adares knelt beside him, and even smiled. "Only a minute ago you swore you would never drink wine again," he said. His voice sounded hoarse and constricted.

"This is for you," said Adares, holding out the cup. "Can you manage, or shall I help you drink it?"

"I can manage." He pushed himself up a little and took the cup from Adares. He held it carefully in both pale hands and drank down half of its contents before he had to stop, coughing and gagging. "Do I—I suppose I—have to finish it?"

"Afraid so."

"Ah. All right." He took another resolute swallow. After he had sat with his teeth clamped shut for a moment, he asked, "What is it?"

"Physostigma, four grains, in some really terrible Pyrian wine. It's the antidote for atropa poisoning."

"You are very chakin—very … knowledgeable."

"Not really. It was written down in the pharmacy. There was a scroll labelled *Antidotes*."

"Well." His lips twitched in a weak smile. "You know how to read."

Adares laughed. "Yes. I did know physostigma was the antidote—it's a bean from Gylphos, I think, but they had it ground up in a jar in there, also labelled, thankfully. I just wasn't … *quite* sure about the dosage. Have you finished that? Do you want some more of this dreadful wine to wash it down with?"

The Luth held out his cup. "Yes, please. It cannot possibly taste any worse."

Adares refilled the cup and waited for him to drain it again. He was still looking frighteningly ill. But, Adares reminded himself, it was too soon to expect the antidote to take effect. Probably.

"We had better get this out now," he said, moving a fold of the cloak to expose the crossbow bolt.

"I don't know," said the Luth, rolling up the edge of his kilt with fingers that were visibly shaking. "I am getting used to it, vecha."

Adares smiled. "Better to have it out, though, on the whole. Before we lose the light altogether."

"Ah, all right, then."

By now Adares found he had begun to feel quite confident. He was remembering things from the basic medical training he had got in his days as a student in the Phemian diplomatic corps that he thought he had forgotten altogether. He fetched a knife from the pharmacy and a curtain that he had seen flapping from the open window of a temple outbuilding, made his patient lie down, and tore the cloth into wide strips for bandages. He rinsed his hands in the vile Pyrian wine and began stripping the flights off of the crossbow bolt with the knife.

The Luth watched him with a sort of calm wariness. He lay still while Adares drew the length of the bolt—disgustingly slick with blood—out through the exit wound in his thigh. He made only one small noise of protest, a soft, sobbing moan, as the wound began to bleed in earnest. Adares thought he had fainted, but his blue eyes flickered open before he turned his face away.

Adares had folded-up wads of curtain ready to press over the two holes made by the bolt, and he had already arranged the patient with his knee bent to raise the wound above the level of his heart, which he felt quite proud of himself for remembering. When the flow of blood had slowed, he washed the whole area with wine and wrapped strips of curtain around to hold the dressing in place. He even remembered that one was supposed to wind the bandages from the bottom rather than the top—though he didn't really remember why.

By the time Adares had finished with the bandages, a little colour had returned to the Luth's cheeks, and he was breathing normally again. Adares was so relieved that he felt an impulse to lean over and kiss the young man's pale, untattooed forehead, in much the same spirit as he had kissed the stone lion's nose. He resisted, just, because he felt sure it would not be well received.

Instead, he rinsed the blood from his hands and sat back against the fountain basin, hugging his knees. It was growing cold as the sun went down finally, and his short, sleeveless tunic did not provide much protection against the damp Karhan night.

In Tios they would be thinking by now that he was dead. It was bad that he was not there at such a time, but he could not see any way he could get back into the city now, with the whole strength of the Luth army between him and the walls.

Looking across the courtyard, he noticed that a door at the back of the small temple to the horse god stood open. The back room, behind the temple altar, would make a good place to shelter for the night—probably the best they could hope for, since the priests would no doubt have locked their house and the main temple doors before they left.

He looked down at the Luth.

"Well, that's one question answered, anyway."

"What is?" His voice came out hoarse, as if with disuse.

"I always wondered whether you wore anything under those kilts or not."

The Luth's eyes went wide, and his hand flew automatically to the fabric between his legs, before he collected himself enough to laugh. But laugh he did.

The answer was *yes*. There was a loincloth of sturdy, good-quality linen under the blue kilt. The tattoos went all the way up the Luth's thighs, further than Adares had any need to expose in the course of bandaging him. Still, it was a closer look than he'd ever had of a Karhan tribesman—certainly of one of the Luth.

Of course he'd had a good look at a few Karhan women

in his years in the province, including a couple as fair of hair and skin as this young man, and even one with tattoos—they hadn't been visible until she took her clothes off, and came as a rather exciting surprise. The young Luth's combination of pale skin with hard, lean muscle was very different, though, and rather beautiful.

"Do you feel better?" Adares asked.

"Yes. Not so sick." He pushed himself up gingerly onto one elbow. "Not so poisoned."

"Excellent. What's more, you haven't got an iron-tipped piece of wood sticking through you. I was just thinking, it's getting cold and dark. There's an open door over there—we should go inside and see if we can find a more comfortable place to sleep."

The Luth nodded and sat up all the way. Adares took his arm and drew it around his shoulders to help him up. They made their way slowly across the courtyard to the open door and into the dimness beyond it. Adares let the Luth down gently onto the stone floor, where he could sit with his back against a wooden chest that stood by the door. He left the door open for the little remaining light from outside.

"There should be a lamp," he remarked, straightening up. "I'll see if I can find it."

After some blundering in the semi-darkness, he did succeed in finding a lamp, which was full of oil. Carrying it carefully, he found his way through the darker end of the room to the door that opened onto the main chamber of the little temple. It was latched on this side, but not locked, and when he opened it, he saw beyond it a faint glow in the tripod at the centre of the ambulatory, where the sacred fire had been banked and not quite gone out. Praise be to Soukos.

He stirred the fire with a poker propped nearby, found where they kept the extra coals, and added some. In the shadows, the votive horse statues that lined the walls stared down at him with blank eyes and flaring nostrils. He thought of his own horse, and of the team of shaggy white Luth horses that had pulled the cart he had ridden into. He lit the lamp from the fire and returned to the back room, shutting the door behind him. He came back to where he had left the Luth, and shut the outer door as well.

In the light of the lamp, Adares could see that the room they were in was part storeroom for temple paraphernalia, part quarters for some temple functionary—probably an assistant priest or votary servant who was in charge of keeping the sacred fire lit and the ambulatory swept. There were barrels and piles of folded linen near the far wall, a heap of empty lamps and bronze censers, a little shelf with a dish of dried figs, a bowl of apples and walnuts, jars of oil and honey, and a few other things on it, and pushed up against the left-hand wall, draped with striped blankets and a warm fur rug …

"A bed! Look—could one ask for more?"

Adares fetched down the dish of figs and came over to sit beside the Luth. He set the lamp on the floor and offered him the dish.

"I'm Adares, by the way. Do you feel up to telling me your name?"

"It's Rus." He took one of the figs and looked at it dubiously. "What is this?"

"A fig. All the way from Pheme. They're good."

"They're food?"

"Why do you think I'm eating one?"

"I don't know," said Rus drily. "You are a Phemian. I hear strange stories." He took a bite of the fig and chewed appreciatively. "It's nice. Sweet. This is one of your holy places, is it?"

"Yes. Well, this is the back room, the holy part is out front.

But the whole complex is temples. I suppose your people don't build temples, do they?" Nobody in this part of Kargania did, and he knew the Luth were at least semi-nomadic.

"No. We have sacred hills. Built by the gods. It makes more sense."

"When you put it like that. But we build stone and brick houses for ourselves, with tiled roofs and paved streets and fountains in the gardens. It would look bad if we couldn't do at least as well for the gods we worship."

"Fair enough. We do make stone circles—you know, with standing stones. But they don't keep you dry when it rains."

"I guess they wouldn't."

"No, they just … stand."

"In a circle?"

"Mm. It must be nice, not having to do sacrifices in the rain."

"I guess it is. We do a lot of processions in the rain, though. Not in Pheme—it doesn't rain all that much in Pheme. We haven't quite adapted to the Karhan climate."

"It is not to 'adapt.' Only to 'put up with.' But it makes you strong." He made a fist, with a satirical expression. "That is our … what we tell ourselves, what the old men tell the young men. Hathavi virhavi."

"Propaganda."

"That may be it."

They ate several more figs in silence.

"What have you heard?" Adares asked, by and by. Rus gave him a questioning look. "You said you had heard strange stories about Phemians."

"Ah. The strange stories. Well—is it true that you make a kind of … " He made a face, half disgusted, half apologetic. "A kind of liquor out of rotten fish. That is not true, is it?"

"No … well, it's not a liquor, it's a sauce—it's for seasoning food."

"It's made of rotten fish," Rus repeated, deadpan.

"Well, fermented. Like you do with grapes, you know, for wine—or barley or whatever."

"Mm. But fish."

"Yeah. It's surprisingly delicious."

"Surprising. Yes. Well … we eat raw meat. Not because we are savages and don't know how to cook, you understand."

"Of course. Do you eat it raw for … ritual purposes, or something?"

"No. We eat it raw because it tastes good. You don't just eat a big piece of raw meat—you cut it up very fine, and mix it with some hasha—I do not think I know that Kosoth word. It's a kind of thing that you grow, in the ground, and it's red on the outside."

"An apple," Adares suggested.

"You grow apples in the ground in Pheme, do you?"

"Oh. A strawberry."

Rus frowned at him. "Radish. I think. Radish. You mix it with the meat, and you eat it—right away, while it's fresh. It's very good. Delicious. Like your fish wine."

"Right. Sounds disgusting."

"It would be, with strawberries."

They looked at one another and dissolved into laughter again. When they stopped laughing, they sat in silence.

It was strange, and it wasn't. They had fallen into an easy friendliness, as if they had known each other for years. It would have been something remarkable if they had been soldiers serving together or two people introduced by a mutual acquaintance at a party. But they had been on opposing sides of a battle a few hours earlier. This felt far more natural than that.

Adares got up and fetched the apples and walnuts from the shelf. Rus took an apple and bit into it.

"Your Pseuchaian is beautiful," Adares remarked, as he tried and failed to crack a walnut.

Rus gave him a suddenly wary look. "My what?"

"Your—uh—the language, whatever you call it. You speak it very well." He also had a deep, musical voice, and a fascinating accent: growly barbarian consonants mixed with elegant Kossian vowels.

"Ah."

And, for that matter, a handsome face, with a wide, shapely mouth, high cheekbones, and a nose that must once have been straight but had been broken and healed with a slight kink. He was clean-shaven, and though he didn't remove the hair of his body like a Pseuchaian man, it was light, and as blond as the hair of his head, so it did nothing to obscure his tattoos.

"What did you think I meant?" Adares asked.

"I don't know." It was hard to tell whether that was true or not. "I am tired."

"We were in a battle," Adares reminded him.

"We were."

"We almost died."

"We did. Almost." After a moment's silence, as if he had been reviewing the conversation in his head and got back to the relevant part, he said, "Thank you. What you said about the language."

"Oh, you're welcome. Do you know how to get these open?" He held out the walnut he'd been trying unsuccessfully to crack while they had been talking. "I usually use a thing … you know … but I didn't see one."

"You use a thing," Rus repeated.

"I'm tired."

"Ah, yes. We were in a battle."

"That's right."

"You have to take two of them and squeeze them together."

"What?"

"The walnuts. Give them to me."

Adares handed over the dish, and Rus took two nuts in one long-fingered hand and cracked them, apparently without effort.

"Will you look at that?" said Adares.

Rus handed him a cracked walnut.

"Of course," said Adares, picking the meat out of the walnut, "I knew that your people traded with the old Kossian colony at Sapha, before it was abandoned. But that was decades ago. I didn't realize anyone among the Luth would still speak Pseuchaian."

"Ah, I see. We had many books from the Kossians, books of science and learning. We have no writing of our own, so we have kept the Kossian speech to use when we study their writing. Few of us speak it, only the kahar, but we use it among ourselves, as a dashak, a mark of distinction. Tch." He shook his head as if annoyed with himself. "We mix in a lot of Luth words when we speak, and I have to remember not to do that with you." He yawned suddenly, hiding it behind his hand.

"I'll help you to the bed," Adares suggested, brushing fragments of walnut shell off his hands. "You'll be more comfortable there."

There was a moment's pause. "Where will you sleep?"

"I'll take that fur, if you don't need it, and put it on the floor."

"Ah, all right."

Adares supported him across the room to the bed, helped him take off his boots, which fastened with odd, barbarian-style thongs and toggles, and spread the blankets over him, at his request, when he had lain down. Rus fumbled with something under the blanket for a moment, then pulled out his kilt and tossed it onto the floor. It was a single length of cloth that had been fastened with a heavy gold pin. Adares was privately amused that he'd felt the need to take it off under the blankets, especially since he had a loincloth under it.

"Comfortable?"

"Yes." Rus settled himself carefully, to avoid moving his injured leg. "Look," he said, patting the blanket beside him. "There's room for two. Don't sleep on the floor."

Adares hesitated. He thought he'd got Rus's measure a minute ago with all that fuss over the compliment he hadn't understood, and then the coy little display of undressing under the covers.

It was no more than he'd expected. The Karhan tribes were dead-set against what they called "unnatural lusts" and "men making themselves into women." They all had different names for it, which they used as terms of the gravest insult, and every tribe accused the others of practicing it or secretly tolerating it, but the truth was they all hated it about equally. Did that mean, by some kind of backwards logic, that for a Luth to invite another man to share a bed—not a big bed, meant for sharing, but a cozy single bed—was entirely innocent, because anything else was unthinkable?

It wouldn't have worked that way in Pheme, or Tios. You'd have to be specific—"Just to sleep, mind you!"—if that was really all you intended. "I'm a ladies' man, mind you," was what Adares would have said himself to convey the message. It was perhaps not strictly true, but it was what he would have said. As it was, he didn't care to be the one to raise that subject. And, at the same time, he didn't want to sleep on the floor.

"Thanks," he said finally. He had vague thoughts about washing, changing out of his muddy tunic, seeing if he could find soap or clean clothes in the priests' quarters, but all of that seemed suddenly impossibly tiring. "I do think I could sleep," he said, sitting down on the edge of the bed to unfasten his boots. "I thought I might need wine, but now I think I could sleep without it. Do you need wine?" He looked back at Rus, who was silent, trying to look noncommittal. "I'm sorry. Of course you do—you've just had a crossbow bolt taken out of you. What am I thinking?"

He retied his boots, fetched the lamp, and went looking for more wine. He found a bottle of something a bit better than the wretched Pyrian, and brought it back to the storeroom along with the cup that they had left out by the fountain. Rus propped himself up on one elbow to drink. Adares drank too, though not as much. Then he tugged his boots off finally, put out the lamp, and they lay down together. Adares did not undress, outside the covers or under them. He pulled the fur rug over himself and lay facing out into the room, his back to Rus, the blankets separating them.

"Don't try anything funny," said Rus drowsily. "I know about you Phemians."

Adares laughed and thought he would say something witty in response, as soon as it came to him. He would think of something in a moment.

Before the moment was past, he was asleep.

CHAPTER III

HE DREAMT OF huge, muscled animals with glistening black hide and long, curved horns charging down hills, their heads thrown back, their eyes wide and white while they bellowed and snorted and tried to shake off the blue-and-white riders who clung to their backs. It was something he could not have dreamt before that day, when he had seen it, exactly like that.

He woke from that dream, mercifully, and slept again, this time more peacefully and for much longer. When he finally woke again, it was light. He was aware of a comforting warmth, a feeling both familiar and unfamiliar, but entirely pleasant. His head was filled with a smoky, foreign smell, mingled with the tang of sweat, and his face was buried in something soft and scratchy. He opened his eyes. He must have rolled over in his sleep; he was lying with his face in his bedfellow's long, curly hair. And—it took him a moment longer to realize it—he had thrown one arm over Rus's waist and was lying tight up against his side.

He froze, holding himself in place carefully. The blankets were still between them. He would roll away as slowly as possible to keep from waking Rus. He held his breath and started slowly to lift his arm.

Rus put his hand on Adares's wrist, tugging it gently back

down. He stirred and opened his eyes, and after a moment turned his head slightly to look at Adares. In the light, at such close quarters, Adares could see the faint glint of blond stubble on his jaw and the individual pin-pricks of blue ink that made up the tattoo over his cheekbone. He thought again what a strong, open, attractive face the young Luth had, and that the barbarian decoration just enhanced it, somehow. The blond curls were coarser than a woman's, but still in their way quite lovely.

"Comfortable?" said Rus.

"Yes, quite. Um." He pushed himself up and back a little. "This is just the sort of thing you were afraid of, isn't it? If it's any comfort, I did this in my sleep, and it's not my normal—I mean, I was asleep." He realized in time that saying, *Generally, I prefer women* might not be quite as reassuring as he would intend it to be.

Rus let go of his wrist, and Adares rolled away from him—as much as the bed would allow—and sat up all the way. His stiff, sore muscles howled in protest, and he gritted his teeth against the pain.

Rus said, "I wasn't afraid."

"Hm? No, no. No reason for you to be. Ugh. I feel as if I was run over by a cart. Oh, wait ... "

That earned him a tired laugh. Adares looked down at Rus. He had the kind of colouring that couldn't conceal fatigue or illness at all. He was certainly in worse shape than Adares, but as Adares looked at him, he smiled cheerfully, a warm, uncomplicated expression, as if everything about that moment made sense to him, and made him happy. Adares thought that if the two of them had met on the battlefield yesterday an hour earlier than they did, there was every likelihood that one of them would have killed the other. He felt suddenly sick.

"Did you have bad dreams also?" Rus asked, his smile fading.

Adares nodded. "I dreamt about the bull-riders."

"Ah."

"They were terrifying. They took us by surprise, even though we knew to expect them. It's one thing to hear that the Luth ride wild bulls into battle—it sounds fanciful, frankly, like something out of an overwritten novel. It's another thing entirely to be faced with them actually charging across a valley at your army."

Rus was silent for a moment. "We have hunted the bulls and their cows on our land for many, many generations," he said, looking up at the ceiling. "We know their ways better than any of the southern tribes. We know that the spirit of Genhath—the god of rage and bloodshed, whom you would call Nepharos—that he enters the bulls when they are taken from the herd and deprived of their cows. Their rage is unquenchable, and if you know how to control it, even a little, you can terrify your enemy."

"Well, it worked on us. My—we—everyone went to pieces. I'd say it cost us the battle, except we were also outnumbered and outclassed."

"Yes," said Rus simply. "Are you new to it?" he asked after a moment. "Warrior life?"

"I'm not a warrior, I'm—an administrator. I have a, uh … an officer's rank—legate of the colonial legion—because of my post, and obviously I've had training, but never had to use it. Yesterday was the first time I ever saw battle."

"Ah, I see."

"That's why it's hit me so hard, I suppose. Career soldiers must have their ways of coping, but … " He let the sentence trail off.

"I am sorry," said Rus quietly.

Adares sat silent for a few minutes. "I'll heat some water," he said finally, turning and swinging his legs over the edge of the bed. "Then we can wash properly, and I'll rebandage your leg. In the meantime, I'll get you some food." He stood up and stretched, though it didn't help much.

On the shelf he found a jar half full of dry oat biscuits, the sort that people lived on when they were fasting for purification. He put a couple of biscuits in the dish with the walnuts and the rest of the figs, and brought that over to the bed along with the jar of honey.

"These things are awful," he said, indicating the oat biscuits, "but they're very wholesome, and if you dip them in honey they don't taste quite so much like sawdust. Don't do that," he said quickly, as Rus tried to push himself up onto one elbow to eat. "I'll get something for you to lean against."

He folded up the fur rug and a bundle of curtains, and piled them at the head of the bed, then he lifted Rus gently and propped him up on this arrangement of makeshift pillows. He set the bowl of figs and biscuits in Rus's lap and uncorked the jar of honey.

"You know," said Rus, taking one of the biscuits, his tone rather careful, "if it is to be thought of in terms of an exchange, you have repaid me for saving your life already."

"I guess so. Have I?"

"*If* it is to be thought of in terms of an exchange. But perhaps that is not the right way to think of it."

"No, maybe not. Here." He held out the jar. "Seriously— they're almost inedible without honey. If you're suggesting that I should leave—"

"No."

"Good, because I don't think I'm feeling all that much better than you, honestly, and I'd just as soon not go anywhere."

"I've no wish for you to. Mmgh—Phemians must have good teeth, these things are like rock!"

"Stick it into the side of your mouth—it's easier to gnaw off a piece that way. I'm not sure where I'd go, anyway."

"There is that."

"So I might as well look after you while I'm here." He shrugged. "Right?"

Rus gave him a thoughtful smile, as if to say that he could tell this was just a story Adares was making up, but couldn't figure out what it was a substitute for. Adares didn't really know himself.

"So long as it does not put you at risk," Rus said finally.

"At risk? Oh, you mean … what do you mean?"

"I mean would your people think you a traitor for this?"

"What?" Adares was genuinely surprised. "No, they'd … " *They'd think you a hero for saving my life. They'd want to look after you too.* "I think they would see it as I do. You cancelled the enmity between us when you pulled me out from under that cart and let me go."

Rus widened his eyes sceptically. "My people would not see it that way."

Adares hadn't thought about that. "You didn't know whether I was a Luth or a Phemian when you dug me out of that hole."

"Ah, well—you'd fallen on a field where more Phemians than Luth went down. I knew you were more likely a Phemian than not. I didn't care. I knew how you felt—probably young like me, and having to stare down your death, waiting for it miserably, instead of meeting it quickly in battle, when there is no time to think." He shrugged. "I must have done the right thing—I didn't know it would save my life too. Do you know, if you soaked these things in milk, they would not be bad at all?"

"I wonder if the priests left any of their goats behind. It seems unlikely—but it's worth a look."

Rus yawned. "I wonder," he said drowsily, "if you are here caring for me because it was your first battle and you don't know how warriors cope. But this is how you cope."

"Huh. I don't think I have anywhere near that kind of subtlety. I should go bring in some water."

He found a copper tub in one of the other outbuildings, dragged it into their room, and filled it halfway with jugfuls of cold water from the fountain. He brought back one more full jug and set it in a corner while he went through into the temple to light a taper from the sacred fire. With this he started a fire in a small brazier in the storeroom and heated the water in the jug so he could have a warm bath. By the time he had done all this, Rus had fallen asleep again. Adares stripped off his muddy black tunic and his loincloth, poured the hot water into the tub, stepped in, and took his time scrubbing himself clean.

Climbing out when the water had cooled completely, he dried himself and rummaged around in the piles of linen at the back of the room until he found a couple of clean white tunics, oversized and worn soft and nearly transparent. He slipped one of them on, emptied out the dirty bathwater in the yard, and put another jugful of water on the brazier to heat.

Rus woke when Adares folded back the blanket over him, almost reached out to snatch it back, but caught himself in time. He stayed awake—and tense—through the washing and rebandaging of his wound.

"Honey is good for wounds," he said.

"Good how?"

"Prevents it … going bad, however it does."

"No, I mean—what do you do with the honey?"

"You just smear it on, I think, and then put the dressing on over top."

"All right. We can do that." He went over to the shelf where he had replaced the jar of honey, and rummaged about for an empty vessel. He found a small pot and poured some of the honey out into it. "From now on," he said, putting the jar back on the shelf, "this is the food honey, and this," holding up the little pot, "is the medicinal honey."

"Is that important?"

"Yes, it is. It's important to me."

Rus gave him a look that suggested this made about as much sense to him as temples and fish sauce, but he said nothing.

"It's lucky it was such a tidy wound," Adares remarked, sitting down on the bed again with the medicinal honey. He dipped two fingers into the pot. "Won't disrupt the symmetry of your tattoos." The blue lines were continuous from flank to thigh, interrupted only by the band of linen holding up Rus's loincloth. The holes made by the crossbow bolt missed the main part of the design. Adares dabbed the honey gently around the wound. He wiped his fingers and began wrapping the fresh bandage.

Rus swallowed. "Sometimes the warriors of the Luth have new tattoos made around their scars—to show off all the wounds that they have survived." He winced slightly as Adares tightened the bandage.

"All done." Adares took away the basin of water and the dirty bandages, and he set the pot of medicinal honey at the opposite end of the shelf from the food honey. He returned to sit on the edge of the bed, tossing the cover casually back over Rus. "Are you not a 'warrior of the Luth' yourself?"

"No, of course ... " Rus looked puzzled for a moment,

then he laughed. "Of course, you cannot tell. No, I am not a warrior … "

Adares raised an eyebrow. "What are you, then? You have a lot of tattoos. Don't Luth men accumulate tattoos over the years, as they accomplish things?" He knew nothing about it, but this seemed logical. It was how it worked in some of the other tribes, anyway.

"Usually."

"But you can't be much more than twenty."

"To be truthful, a little bit less. I am kahar—the Kosoth word is … I don't know. What it is, is a servant of the gods. We get the tattoos all at once, when we have our initiation."

"A servant of the gods," Adares repeated. "A priest?"

"That is the word."

"What were you doing on the battlefield?" But even as he said it, he guessed.

"Bringing the wrath of Genhath to fall on our enemies." He didn't sound happy about it. "I did not think, until you told me about your dream, that you did not know it to look at me. Among my people, it is obvious."

"You're one of the ones who rides the bulls."

Rus nodded. "I am sorry."

"Don't be!" It came out rather forcefully. "No. You served your people very well. And it must take some skill. It looks difficult."

"We train for a long time." He hesitated, and Adares thought he was trying to decide whether to apologize again or to change the subject, wondering which one Adares wanted. Finally he said, "Staying on the back of a bull for the length of a charge is … it's very difficult. And then to defend yourself from the enemy at the same time? Nearly impossible. A lot of us are killed. A lot of us have been killed in this campaign. I don't know, when I go back, how many of us there will still be."

"I remember seeing one of the bulls without a rider. I suppose … "

"We usually try to get off. Your best bet is to get off as soon as you can take down one of the enemy and get onto his horse."

"From the bull's back?"

"It can be done. It is not as difficult as it sounds."

"I'm not sure *difficult* is even the word I was going to use. That sounds like one of those things out of an epic with talking horses and chariots that fly."

Rus frowned. "Phemian horses don't talk?"

"Well, you know. Only under special circumstances."

"Ah. And you don't have the same kind of wild cattle in your homeland either, do you?"

"No. In fact, no. Joking aside. Only some of their small, tame cousins, with much shorter horns. Good for milk, but not much use in a fight."

"Mm. The people in Karhan have never tried to tame the bulls. We are the only tribe that rides them in battle."

"Which causes you to be feared by your neighbours—I know all about that."

"You know a lot about us, I think."

"I really don't. I should know much more—to do my job properly."

"What is it, your job?"

"Oh, it's not interesting." That was a lie, and Adares felt ashamed of it immediately. There were plenty of secrets he would have been glad to share with Rus; this wasn't even a secret, but to reveal it would have been irresponsible in the extreme.

Rus made no comment and did not ask the question again.

"I ought to know your language," Adares said. "You put me to shame, speaking mine so well."

"Ah, but that is only a coincidence. I thought it was just the language of Kos, remember."

"That's the sort of thing Kossians would be proud to hear. They like to think they invented civilization, single-handed."

"Do Phemians think the same?"

"No, not really. We're better known for our navy."

"I've never been on a ship … " Rus had closed his eyes.

"There's nothing like it," said Adares softly. "When the wind is in the sails, and you are so far from land that all you can see is a dark line on the horizon, and then just blue, glittering blue, far off into the distance, further than any man can see. And you see gulls sitting on the waves, and taking off into the wind, and fish that jump out of the water sometimes, and splash back down into the foam. And you can feel the waves rocking the ship as the wind drives it on, gently, on a calm day, rocking it back and forth … "

At home in Pheme—in the days when he had thought of Pheme as his home—he used to put his little brother Chares to sleep sometimes by telling him stories. He had developed a knack for it, and Chares used to request his stories. It was not long before he could tell that Rus was asleep again. Adares got up from the bed, wishing he had someone now to tell him a story that would put him to sleep, maybe even to give him pleasant dreams while he slept.

He walked out of the temple storeroom into the sun-lit, honey-coloured courtyard. The morning air promised a warm day, but warm for the mild Karhan climate, nothing like the heat of high summer in Pheme, where some days even the wind off the sea seemed hot. His first visit home from Tios had been in the summer. "Don't you get home-sick?" people had asked him, slouched in the shade on the balconies of their cramped city apartments, fanning away the flies, and draining cups of sour orange juice and weak wine because of the water shortage. "Are you mad?" he had been tempted to reply.

He turned a corner into the outer courtyard, and the temple of Anaxe, the central building of the complex, presented its broad, colonnaded front before him. There was a gallery below the carved and painted pediment, where the priests could stand to watch processions coming up from Tios. The view from there would be good, Adares thought. He would be able to see how the siege was progressing, and gauge whether there was any hope of getting past the Luth and back into his city.

He entered the hushed, dim porch of the temple and found the stairs that led up to the gallery. Emerging at the top, he leaned in the sunlight on the stone rail and looked out past the walls of the temple complex, across yesterday's battlefield towards the city.

The smoke of funeral pyres clouded the air—the Luth respectfully cremating the fallen Phemians, that must be, since they did something else with their own dead, buried them or something. He could ask Rus if he really wanted to know.

The walls of Tios in the distance seemed to glow, as if lit from within, the yellow stone soaking in the sunlight. From here it was impossible to tell the state of their defences. The Luth seemed to have settled down around the walls, pitching clusters of hide-covered tents at a safe distance. He could see the bulky shapes of their remaining siege-carts standing ready. The real assault had not yet begun.

He thought again about his dream, about the beasts charging at the head of the Luth cavalry, the riders clinging to their backs. One of them had been Rus. Strangely, he realized he found it comforting to know that. It was as if a frightening shape in the dark had been revealed, at the lighting of a lamp, to be something familiar—an ally, a friend.

CHAPTER IV

RUS WAS AWAKE when Adares finally came back into the storeroom.

"Sleep well?"

"Yes … " He stirred, pushed himself up slightly, then collapsed back against his pillows. "You're back. I thought perhaps you had gone. I wouldn't have blamed you," he added quickly. "You have helped me, and it helped you to collect yourself after the battle, but when you learned I was one of the bull-riders … I thought maybe it was too much."

"No, not at all." Adares sat on the edge of the bed. "You're one of them, sure—but you're the one who pulled me out of that hole. I know you think I should have got over that by now because I repaid you and blah blah honour something something—I know what you tribesmen are like."

"Clearly."

"Anyway, I was brought up not to do that sort of thing. Slink away while the other party's still asleep. Bad manners."

Rus blinked up at him uncomprehendingly.

"Uh, it's a joke. Never mind."

"What were you doing all this time? Did you find the goat?"

"No, there's no sign of a goat. I did have a bit of a look around—then I fell asleep in the sun by that thrice-blessed fountain. I've brought you in some more water, by the way. Before that I went up to the top of the big temple to see how your people are going about besieging my people."

"I do not think that will work," said Rus, hoisting himself up onto the improvised pillows again so that he could drink from the cup of water Adares offered him. "We have never attacked a city with stone walls before, only the wooden strongholds of the Karhan tribes. And you are at the top of a crag, with cliffs all around."

"Only on this side—on the other side, where the main gate to the city is, there's a much gentler slope down to the coast. They'll have discovered that by now. Anyway, even if your people can't break down the gates or breach the walls, they can still starve Tios into surrender. They'll have cut off the route to the port by this time. I only hope that we bought enough time, meeting your troops on this side of the city, to allow the women and children to get out to the ships. We knew an attack was coming, but we were not ready for it so soon. We had ships at anchor in the harbour, but the people were all still in Tios when we got word that the—your people—were in the woods just north of the city."

Rus nodded. "I know that we were not planning to come south to the coast so soon, but there was a report that you were building walls from Tios down to the harbour, so that no one could surround you and keep you away from your boats."

Adares laughed. "You could have waited, even still. It's a big job, and the walls are months from completion."

"We have heard that Phemians work fast. Our headman did not want to take chances."

"Gunthanaruth—that's your chieftain's name, isn't it?"

"You can pronounce it—I'm impressed. Part of your uninteresting job again, I guess."

"Mm. He may do a creditable job of besieging Tios.

He dealt with the Getti very efficiently a few months ago. And he's got some impressive siege equipment. But our real weakness is the harbour. The first colonists built Tios to be defensible from land—within easy distance of a good harbour, but not a port city like Pheme. The harbour is easy to defend itself. It's shaped sort of like this—" He gathered up the bedclothes to describe a tight horseshoe shape, the two ends nearly meeting.

"On either side are high cliffs—the narrows, here, are just wide enough for a ship to pass through. We only started to build walls to the harbour a few months ago—if they were done, they would not only protect us in case of a siege, but allow us to bring in reinforcements from Pheme by sea. Since they're not, Gunthanaruth can surround Tios, and, by taking the cliffs, he can defend the harbour against Phemian ships, just as we would have defended it against enemies."

"Tch. I see. Has he taken the cliffs?"

Adares nodded. "I could see blue banners flying from the watchtowers. I can only think of one route to get back into Tios, but it's cut off—your people are swarming all over it."

"What is it?" Rus asked curiously. "How would you get back?"

"Well … "

When he hesitated, Rus quickly held up a hand. "You do not have to tell me," he said seriously.

"What? No, I'll tell you—I'm just thinking it through myself. Unless … I mean, if you don't want to know … "

The line of one of the tattoos around Rus's wrist curled up just slightly into the base of his palm, where it trailed off in a couple of blue dots. He dropped his hand.

"Ah, no, I *do* want to know—I want to appreciate your brilliance."

"Yeah, you'd better. So here it is. There's a little fishing

village, Ikthyra, on the other side of the woods just east of
Tios—they supply most of the fresh fish for the city—anyway, it's small enough that the—your people … Can I just
say 'the Luth'?"

"Please."

"Well. The Luth probably don't know about Ikthyra—
would you say this is true?"

"I'd say most of us couldn't pronounce the name even if
we had heard of it."

"Yeah?"

"Ik-thy-ra. But I told you, I am kahar, I am special."

"Right. Well, the place will be half-deserted now, just a few
fishermen left—all the women and children are inside Tios.
But there would be small boats there—and in a small boat,
I could sneak under the cliffs at the narrows by night. Once
I got into the harbour … well, it would be tricky. I would
have to stay out of sight until low tide, and then I'd have to
move fast. The main drainage system from Tios lets out into
the harbour, and it's quite a big tunnel—big enough to row
a small boat up, certainly. There's a grate at the end, but it's
possible to open it. And of course it leads all the way back
up to the city." He paused, feeling a little ridiculous knowing
so much about sewers. "I had a job with the department of
public works when I first came to Tios," he explained. "That's
how I know all this."

"Ah."

"Anyway, there's a Luth encampment sitting between me
and the road to Ikthyra." It was where he had seen the smoke
of the funeral pyres. "I don't think I could get by."

"So you can't go back into your city to be besieged with
all the others."

"Yes, well … I admit it sounds like a lot of effort to go to just to find a place to starve. But I'd be more use inside Tios than not."

"I can't agree. I'm finding you very useful here. Can I have some more water?"

Adares laughed and fetched the jug to refill his cup.

"In truth," Rus said, after he had sipped his water, "I understand why you want to return to Tios, even though I am not in the same hurry to return to my camp. Your cause—the Phemian cause—is more just. You were defending your home, and I cannot find fault with that. We were attacking you."

"Sure, but we're interlopers in Kargania—Karhan, I mean. We annexed the good goldmine and the quarries, we've coopted the Getti, who used to be your allies, and allied with the Daine, who've always been your enemies. You're right to see us as a threat—maybe even right to try to drive us out, based on what you know of us.

"There's more that you don't know—the reason you defeated us so easily yesterday is that we've only got one legion, and not even a very good one, the Fourth Colonial. Pheme refuses to send more troops until … well, there's a lot of politics involved, but the thing is, so long as we've only got the Fourth Colonial, we're not going to mount a campaign against you up in the North. Pheme's not interested in expanding in Kargania these days. The colonies are falling out of fashion. We could settle down and just be a presence in the territory, a link with the Pseuchaian states, trading with the tribes—you could get more books from Kos—but if this siege turns into some kind of massacre, if Phemian civilians die … "

"Pheme will send the legions," Rus finished for him. "Marching into the North for revenge. Years of bloodshed.

And your people would become merchants of war after all, which is what you do not want to see."

"So desperately. I can't tell you."

"You do not have to. I could tell that is how you felt. It is why I thought you might have left, before."

"But you understand all that. I guess that's why I didn't."

They were silent for a few moments, not looking at one another, the mood solemn and serious.

"No," said Rus finally, "I think you just enjoy laughing at me about fish wine and medicinal honey and things."

"Actually, you're right."

"Tell me," Rus said, "what was propitious about this place? Why did your holy men choose it for their temples?"

Adares gave that a moment's thought. "Honestly, I've no idea. It was built long before I came to Tios. I'm sure there must have been some reason to pick the site, but … well, it's just traditional to have temples outside the city—we do it in Pheme—that you process to on festivals. We have temples inside the city as well. Sorry, I'm not a religious specialist like you, so I don't know the details."

Rus sighed. "And this temple we are in now—who is it dedicated to? I suppose you know that much."

"Soukos. Our horse god."

Rus gave him a look. "He's not *your* horse god, Phemian. He's *the* horse god. We call him Gurhat, and we worship him differently—but that is only a difference in language and custom. The god is the same."

"I know that. We know that—Phemians know that."

"But you thought the barbarians didn't. You are quite wrong. It is not just I, because I am kahar and a 'religious specialist'—it is not just the Luth, even, it is all the people of the Karhan who know that you worship the same gods on your islands as we do here. It is commonly known. Do you think anyone would have let you stay in this land as long as they have if they thought you worshipped false gods? We would have been down here besieging your city long before now if we thought you spread lies with your religion."

"That was an interesting tirade, but you misunderstood me. I didn't mean to suggest that your people don't know—I just meant that my people do. I said 'our horse god,' but all I meant was 'our name for the horse god.' You're a bit of a nitpicker, Rus."

He nodded. "That's fair. It is too bad you don't speak Firhat Luth. For me, Firhat Kosoth is the language of, as you say, nitpicking. I am not like that when I speak my native language. Well ... not so much."

"I'm not sure I believe that. But I never had much incentive to learn your language. Not very many Luth have been willing to speak to Phemians—or come near us, really. I know the languages of the Getti and the Daine, well enough to get by, and I have a smattering of Tak—those are all the tribes that we've had friendly dealings with. Not that we've been able to do them much good."

"You did help the Daine, last summer."

"Yes. Against the Hurs. Gunthanaruth's pet tribe, as I hear."

"He married his daughter to the Hurs headman last year."

Adares nodded. He ran his fingers absently over the cool clay handle of the water jug sitting beside him on the bed.

After a while Rus said, "I'm sorry I was rude about the horse god."

Adares looked up at him, surprised. "You weren't. Well—if you were, I didn't mind. I was just ... remembering. That skirmish with the Hurs last summer was a disaster. That was when our archon, Hesteios, was killed."

"Your what?"

"Archon. Elected leader. Sort of like one of your chieftains—I think you elect your chieftains?"

Rus wrinkled his nose and opened his mouth to nitpick again, then appeared to think better of it. "In a way. The lords of the different hearths elect a new headman when the old one dies. Do your archons rule for life?"

"No, they're elected for five years. In Pheme they govern three at a time and rarely get more than one term—but the colonies only have one archon apiece, and quite often they're re-elected. Hesteios had been archon of Tios for nearly twenty years. He was a superb leader, and a good man, too. It was a sad way for him to die—far away from Tios, in an unimportant little battle."

"I'm sorry." After a moment he added, curiously, "Your ruler now—his name is Fy-something? I have heard Gunthanaruth say his name, and then spit."

"Charming. His name's Phyleros."

"And is he also a good man?"

"I don't—I'm not really qualified to say. He's too young to be archon, that's one thing."

"How young?"

"Twenty-four."

Rus frowned as if that didn't seem excessively young to him. It was hard to remember that he was a teenager himself.

"In Pheme you can't even stand for the office until you're thirty-five."

"How did he get elected, then?"

"He was chief assistant to the archon under Hesteios—he took over as acting archon after Hesteios died, as a matter of course."

"Ah, so he was not elected."

"Well, but he was, eventually. In Pheme there would have been an election right away. But Tios is a colony—we'd had our archons elected for us in Pheme, in the past, and sent over. Of course, it had been nearly twenty years since we had needed a new archon, which is a long time in the life of a new city. While Hesteios was willing to stand, they just kept reappointing him every five years. But after he died, we were notified that a new archon would be chosen for us in the usual way. Then, for a whole variety of reasons—a change of government in Pheme, some bureaucratic screw-up with counting votes, and a season of storms that almost shut down sea travel—it was a full year before the new archon was sent over. In the meantime, Phyleros was in charge, and—people got used to him, I suppose."

"Got to like him, you mean."

Adares shrugged. "Took leave of their senses, maybe. Anyway, when the man from Pheme did arrive, the citizens' council had decided that they wanted an election in Tios after all. There was no precedent for a colonial council to make that decision for itself—it was almost an act of rebellion, but they did it. I'm not saying it was a bad idea, either, as far as that goes. The man Pheme had sent was put out, of course, but he couldn't take over without the acclamation of the council. He hadn't had the forethought to bring a legion with him to support his claim. So they held an election, the first ever in Tios. They waived the age requirement—someone gave an eloquent speech about a young city deserving a young governor—and they elected the acting archon. Phyleros."

"You don't think it was a good decision," Rus observed.

"I think the people were off their heads," said Adares, with conviction. "Well." He got up from the bed. "Never mind that. I'll heat some more water, and you can bathe properly. There's another clean tunic like this one that you can put on afterwards—if the idea of wearing Phemian clothes isn't too revolting to you."

If Rus was disconcerted by the abrupt change of subject, he didn't show it. All he said was, "Your clothes look comfortable in this warm weather."

Adares built up the fire in the brazier and put some more water on to heat. He refilled the tub from the fountain and dragged it over near the bed. Rus pushed himself up shakily into a sitting position.

"Here, I'll help you," said Adares. "I can even close my eyes, or look away, so as not to offend your barbarian modesty."

"Ah, but I'll bet you can't, actually. I'll bet you are too curious to know exactly how much of me is tattooed. Aren't you?"

Adares looked at him. "Now I am."

Rus grinned. He moved the covers aside and pushed himself towards the edge of the bed, drawing in his breath sharply as he moved his injured leg. "I don't mind you knowing. If your people are like the Kossians, I think you are not ashamed to go naked when you play sports, or to have big bath houses where everyone sees everyone else without his clothes?"

"Civilized. Yes."

Rus snorted. His long, pale fingers unpicked the knotted ties of his loincloth. He stripped it off in a quick, economical motion. Then he didn't seem to know where to look.

"Blessed Orante. I thought you were bluffing."

Rus laughed, as merrily as the day before at the fountain, and blushed. He sat on the edge of the bed with his feet on the floor. He was still embarrassed, and couldn't meet Adares's eyes, but sat looking away, one hand pushed shyly up into his hair.

Adares looked at him appreciatively. He really was attractive. The tattoos on his chest and stomach coiled down over his slim hips and onto his thighs, an unbroken pattern, but his dick was just circled by two spiralling, parallel lines, unconnected to the rest. It was also thick and rosy and very nicely proportioned.

Suddenly Adares realized how odd this whole situation was, with Rus unmistakably displaying himself and looking bashful about it—as well he might, with a body like that. It was like the invitation to share the bed, which seemed so boldly flirtatious that it had to be innocent. Adares felt again as if he should say that he was a ladies' man, and had to remind himself again that it would probably make matters worse. Also, in this situation, it was starting to feel like it would have been a lie.

"How long did it take to draw all that?" he said instead.

"To *draw*? A couple of hours. You mean how long did it take to ink it." He shrugged. "I don't know exactly. They do it in stages over a week, and I was, what do you call it? Drugged—most of the time."

"Drugged?" said Adares, intrigued. "Really?"

Rus nodded. "Part of the initiation. Our healers have a great knowledge of such things—and they did not get it from the Kossian books. The drugs for the initiation—that's when I had the tattoos done—they're part of the ceremony, to make it easier to feel you're giving yourself up to the gods. It's supposed to be a good feeling."

"Supposed to be?"

"I didn't like it." He brushed past that quickly. "The initiation drugs are sacred, you're not allowed to use them again. But we do have others—just different combinations of the same things, and they are for pain of all kinds. Our healers are good. Though," he added, running a hand gingerly over the bandages on his leg, "I think yours must be good too."

Adares frowned. "I didn't know. I mean, that you had drugs and so on."

He went to check the temperature of the water on the brazier, though he knew it would not be hot yet.

"You could use some of those drugs now, couldn't you? All I can give you is wine, and it's not much use."

"That's all right. If I were drugged, we couldn't talk." He had drawn his good leg up and wrapped his arms around it, so that the blue curls on his forearms lay across the matching designs on his shin. He seemed more at ease now.

"You're not thinking that I should have left well enough alone and let your own people take care of you?" said Adares, only half jokingly.

"Adares. You saved my life. Our headman knows that the bull-riders win his battles for him—if we don't die on the field, we are taken care of. And our healers know some things about Phemian ways. They looked at the arrow in me, and they said, 'It's poisoned. You won't live.' When I found you, I had been left to die, the same as you had. I … went looking on the battlefield for survivors, to be useful in the time I had left." He mentioned this almost apologetically, and Adares thought he did not want to be praised for it.

"In all fairness," Adares said, "my people didn't really leave me to die. Or … I wouldn't think so. I think they must have believed I was dead already."

"They probably did not even know where you were," said Rus reasonably. "You were completely hidden under that cart." He looked at Adares thoughtfully for a moment. "I have not stopped to wonder how you got there in the first place. Now that I think about it, it is something rather strange."

"I ran into it," Adares said simply. He was surprised not to find this more difficult to talk about. "On purpose. I can remember *why* I did it—we were trying to take out as many of your siege machines as we could, as a kind of last-ditch strategy. And I could see that if this one went down, it would break up the charge, like a big rock on the shoreline—the wave would break on either side of it.

"All that more or less makes sense. What I can't remember is whether I had any idea of surviving after I charged into the thing. I don't suppose I did. I was riding downhill—I was on the right flank of the division that was trying to retreat, just in front of where this charge was coming across—and I just galloped straight at the thing, which took the driver by surprise, as you can imagine. He tried to get out of the way, but he couldn't turn his horses sharply enough, and the whole cart pitched up onto two wheels—I suppose the men inside were thrown out, if they hadn't jumped clear already. I couldn't stop in time, of course—my horse was killed when she slammed into the cart, and the whole thing just came down on top of both of us. I don't know whether I ended up buying enough time for the retreat or not."

Rus sat staring up at Adares in silence for so long that Adares finally said, "What?"

"I thought you said you were a … what did you say you were?"

"An administrator. But I had military training—I did say that."

"And great courage—that is what you did not say. To sacrifice yourself on the battlefield like that—I do not think that is the normal job of an 'administrator.'"

Adares laughed. "Oh, well—in the colonies it sometimes seems nobody does just their normal job. When I first came to Tios, I was landed with that awful post in the public works office. I came expecting a job as a junior assistant to the archon, and ended up working for the man in charge of inspecting public drains."

Once again, Rus accepted the change of topic with equanimity. "What would they be, public drains?"

"Big pipes, laid under the streets, where the waste water from the gutters, and the fountains—and the public toilets, but you won't know what those are either—is all collected, and channelled into the main drain, which empties out into the sea."

"And that is how you thought you could get back into Tios—from this drain."

"Yes."

"And the public toilets?"

"Here," said Adares, hoisting the jug of water off of the brazier. "This should be warm enough now."

He emptied the jug into the half-full tub by the bed. Rus shifted over on the bed and levered himself down to sit in the tub without assistance, while Adares hovered. When he was seated in the water, he looked up at Adares with a little, wry smile.

"Here," said Adares, offering him a cloth and the glass vial of soap that he had found in the pharmacy. "You wash, and I will regale you with the wonders of Phemian public toilets."

He sat on the stone floor by the bed, while Rus scrubbed the grime of yesterday's battle from his skin, and he explained not only public toilets, but also communal bath houses and their heating systems, aqueducts, public fountains, and running water in houses.

"You have many ingenious ways with water," said Rus archly. He gathered up the mass of his hair and pulled it over one shoulder.

"You want a hand?" Adares said without thinking.

"If you don't mind," said Rus after a moment, holding out the cloth and the soap.

"Not at all." Adares took the cloth, wet it again, and poured some soap onto it. He smoothed the soapy cloth over Rus's back, the suds obscuring the blue lines that curled over his shoulder blades.

"What do your women use to wash their hair?" Rus asked, combing through his own hair roughly with his fingers.

Adares considered that for a moment. "I have no idea. All of the women I've known—even the ones I've known pretty well—have been terribly secretive about that sort of thing. Probably afraid that I would think less of them if I found out there was any kind of artifice involved—any dye or curling irons or whatnot. It's a typical Phemian weakness—we expect everyone to look beautiful, but we look down on any art used to achieve beauty." He wet the washcloth again and rinsed the soap off Rus's back. "I don't think your people have the same trouble."

"No. We believe in decoration. The more art the better."

"Why do you want to know about Phemian women's hair?"

"I don't. I want to wash *my* hair."

"Oh, right. Can't you use soap?"

"If I have to." He sounded dubious.

"Do you know, in Pheme they don't even have soap?"

"What's that, then?" Rus indicated the vial that Adares had just set down.

"That's a clever new idea introduced to Tios by the locals."

"And how do Phemians wash?"

"With oil. You smear it on and scrape it off."

"That's foul. That can't possibly make you clean." He gave Adares a comically disgusted look over his shoulder. "Dirty barbarians."

"Your precious Kossians do the same, you know. In between exercising naked and writing poetry about—uh, loose women," he finished rather hastily.

"About boys, I thought," said Rus after a moment, his tone strangely diffident.

"That too." Adares got to his feet. "Can you get out on your own? I'll get you something to dry yourself with."

CHAPTER V

WHILE RUS DRIED himself and dressed in the other oversized white tunic, Adares stripped off the dirty sheets and replaced them with clean ones. He helped Rus back onto the bed, where he lay back gratefully and for a moment closed his eyes. The blue of his tattoos showed faintly through the worn linen of the tunic. Adares thought he was going to go back to sleep; but he seemed to want to talk instead.

"I have seen the walls of Tios, and I have read a little about the cities that you have on your islands in the West. But I have never seen the inside of a city. It is something I would like to see. I guess you know what our halls and houses are like—you would have been to some in the Karhan, for your job, I think."

"Yes, but never as far north as the Luth territory. I hear that Gunthanaruth's hall is a marvel." He'd heard that from other Karhan tribesmen, of course. It might not have impressed him.

"I doubt if you have seen a house like it," Rus said. "It has sod growing on the roof, and great beams carved like snakes and birds holding it up. But not real snakes and birds, not the way you would carve them on a Phemian temple, so they look like they might jump off and bite you—these are Luth carvings, all made of patterns. Like mine. This is to show not what they look like, but how they are—in time, in the web of everything. Just as my patterns show what I am, how I fit."

He paused, looking thoughtful for a moment. "Also, we just like to decorate things. The hall is at the top of a hill, in the headman's summer village. There is a wall around it—around the whole village, a wall of sharp stakes. And at the bottom of the hill there is the house of the kahar, and it is also probably not like anything you have seen. It is round, and made of wood too—we build everything out of wood—but the outside is covered in … a sort of white clay, I'm not sure what you call it. And we paint around the outside in blue, patterns that don't make up anything you can see—not snakes and animals, like we use to decorate other things. We say that a pattern like that is part of the Great Pattern of the world, Heva, which is so large that we can't see all of it. We have to repaint the house every year, because the patterns wash off in the rain—but the repainting is important, it is also part of a pattern."

"Is that where you live, in this round house?"

Rus nodded. "Since I was eleven. I was born in a village on the other side of the mountain to the east of Gunthanaruth's stronghold. My father is the hearth headman of our clan—he has herds numbering in the thousands."

"So you're what we'd call an aristocrat."

"I know what that is. Skar, we call them. Sakar, skar, kahar—those are the three classes. The owned, the owners, and the set-apart. My family belongs to the skar. Their land is in the foothills of the mountains. Adares, have you seen mountains?"

"Certainly. The island of Pheme is mostly mountains, inland."

"Ah, I see. I thought somehow that you would only know the sea, which I have never seen yet."

"You can see the sea from here—from the gallery of the temple of Anaxe, anyway. When you're back on your feet … " It would be a while before he was well enough to want to climb stairs just for a view, and would he still be here then, idling about the temple complex with Adares? It seemed unlikely.

"Mountains are different, though." Rus ignored the awkward topic, as usual. "They don't do anything—they just are. It takes a whole week to travel from the headman's village to my father's summer pastures, because it is so difficult getting through the mountains. So I do not see my parents often. And you? Are your parents alive?"

"Yes. In Pheme. It takes a week to get there too, by sea, if the wind is in your favour and you have a good pilot. I used to go home more often, in the days when I could still take a whole month off to make the trip."

"Do you miss Pheme?"

"No. My family writes me pitiful letters. Yours?"

Rus gave him a look. "They don't read."

"Oh, right—that's just you with your set-apartness. To tell the truth, I do miss my family, when I'm away for too long. Not the city they live in, just them."

"What do they do?"

"They're aristocrats. They're like the mountains—they don't *do* anything, they just are."

Rus laughed. "But you left home to come to Tios and do things."

"More or less."

"Is Tios like Pheme?"

"Not very much. Pheme is bigger, of course. The biggest city in the world. And it's crowded—there isn't much space to expand, between the coast and the mountains. The buildings have four and five storeys in some places, all carved up into apartments—rooms, you know, that people rent."

"Up, off the ground?" Rus gestured, looking rather alarmed. "One on top of another, you mean, stacked up?"

"Yes, exactly—stacked one on top of another."

"Is it safe?"

"Not entirely, no. But Tios isn't crowded like that—they built the walls deliberately with plenty of space inside for new streets and more houses. Then they ran out of money before they could build walls all the way out to the mouth of the narrows—but that's another matter. Tios is a different colour than Pheme, too."

"Ah, is the stone different?"

"That's right. Here it's yellow limestone. In Pheme they build mostly in brick, pinkish brick—and the temples and civic buildings are made of imported marble, which is white, so the painted carvings show up better than they do here. But I like the limestone. It has a warm look. I like the way Tios looks."

"It is your home. You love it."

"It's true. I've lived here for five years. I came here when I was your age, and I knew right away that I wanted to stay. My parents have never really understood. Every time I would try to explain to them that I wanted to stay in Tios, they would think it meant I was in love with a local girl. They thought that was the only possible reason I could want to stay here. They would tell me, 'You should bring her back to Pheme— she'd be much happier.' They don't understand—*I* am much happier in Tios, and there is no local girl.

"I mean, there are local girls, of course—it wouldn't be much of a place if there weren't. There are lots of wonderful girls, in fact, lots of daughters of colonists who were born here, and like it here, and lots of women in the local tribes who are quite charming. When I have time to catch my breath between one crisis and the next, I am sure … you know … I probably *will* fall in love with one of them. But I made up my mind about Tios without falling in love with anybody."

Why had he found it so awkward to say that about the local girls? He'd got halfway through his explanation and felt as if he was talking unnecessarily loudly.

Rus nodded but didn't immediately reply. Finally he said, "I think I know how you feel. Not about the girls, I mean— about your parents."

"Tell me."

"I also wanted a different life than my parents, and I did what I could to get it—and they do not understand, not really. I told you we have the three classes, and the kahar, we are supposed to be at the top—set apart for the service of the gods. And so it is in Heva—in the Great Pattern of the world—but in the minds of men and women it is not so simple. My parents respect the gods, yes, but they distrust men who answer only to them—many people do. I was chosen, when I was eleven—it is a competition, you have to enter and do well, in order to be chosen. My father gave me permission to enter, but neither he nor my mother liked it when I was chosen. Still they don't like it, and it has been eight years.

"It isn't irrevocable until the initiation—you have to stop growing before you can have tattoos. That was three years ago for me. So there is no going back, now." He held up his hands against the light for a moment, looking at them thoughtfully. "I am what I am."

"Indeed you are."

"Adares," said Rus, folding his arms behind his head, "do you think me ugly?"

"Do I *what*?"

"Ah, you don't." He started to blush. "I just thought … What you said about artifice … "

"Oh, you mean the tattoos? Immortal gods, no. They're gorgeous." He reached out a hand, intending just to smooth down the fabric of the white tunic so that the blue lines would show through clearly. But he stopped and did not complete the action. "Really, honestly. I think they're beautiful."

They were unlike any art that Phemians used to decorate their belongings: curling, twisting lines that flowed into each other, intersecting, diverging, breaking up, and trailing off into patterns of individual dots, not describing any particular shape, just covering the surface of his pale skin with pattern. But he hadn't needed any artifice to be beautiful.

"What do your local girls think?"

Rus gave him one of his blank looks, this one apparently sincere. "What do they think about what?"

"About … " Adares started to make a gesture, indicating Rus's appearance, tattoos and all, when something suddenly occurred to him. He wasn't sure why he hadn't thought of it before. "Oh. This business of being 'set apart'—would I be right in thinking it involves a vow of celibacy?"

"A vow of … I don't think I know that word."

"It means not marrying, or … "

"Or getting children—yes, that is it, of course. That is what it means to be kahar. It is not a *vow*, that is something you speak—this is written in my skin. For me to do what is forbidden to us would be to make myself a lie. Ah, I see! You were asking, do the local girls think that my tattoos look good—but of course they know what they mean, so … "

"That was like asking if a Maiden of the Sacred Loom gives good head or something. Yeah, no, you don't know what that means either—never mind."

"I can roughly work it out." Rus frowned disapprovingly.

"Of course, many of the girls at home have died of heartbreak … "

Adares shouted with laughter. "Yeah?"

"Ah no, I don't know, Adares. They might have—I have not paid attention. I don't pay attention at all to girls."

"I suppose you can't, can you?" A sobering thought.

"No, you see I … I never did." He said no more, and he put his hand over his mouth as though he wished he could stuff the words back in or was afraid of others escaping. "You understand?" he said finally, from behind his hand.

"Of course," said Adares. "Lots of fine men are like that, you know. At home … " He stopped. He realized Rus was way ahead of him here.

"Yes."

"You know all about it, don't you? They do as they like, for the most part. Of course there are still some difficulties—people think you're not fully a man if you don't marry, and they don't like an 'unmanly' man running for public office or leading the army or things like that. But nobody thinks twice about a good, manly man with a wife doing what he likes on the side. I don't think that's right, personally—I'd rather reward a man for faithfulness in love and honesty about what he wants."

He shrugged. "That doesn't make me a radical—you could find plenty of people to agree with that sentiment today, but the traditions are strong, and that's how it is. Of course, things are a bit different in Kos, which you probably … "

"Which I know," Rus finished for him. "Which I have read about, and wished that I could go there. I have never told anyone that."

"I guess not."

The whole thing made him suddenly very sad. Rus was such a fine person. Why should he have to resign himself to a life of loneliness? Adares realized he had not thought about how the taboos of the Karhan tribes would affect men like Rus.

"I used to think, before I read about the Kossians, that I was the only one in the world like this," Rus said. He smiled ruefully. "I learned so much when I learned to read Firhat Kosoth. But I did not think that Kos was a paradise—most of what you have just told me about Pheme is familiar to me, although, as you say, it seems it is a little different from one city to another. Just as from one tribe to another in the Karhan. None of them would harbour a man who polluted himself with other men, but I hear that what they would do to him would be different. Some would put him to death, some would only exile him. The Luth would do both, in a way—they make you an outlaw, which means no one will take you in, and you most likely starve or freeze alone in the mountains when winter comes."

Adares wanted to ask, without quite knowing how, whether Rus had chosen the set-apart life, the tattoos and the initiation and riding bulls into battle, strictly because he thought it was the only course for someone like him, and whether he regretted it. From the way he spoke, he seemed not to. Adares hoped that was true.

"What I did not know," Rus went on, "until I heard you speaking the language of Kos yesterday, was that the Phemians we were attacking belong to the same civilization—I did not know I would be fighting the thing that I admired." *Oh, of course*, Adares thought. Of course it got worse. "I am not sure what I could have done if I had known—the stathan, the leader of the kahar, had already spoken against the campaign, called it needless."

That was unexpected—and interesting. "Did he really?"

"But he was overruled by Gunthanaruth. The headman's word is law, even over the kahar."

"Did he have much support, though, the whatyoucall, the chief priest?"

Rus nodded. "I think most of the kahar would have sided with him, some of the skar, too—nobody cares what the sakar think, but in truth they never favour war, it is not their business."

"Huh. I didn't realize the Luth were divided like that." He was about to say more, but he realized he was getting distracted by talk of politics from the more important topic of Rus's life. He said, "I'm sorry if I've made things more difficult for you than they needed to be. I mean, with anything I've done here ... And if you want me to sleep on the floor, you don't even need to explain, I'd be happy to just ... "

"I am very used to controlling myself, Adares. We often share beds at home, because of the cold—and there are *so* many jokes, and they are not funny if you really ... " He made a vague but eloquent gesture.

"It sounds wretched."

"But you—you have been very honest with me. You like women—you made that clear, very politely. I didn't think ... that you would be like me, but ... " He was looking embarrassed again, but this time as if he was about to laugh at himself. "I think I must have thought that Phemians just ... make love to anyone at all, whenever they like."

"That's not far from the truth."

"Ah, is it not?"

"No, I mean ... I'm a pretty average Phemian man, and I got interested in girls when I was quite young, but I messed around with some of my school friends, too, and with one of the household slaves. He was willing," Adares added quickly, "as much as you can be sure of that with a slave—at least I felt sure of it at the time. And I had a lover when I was a teenager—a man, I mean. He went on to an impressive career in politics, but as a lover, honestly, he wasn't that great. Since then I've only been with women, but not, you know, purposely. Just the way it's happened, I guess. On the whole, I prefer women, but … " He realized he was giving a summary of his sexual experience to a consecrated virgin. "This isn't really helpful, is it?"

"I may make you sleep on the floor after all, out of pure spite." Then, after a moment, as if he couldn't resist asking: "How many women?"

"I don't know, I haven't kept a tally!"

"So many you can't *remember*?"

"No, I'm sure I could give you a rough estimate if I … if I took time to think about it."

"Bah. Do not trouble yourself, Phemian."

Adares was still snickering about that as he got up to wash their muddy clothes. He hung them by the fountain to dry. Returning inside, he fetched out the biscuits and honey again, and they ate, and then spent the rest of the afternoon sleeping on the clean sheets of the bed, side by side as before.

He was woken, in the dim, purplish evening, by a crash. It had been caused by Rus dropping the wine jug when he tried to get out of bed and get himself a drink without waking Adares. Rus was miserably annoyed with himself and tried to apologize for everything: waking Adares, not waking Adares sooner, spilling the wine, causing his wound to bleed again.

"All right, all right," said Adares, kneeling beside him on the floor and making shushing gestures. "You're sorry. I get it. Calm down."

Rus gave a little snort of laughter, and Adares thought how good it was when you could make someone feel better so easily.

The sun had gone down completely by the time Rus lay quietly on the bed again, his leg rebandaged, wearing Adares's newly washed black tunic, which looked strange on him. There was no more wine; Adares had searched the temple complex, by the light of his lamp, and returned with this discouraging news.

"If I were in Tios now, I would be thanking the priests for being so thorough and bringing everything with them. But here I am wishing they had been just a bit more careless. Dreadfully ironic."

It was worse than ironic; it was worrying. He did not want to trouble Rus further by mentioning it now, but the priests had taken away more than just their wine. By luck, the two of them had stumbled onto the one place that the priests had forgotten to clear out before they left. Once the figs and the oat biscuits were finished, there would be nothing in the whole temple complex to eat.

He sat down on the edge of the bed by Rus, who looked as though he badly needed more wine and wanted to say he was sorry yet again. Rus levered himself up, with considerable effort, in order to move over and give Adares more room on the bed. Adares slipped in next to him and rearranged the covers. Rus moved restlessly, turning to lie on his stomach, trying to find a comfortable position. Adares reached out a hand and stroked his back. He felt Rus tense, and then slowly, probably with an effort of will, relax into the simple offer of comfort.

"Want me to tell you a story?"

Rus laughed softly into the pillow. "Is it a true story about one of your countless women?"

"Of course not," said Adares, and immediately thought of an anecdote involving the man who had been his lover when he was sixteen. "It's a story my nurse used to tell me when I was little."

"That sounds good," said Rus, relaxing further.

"Well, it begins on an island, in my part of the world, where the sea is full of islands. And this island was ruled by a king, and this king also held dominion over many of the neighbouring islands, and a bit of the mainland as well, and every year he would exact a great tribute from the peoples that he ruled … "

CHAPTER VI

"YES! GO IN! Come on … No! Blast! Missed again."

"They don't roll straight, because of the handles."

"I know, that's what makes it a challenge. All right, this is my last shot—this one had better go in."

It did, though it was a bad throw that should have missed. Rus laughed. And the whole thing was really about making Rus laugh, so that was all right.

It was the second morning of their friendship. Rus was lying in the sun outside the back door of the temple of Soukos, on the fur rug and Adares's cloak, propped up on one elbow to watch Adares, who had improvised a game of bowls for himself with a bronze cauldron as a target and a number of round bronze censers as balls.

The censers made a satisfying clang when they went into the cauldron, but because they had small loops on either side for hanging, they had a tendency not to go where they were aimed, even across the smooth pavement of the courtyard. Sometimes the two halves would come unfastened as they rolled, and the ball would fall apart before it reached the target. Still, when Adares had thrown the last of them and went to gather them up, most of the censers were inside the cauldron.

That morning when they had awoken, they had been

nestled together again, but Rus had been turned away from Adares, toward the wall, curled slightly in on himself.

"You're a good shot," Rus admitted, as Adares dumped the armload of censers next to him and sat down to repair the ones that had fallen apart. "Not as good as me, but … "

"Talk is cheap—but I'm not going to let you overtax your leg proving yourself a liar."

Rus snorted. "But you are a good shot. Do you hunt?"

"Not if I can help it. I grew up hunting rabbits and wild geese with a bow on my family's country estate with my cousins, and that was fun. But the hunting around here—boar, and deer, and worse—it's too rich for my blood. I am always getting invited out by these hot-blooded Getti lords who make a whole day's business of it, sunrise to sunset, charging about in the rain half the time—and one has to accept, at least now and then, to be polite."

Rus chuckled. "At least they haven't asked you to play fingin with them—I think that is what they call their ball game. Or have they? I don't think they would let a foreigner join—they take it very seriously."

Adares picked up one of the censers and bowled it across the pavement towards the cauldron. It went in with a resounding clang.

"No, they haven't asked me to join. I've been a spectator, and it looked … I mean, I like ball games, at least the kind we play in Pheme. But I honestly couldn't tell what was going on with that game. And whatever it was, it went *on* and *on*. I'd have preferred listening to one of their epics—which is saying something. The Luth don't play that, do they?"

"We have a version of it. Hargan. It's rougher than the Getti version—and it takes longer to play."

Adares gave him a sceptical look. "I'm not sure how that's

possible. There are only so many hours in the day. Do you play?"

"Of course."

"Well, you'll have to explain the rules to me some time. I'll try to stay awake." Adares bowled another censer and missed this time.

Later, he climbed to the gallery of the temple of Anaxe again, to check the progress of the siege. The Luth siege-carts had been moved around the walls to the far side, to attack the main gate, but the rest of their camp looked quiet, as if they were resting between assaults or while refining their strategy, or just taking their time.

Inside the temple complex, the food situation was close to becoming desperate. Adares made another, thorough search of the outbuildings, by daylight now, and managed to break into a door that had previously resisted him, but there was no food on the other side of it. He and Rus had stayed up most of the previous night, telling each other stories, and Rus had got hungry at one point, so Adares had fetched more biscuits for him; and then Rus had been reluctant to eat if Adares was not going to eat too, and since he had not, in perfect honesty, been able claim he was not hungry, he had eaten a biscuit himself. Now there were only four broken pieces of biscuit left, and a half a dozen figs to go with them. And the sun was high in the sky, and Adares was feeling hollow with hunger.

He mentioned none of this to Rus when he returned to the storeroom, where Rus was lying down again. He did not bring the whole jar of biscuits over to the bed, to avoid letting Rus see that it was almost empty. It was amazing, when he stopped to think about it, how protective he felt of this young man, who could no doubt take care of himself very well under normal circumstances.

"I have been thinking, Adares," Rus said, looking down

over the side of the bed at Adares, who was sitting on the floor to eat. "These walls to the harbour that are not finished—you said that they were started a few months ago. So it must have been Phyleros, this archon who is too young, who gave the order to build them."

"Yes."

"That is not so bad."

"No! No, but it's not spectacularly clever—anyone could have thought of it."

"Ah. Anyone."

"Yes, I know. That's easy to say."

"It is," said Rus, but he let the subject drop.

In the afternoon, when Rus had slept again for a while, he was restless and began asking questions about Phemian temples. Adares had discovered that morning that it was possible for him to carry Rus a short distance, without any harm coming to either of them. They relocated, for a change of scene, to the small, dim sanctuary of the temple of Soukos.

Rus, for all he had declared temples to be less sensible than sacred hills, seemed impressed with the place. He was also extremely respectful, and would not sit with his back to the altar or speak above an undertone. He made a joke of worrying that Adares was going to behave impiously; but there was something in it, besides teasing. Adares did not swear much, but by now he was pretty sure that Rus did not swear at all, even in his native language. He had been restrainedly scandalized by Adares's use of the censers that morning, though he had got over it eventually.

"Is it true," Rus asked, looking up at the frieze of painted carving around the top of the sanctuary walls, "that your people believe you can make the spirits of the dead speak by offering them a big dish of blood?"

"Well … no. I wouldn't say it's something people believe,

as such. It is said to have worked for some ancient heroes—
it's in a couple of famous poems, as I'm sure you know. But
it's not something actual, sensible people would really *try*.
Philosophers would say that sort of thing was made up by
the poets—or, if it does represent something real, it was so
badly garbled by the poets that it doesn't bear much resem-
blance to the truth any more. Philosophers are often rather
hard on the poets." After a moment, he asked, "Is it true that
your people put important questions to the judgement of the
gods by making a man fight against a bull?"

Rus laughed softly. "Ah yes, we do. Look."

He hooked his thumb under the gold torque around his
neck, to lift it off his collarbone a little. Underneath, three
matching blue designs curved around the base of his throat,
as if forming part of an unfinished torque of ink.

"I told you that all the tattoos were done at the same time.
It is not quite true. These ones are newer. One for each bull."

Adares hastily bit back an oath. "Not—really? You fight
them, as well as riding them?"

Rus nodded. "It wasn't always the custom. In the old days,
they used to choose an ordinary man—a sakar, of course, a
serf or a hearth-guard—give him a horse and a weapon, and
set him against the bull. If he won, the gods were with us—if
he lost, they were against us."

Adares whistled. "That sounds … well, brutal. Like human
sacrifice, almost."

"Something like that. They didn't do it often. But it was
fair, in a way, when they did do it. The odds were even—the
man was smarter, the bull was stronger, neither was trained in
the best ways to kill the other—the outcome was in the hands
of the gods. Now, the ceremonies happen all the time, and the
men who do the killing are like me—trained bull-fighters. We
rarely lose—we know all the tricks, and they don't let us fight

in a real ceremony until we are well practiced. So the odds aren't even any more, and the fights don't prove anything. It's not that the gods are always with us these days—it's that we're not really asking for their allegiance any more."

"Don't your priests realize this?"

Rus's eyebrows went up. "We do—it's the skar and the headmen who don't. Or they don't care. The kahar began reading the Kosoth philosophy generations back, and said the bull ceremonies should stop, that they made us uncivilized, but the skar like them. Using the bull-riders in the ceremonies was … a compromise."

"So you've killed three bulls."

"Three for the ceremony—for divination. But we go out and take bulls down in the hunt, when they are with the herd and are not possessed by Genhath. It is good practice—and of course you get the meat. So I have killed many more than three. We are responsible for capturing them, too, for the ceremonies."

"I see. So when I said hunting boar was too much excitement for me … "

"They are a bit smaller, aren't they? But I hear that they are fierce."

"Oh, very fierce, yes."

"Rabbits, now … "

"Less so. But geese … "

They sat a while longer in the sanctuary. Adares explained the subjects of the decorations, since Rus wanted to know about them. In exchange he got several interesting stories about the Luth horse god, Gurhat—that is, *the* horse god, whom the Luth called Gurhat—lengthily augmented with commentary.

At sunset, they went out to sit on the steps of the temple and look at the sky, where streaks of cloud stood out dark against brilliant orange and purple. Rus was wrapped in Adares's military cloak again; Adares had brought one of the blankets from the bed. They did not talk.

When the sky was dark, they went into the temple baths, which were on the other side of the door that Adares had broken down earlier, and they bathed by lamplight, with considerable silliness. Rus had apparently never seen a grown man entirely without tattoos, and said he found the sight unnatural, which Adares said he found insulting. He wasn't insulted. He thought Rus wanted an excuse to look at him, and Adares couldn't see why he shouldn't.

Dried and dressed, they returned to their room, where they sat on the floor and drank water, pretending it was unmixed wine. They began singing loudly. Rus taught Adares a Luth song with a very peculiar tune, full of sounds that Adares could not properly pronounce and untranslatably subtle synonyms for "honour." Adares tried to teach Rus a pornographic hymn to the embarrassing Boukossian god Psobos, but Rus refused to sing it. Adares sang him another, much nicer hymn to Anaxe, and when he looked at Rus after he had finished, the lamplight showed what might have been a sparkle of tears in his eyes.

He put Rus to bed soon after that, and then he went outside for a while to look at the stars before coming back to join him.

He woke, some time later, because Rus had moved fretfully in his sleep. Adares turned on his side to look at him. In the moonlight, his face looked flushed, and not from embarrassment this time. Adares put out a hand and felt Rus's forehead. He was feverish.

Adares sat up on the bed and rubbed sleep out of his eyes and tried to think rationally. At this point, it could not be the atropa poisoning. Could it? Fever was common after a wound—but of course it wasn't a good sign. When he had changed Rus's bandages that evening, he hadn't noticed anything off. He wondered what medicines the Luth might have to treat fever. For that matter, there might be something in a jar in the priests' pharmacy that would help, but he wouldn't know what he was looking for. He got up from the bed and spread all the blankets gently over Rus. He went out to get some fresh water from the fountain and wet a cloth to lay on Rus's forehead.

Rus woke and pushed the cloth away as he twisted restlessly on the pillow. He muttered something in his native language. He seemed to be aware that Adares was there, but he had forgotten who Adares was, or that he did not understand the Luth tongue. Adares felt frantically, monstrously alone in the dark temple complex.

The night went on and on. Adares fell briefly asleep, kneeling by the bed, and woke to find his knees cramped on the cold stone, and Rus not improved. He got to his feet, gave Rus some more water to drink, and wet his face. When Rus seemed to have fallen back into a fitful sleep, Adares found his cloak, pulled on his boots, and went out into the moonlit courtyard.

He had not been inside the temple of Anaxe yet, and now he did not know what he would have done if he had found the big gilded doors locked. He might have sat down on the steps and wept. But the handle turned under his hand, and the door creaked inwards.

The interior of the temple was dimly silver with moonlight from the high, narrow windows down its sides. Adares followed the brighter wedge of light cast on the floor through the open doorway down the outer hall and up the steps into the inner sanctuary. Behind the screen at the top of the second flight of steps, he could just glimpse the tall gold and ivory-clad figure of the goddess. He knelt on the lowest step, made an awkward, unpracticed prostration, and sat back on his heels.

"Divine Anaxe," he said aloud, "I know that you understand friendship."

His voice echoed in the empty sanctuary. He looked up at the shadow-masked face of the statue, barely visible beyond the screen.

"You had a friend in the mortal Aradne, and you took her into the Heights with you and made her immortal," he said, following the formula of invoking the deity's history before presenting his petition. "I don't ask for that much. I only ask that he may live out a full life on earth. Think of how you love your friend and pity me, and let him live."

There was something a little, well, *off* about petitioning the chaste goddess with an invocation of her earthly friendship, given the way he knew he had started to feel about Rus. But he forged ahead. Friendship was—undeniably—what they had, and it felt miraculous, and he was grateful for it.

"I thank you for granting him to me, divine Anaxe. I never looked to have a friend like this—I didn't know what my life was lacking. And I'm not a fool, divine Anaxe—I know that he will have to go back to his people, as I will go back to mine, and we may never meet again after we leave here—and he will probably forget me. But please, holy goddess, let him go back, not to the funeral pyre, not with the men of his kin that I killed, but alive—please, even if it means he must ride against my people again in another battle."

Even if it means I lose my city and go back to Pheme and start over. He did not say that out loud, but he was startled to find it in his mind. And, because there was more in his mind than that, he forced himself to go on.

"I do … I do want him—I'd be lying if I said I didn't, and

I can't lie to you. He's so different, so vital and captivating and ... *lovely*. I do want to touch him, I want to know what it would be like to kiss him, to be the first man who's ever ... I mean, how could I not want that? But what we have now ... it's good. It's more than good." He cleared his throat.

"According to the custom, this is something of his, which I give you as an offering." He laid the heavy gold object on the step above him. "I am sure you know him already—he is your servant, and the servant of your divine brothers and sisters. If not for my sake, maybe you will protect him for his own—he worships you, I am sure, with more reverence than I ever have. He calls you something different—I don't know what it is, it probably has a sort of phlegmy 'h' in it somewhere ... "

He stopped. He found himself—as if the impulse had been thrust into him like a sword's point—suddenly about to laugh. He looked up at the goddess's half-hidden face again with surprise.

"Thank you, my lady," he whispered.

He went back to the storeroom behind the temple of Soukos. He would check on Rus, see that he was comfortable, then go and see what he could find in the pharmacy. He felt calmer now; the panic of earlier had ebbed, as if the hand of the goddess had smoothed it away.

Rus woke at the sound of the door closing, and as Adares approached the bed, he asked something, softly and hoarsely, in the Luth language.

"What can I do for you, Rus?" Adares whispered, leaning over him. He did not expect an answer that he could understand.

Rus blinked up at him for a moment. "Like last night," he said finally, evidently finishing a sentence. "Have I been speaking the wrong language?"

Adares almost laughed with relief. "Yeah, but it's my fault—I didn't try to get you to switch. Do you want more water? Then I'll go see whether the pharmacy has anything to help your fever."

Rus shook his head impatiently. "You have to let a fever run its course—even I know that. Get in with me again. Like last night."

"Oh. Of course. Just—just let me put the water by the bed first, so I can reach it if you want any."

Having done that, he lay down beside Rus and reached over to stroke his back, like the night before. Rus fell asleep almost immediately.

CHAPTER VII

ADARES WOKE TO a soft, grey light and a soothing, familiar noise. He turned to see Rus lying awake beside him. In the light, he looked very pale. His eyes met Adares's.

"It's raining," Rus said. He smiled.

"You're feeling better."

"Much better. Thank you, my friend. You have been very kind."

Without thinking, Adares leaned over and put his lips briefly to Rus's forehead. Rus looked startled, but said nothing.

They went out into the rain and washed at the fountain. Rus reluctantly washed his hair with soap, grumbling about how it would be dry and tangled as a result, and Adares laughed at him. The rain stopped and the sun came out, weakly. They went inside to dress, and Rus looked for the pin to fasten his kilt.

"Did it fall down behind the bed?" he asked, trying to peer between the mattress and the wall.

"Actually, I know where that pin is."

"Ah, do you?" Rus looked up at him from where he was draped across the bed, his kilt half-wrapped and not fastened.

"It's on the upper steps in the temple of Anaxe. I gave it as an offering for your recovery, last night when you were feverish. It's a custom, when you pray for someone's health, to offer something of theirs."

"And you offered my kilt pin? To Kahait?"

It did have an "h" in it. And Adares was surprised to see that Rus was turning rather pink about the whole thing. He sat up and gathered up the loose fabric of his kilt.

"We don't usually bother Anaxe in cases of sickness," Adares went on quickly, pretending not to notice Rus's embarrassment. "We pray to her servant, Petteia, usually. But Petteia has no temple here. I was worried about you. I had to do something. The pin was the only thing of yours that I could think to offer—I didn't know how to get that torque thing off, without half choking you."

"Yes." Rus smiled, though he was still blushing steadily. "It's just … I guess it's a good omen. With my people, the pin that you do up your kilt with … it's the sort of thing that might be given sometimes as a love token. And so, when a young man wants to go courting, he will give an offering of his kilt-pin—so that the goddess will give him success."

"Oh. What do you suppose it means, when someone else makes the offering?"

"I don't know. I can't think that it ever happens, ordinarily."

"No, I suppose not. Well … as you say. It is probably a good omen."

Rus cleared his throat. "Usually it is not Kahait that they offer to, of course—she is too stern."

"Well, that and chaste. At least, Anaxe is, in our tradition."

"Kahait has a faithless husband. I always forget that your Anaxe is chaste."

"It's weird, if they're the same goddess."

Rus waved a hand. "It is religion—it doesn't have to make sense like that."

"Riiight. Do you know the story of Anaxe's mortal friend, Aradne?"

"No. Tell me."

Adares sat down on the bed, leaning against the wall. "Well, she was a weaver."

"*Was*? She died? Anaxe let her mortal friend die?"

"No, no. Stand down—let me tell the story. Aradne was a weaver, while she lived on earth, and Anaxe came to her house, at the time when she was fleeing from her brother Nepharos, who had gone mad and was chasing her through the realms of gods and men. Aradne helped her, turned Nepharos's men away from the door, without knowing who Anaxe was—just because she felt sorry for her. They became friends.

"Over the years, Anaxe would come down to earth to visit Aradne, and Aradne grew older, and married a good man, with Anaxe's blessing, and bore many children—and her friend never changed, as the years passed. No one needed to tell Aradne that the woman she loved so well was a goddess—that was obvious enough. But Aradne never asked any favour of Anaxe. She always welcomed her into her home just as if she had been an ordinary woman, and their friendship endured, until Aradne was an old woman and her husband an old man, and their children were all grown men and women themselves.

"Then when Anaxe saw that her friend could not live much longer on the earth, she took her up into the Heights with her, and made her an immortal by her side. Some people say that she did the same for Aradne's husband and her children, too—because divine Anaxe is not one to be jealous of the other loves of the one she holds dear."

Rus was silent for a while. Finally he said, "They are the same, the gods, but we know them imperfectly. It may be that Kahait, when she was Anaxe, was chaste, but it was because she did not yet know how to love. And then she met this friend, and she learned what it is to love another, and after that she became Kahait, and she wanted a husband. Because this had been awakened in her. But then she married Denhath, and he broke her heart with his unfaithfulness."

"Do you think so?"

"I don't know. It may be. You tell that story well, and I am glad to have heard it. Ah, and I am glad you chose my kilt pin and not my necklace—but if the goddess wanted that, it does come off. You have to twist it." He demonstrated how the ends could be forced apart with the right motion, because the solid-looking band of the torque was actually made of tightly twisted gold wires.

"I've always wondered about that," Adares admitted. "All the Karhan tribes wear those, and no one ever explained to me how they get them on."

"I don't usually take it off. It is from my family. A coming-of-age gift. This is their … what do you call it? Their symbol." He fingered the stylized eagle's heads at the ends of the torque.

"This is mine," said Adares, holding up his left hand and pointing to his signet ring. He slid it off his finger. "It comes off like that." Rus swatted him.

They ate the last two oat biscuits and both agreed that they were still hungry.

"I could go out and catch us something, if I had a bow," said Adares. "But I don't. I doubt your spear would be much use against rabbits—and I don't think I can hunt down a deer on my own. Still—I suppose I had better try something."

Rus lay with his hands clasped behind his head, his wet hair spread out on the pillow to dry. "You know, there are other things in the woods besides animals."

"Berries and mushrooms, you mean?" Adares shook his

head. "No good. Some of them are poisonous—and I don't know which."

"Yes, but I do. There's not a lot ripe this late in the year, but I can tell you where to look."

So Adares set out into the woods, armed with an empty jar and an elaborate description of which elements of the local flora and fungus were edible. Rus had even drawn him a sketch, scratched on the whitewashed wall of the storeroom, of one particularly poisonous mushroom, which he said it was better not even to touch.

Adares had never walked in the woods around Tios before, only ridden through them, and he was slightly apprehensive about getting lost. Fortunately, since the woods behind the temple complex were sparse and open, and sloped uphill, it was not too difficult to keep the honey-coloured walls in view.

He ranged further afield than he had at first thought would be safe, seeking out the scattered bushes and clumps of mushrooms. Except for a few birds chirping, and the sound of water dripping from the branches, it was quiet among the trees. All the undergrowth was wet from the rain, and after crawling and wading through it in search of the berries and mushrooms and edible plants that Rus had described, he was soaked to the skin, but the weather was still warm enough that this was not unpleasant.

Getting to his feet after stripping a low-lying bush of its fruit, Adares realized that he had climbed almost all the way to the crest of the hill behind the temple. A short distance ahead, a bare, grassy ridge surmounted the hill. His jar was nearly full by this time, but he forged on a little further through the trees, for the sake of the view from the hilltop. One was always repaid, he found, for the effort of climbing to the top of a hill in Kargania.

Emerging on the bare ridge, he stood holding the jar

against his chest, looking out over miles of green, sunlit valley, with the shadows of clouds moving across the rough carpet of treetops. And far in the distance, in a deep trough between the slopes of two forested hills, the flicker of yellow banners in the air, and a dark shape of massed men beneath them.

They were not marching, but were making camp between the hills; Adares could see tents bulking here and there among the troops. And the yellow banners told him who their owners were. It was the Daine, allies of Tios since the previous summer.

He walked back to the complex, deep in thought. On the way, he encountered a kind of rough track, apparently beaten down by someone or something ploughing violently through the undergrowth. It led in the general direction of the temple walls, so he followed it, and emerged at the back of the complex.

Afterwards, he was never quite sure what caused him to go warily as he rounded the corner at the front of the complex and entered the temple gate. Perhaps he had heard some noise, or caught some new whiff in the air, without fully comprehending it. Certainly, when he looked round the gate which he had cautiously pushed open and saw the horses, he was not aware of having expected them.

There were twenty or more of them, some shaggy, broad-backed Luth horses, others sleek, thin-legged Phemian animals. They were clustered around several bales of hay, eating placidly.

From where he stood frozen, pressed back against the front of the gate, Adares could see that the stable door to the right of the entrance had been left open. But there had been no horses inside; he had been in there already and found it empty. Whoever had brought these horses had evidently dragged out the hay to feed them, rather than putting the horses themselves into the stable. It didn't surprise him. He could imagine what Rus would have to say about stables. Putting animals in a building? It was something only a Phemian would think of.

If the men who brought the horses had left already, Adares thought, Rus was probably gone with them. If they were still here, they might come out at any moment, headed for the gate. That they would take Rus back to the Luth camp seemed a certainty. By his own account he was an elite member of the invading force, and his superiors would be pleased to find him alive after all. They would want to see to his injury properly, give him food and drink, and make sure he recovered. But what would the men think who found him here, hiding in a Phemian temple, dressed in Phemian clothes? Would they think him a deserter? *Was* he a deserter, by this time, according to their standards?

Adares slipped inside the courtyard and shut the gate carefully behind him. Skirting the walls and treading quietly, he crept around behind the priests' house, which brought him to the courtyard onto which the back door of the temple of Soukos opened.

The men who had brought the horses had not left; he could hear several voices, talking over one another in the language of the Luth. He crouched in the shelter of the priests' colonnaded porch, leaving his jar of gathered food behind, and crawled in the shadows until he could see across the courtyard, past the fountain to the storeroom door.

There were three of them, all about his own age, with chequered kilts, coils of blue around their calves and forearms, and gold around their throats. They wore their fair hair long, like Rus, but they had pulled it all up onto the tops of their heads and tied it with leather thongs so that it streamed down behind like horses' tails. It was evidently a fashion, because all three of them had affected it, and from the look of them, they were all young men of fashion.

In other circumstances, Adares would have found it funny how easy it was to get the measure of them. They all had the same stance, legs wide apart, hands either planted boldly on their hips or toying negligently with some flashy piece of equipment. They wore linen shirts with long sleeves, but all three had rolled the sleeves up to show off the tattoos on their arms. They carried spears like fashion accessories. If they had been Phemians, one of them would have had his arm around one of the others; but they were Luth, so of course they didn't.

Rus stood in the doorway of the storeroom, arms folded, listening detachedly to the three newcomers argue. He stood up very straight, which must have cost him a great effort. He had found something to fasten his kilt with, and he had put on his boots and tied back his hair.

Looking at him now, Adares finally understood what was so self-evident to Rus that he kept forgetting Adares didn't know it. He was *obviously* set apart from the other young Luth men, though their clothes and hair and colouring were all similar. His tattoos were completely different, unmistakably marking him out as something other than them, and his demeanour as he stood listening to them said the rest. He was a priest. It was a strange, barbarian priesthood involving wild bulls, but as Rus had said himself, the gods were the same; their servants partook of the same holiness. He was younger than the three warriors, injured and ill and in an awkward situation, but there was a serene superiority about him, a poise that was probably not even a conscious thing. It was part of his being. He was what he was.

Eventually Rus spoke, interrupting the discussion. He

gestured to the temple courtyard, then back into the room behind him. Adares found it strange to hear him speak and have no idea what he was saying. The young men of fashion argued with each other for a few minutes more, then tossed some final remarks in Rus's direction, shouldered their spears, and strode briskly out of the courtyard, heading for the temple gate. Rus remained where he was.

The sounds of the Luth voices receded, until the faint thump of the gate being shut testified that at least one of them had left the temple complex. Rus put out a hand to steady himself against the doorpost and let himself down carefully onto the stones. Sitting there, he sagged against the doorpost and covered his face in his hands.

Adares retrieved his jar from the porch and came cautiously across the courtyard to the doorway. His shadow fell over Rus, who started and looked up.

"You're back," he said. He looked relieved—almost to the point of tears. It was startling. "You're all right."

"Sure," said Adares. He knelt and set down the jar. "I didn't touch any of those white mushrooms. But *you're* not all right—you've been out of bed and walking around, you're not well enough for that."

Rus shook his head dismissively. "There were some idiots from my tribe here."

"Yes, I saw them talking to you. I was hiding behind the colonnade over there—I saw the horses when I came in."

"Ah, you are clever." Rus smiled. "I heard them come in—they were getting something for their horses to eat. I had to get up, to hide your clothes and your armour. I knew they would come poking around. And then I thought I had better not let them know I was hurt—they might want to know who had been looking after me, and they would certainly want to take me back to the camp."

"I expected that they would. I didn't expect you to stop them. They could look after you a lot better there than I can here—they would have drugs, they would have *food*. Divine Anaxe! I've got good intentions, but that's about it." He stopped, because Rus had seized his hand abruptly. He gripped it tightly, and his own hand was shaking. "I'm sorry. I would be lying if I said I wasn't happy you're still here, Rus. It just doesn't seem like the best thing, for your own sake."

"Adares. There is a mad bull in the forest, very near here. It got away from the camp—the men who just left told me. It should have been slaughtered after the battle, but Gunthanaruth ordered the remaining bulls kept, and one of them got away. Don't talk nonsense about what is the best thing for me. If I didn't stay here to tell you, you might have gone out into the forest again by yourself. I did not even know if you would come back this time."

Adares held out his other hand, and Rus took it. Neither of them said anything for a minute. Adares was thinking about the trampled path that he had followed back through the forest, and deciding not to mention it to Rus. He felt rather weak himself at the thought.

By and by Rus said, "They think it was mine—the bull I rode—because it was the fiercest and maddest of the ones we had. They are just beasts, but when the spirit of Genhath has hold of them … Truly, I think that bull would have tried to kill you if it had met you, just to spite me." It sounded to Adares as if he was trying to joke, but couldn't manage it.

"Well, he didn't. I'm here. And so are you, and I'm glad."

Rus looked up at Adares for a moment, a flicker of blue eyes. Then he shifted his hold on Adares's hand, cupping it in his, and drew it up to press his lips to Adares's palm. It was slow and deliberate, as if he had given every aspect of the action careful thought, almost as if it were part of a ritual.

It took Adares completely by surprise. He felt the kiss lance along his nerves like a lightning strike.

Without thinking, he was reaching for Rus, caressing his face, fingers brushing over the lines of blue. He was kneeling over Rus, holding him, one hand in Rus's hair, the other pressed against Rus's bare back.

Rus was rigid in his arms, hands fisted in Adares's tunic. The kiss Adares offered was gentle, tender in a way that surprised even him. It was received like rain falling on parched earth. Whatever else Rus was, he was not reluctant. His mouth opened with a gasp that was not surprise but was more than eagerness, almost desperation.

The kiss turned awkward, unsteady, like a chariot with a loose wheel, but neither of them broke it. And then, as he had done in the night when Adares stroked his back to comfort him, slowly, with an obvious effort, Rus let himself relax. His arms twined around Adares, his long fingers pressing into the small of Adares's back. His mouth softened, responding. The tension in his body no longer felt like resistance—it felt like strength.

He was stronger than Adares, strong enough to have restrained him if he wanted to, but he let go at the first sign of Adares pulling away. He pushed himself back against the doorpost—probably would have moved back further if the doorpost hadn't been there—eyes wide, covering his mouth with the back of his hand. Adares realized he was doing the same thing.

Incredibly—and to Adares's shame—Rus was the first to speak.

"I am sorry," he said. His voice was hoarse. "I know you didn't want it to be that way between us."

"I?" Adares cleared his throat. "Of course I wanted it. I'm always up for anything, especially with someone I like. But

I should never have lost control like that. It was appalling. What you said before, about being set apart—that it's written in your skin, and you would make yourself a lie—I couldn't ever want you to do that, even if—even for—I mean, I care for you too much, I … " This was all both too little and too much. "I'm sorry. I shouldn't have kissed you, and I'm sorry."

Rus leaned back against the doorpost, head thrown back, eyes half-shut, as if all the strength had gone out of him suddenly.

"Adares … what I am set apart from is marriage and getting children. From continuing my line—from the honour of having sons. But I was set apart from all of that by my own nature. And I am not set apart from you. I think my seed would be safe with you."

That—oddly—struck Adares as maybe the sexiest thing anyone had ever said to him. It was a moment before he could work through the implications of what Rus had said.

"Immortal gods! You barbarians! Did they honestly only think to forbid you to have sex with women—and leave you free to do what you like with men?" He started forward, his hand reaching for Rus's thigh, sliding up under his kilt.

"No." Rus pushed the hand away decisively. "No, that is not what it is. I am not *free*—I am an offence against the Great Pattern of the world. But I have always been that, I will always be that, no matter what I do."

"You're—" He stopped himself. It would be flippant and meaningless to protest. He knew nothing about it; he'd never heard of the "Great Pattern" before Rus mentioned it, and certainly didn't believe in it.

Rus smiled rather sadly. "You want to say I'm not. I know. Sometimes I agree with you. Sometimes I know—I seem to know—that Heva is more complicated than we can see, and that I could be, must be, part of it. Sometimes I think it is blasphemy to imagine that I could break the pattern danced by the gods, just by wanting what men in Kos and Pheme have all the time. And then this." He gestured, indicating Adares, the doorway where they sat, the courtyard, the temple complex. "We are here together. The gods brought us to this place together—they have sheltered us in their own house. How could they bless us any better than that?"

"Yeah … " Adares couldn't deny that there was something fascinating, even beautiful, in all this, in hearing the subtleties that occupied Rus's mind. But it left him not knowing where he stood. "So what does all this amount to? Do you or don't you?"

Rus looked away into the room. "They left me some food, since I said I was staying here. Bread, smoked meat, and dried apples. Can we eat? I am hungry."

CHAPTER VIII

ADARES MADE A vague movement, unsure whether he should pick Rus up or take his hand, pretty sure neither would be quite welcome. Rus took the decision away from him by gathering his feet under himself, putting a hand on Adares's shoulder, and pushing himself up to standing. Adares was left to scramble to his own feet.

"How did you get those men to leave you here, anyway?" Adares asked. "I meant to ask that before we—got distracted."

Rus stood, holding onto the doorpost. "I lied. I told them I had been sent to scout the area after the battle—they had been sent to do the same thing, but of course they think my orders came from the stathan, and theirs came from their hearth headman, and so they had to argue, for form's sake, which order should take precedence. I was patient with this only because I was lying—if I really had orders from my stathan, *of course* they would take precedence over the orders of some hearth headman from the eastern plains."

The way he told this story made it clear that he was not in the habit of lying and did not do it lightly. That was only what Adares would have expected.

"But I could not tell them to leave," Rus said, "or to pen the horses somewhere else, and so unfortunately they will be back. They may bring others. We cannot stay much longer."

"Of course. We were living on borrowed time here any-way." His thoughts turned again to the yellow banners he had seen from the hilltop. "I saw something in the forest … "

Rus had turned toward the bed, pushing himself away from the doorpost, and Adares noticed what it was that he had used to fasten his kilt.

"Hey—that's mine."

Rus shot him an overtly flirtatious look over his shoulder. "Is it? I think it's mine now."

It was the pin from Adares's military cloak. It was the badge of his rank, though presumably that meant as little to Rus, or to the Luth warriors who might have seen him wearing it, as the Luth tattoos had meant to Adares. They would have thought Rus took it from a fallen enemy, anyway, and the news that Adares had fallen in the battle would have circulated by now, so that wouldn't tell anyone anything they didn't already know.

But wearing a man's rank badge pinned on your civilian clothes—it was inappropriate, of course, but it was the sort of thing a very bold and open, don't-care-who-knows mis-tress or lover might have done. Of course Rus didn't know that. Did he?

Rus crossed to the bed, limping but not badly, and sat. "You saw something?" he prompted.

Adares shook himself slightly. "Yes. Right. The Daine are camped in a valley a few hours' march from here."

"Ah. Then the help you gave them last summer paid off. They are coming to return the favour."

"And to meet their old enemy, the Luth. They looked like a substantial force."

Rus nodded. "They have been getting strong. We have known this. Some of the hearth headmen were saying the Daine would attack if we threatened Tios."

"Then Gunthanaruth will be expecting it, you think?"

"Yes. He thinks that he has enough men to beat the Daine off and still hold Tios. Some of the hearth headmen don't agree."

"He may be right, all the same," said Adares thoughtfully. "The Daine have more experience defending than attacking, as I understand it. I know that they've fought off sieges of their stronghold several times before. But Hesteios used to say they were weak in a pitched battle. Gunthanaruth would know that."

"He would. He does."

"Well. Anyway. They're there, for what it's worth. I'll go wash the mushrooms."

He took his jar of gleanings and an empty dish from the storeroom and went out to the fountain.

So they would have to leave their hiding place soon—but before then? In several ways he was in uncharted territory here. He had never been with a man who was exclusively attracted to men—or at least not with one who would admit it. He found the idea strangely exciting. He'd never been with an inexperienced man, either, aside from his first forays as a boy with equally unpracticed friends. He wouldn't have called himself inexperienced, by any stretch, but he was certainly out of practice with men. He realized he really didn't know what Rus wanted, how he might want this to go. Except that so far it apparently wasn't going the way he wanted.

Adares piled the washed mushrooms in the dish and rinsed off the berries and leaves that had been underneath them in the jar and got dirty. He spent a moment arranging everything attractively. It looked very nice, like a still life.

It struck him suddenly just how his position with Rus had shifted. There had always been something holding them back before, or at least he'd thought there was, and now there was nothing—nothing except his own potential unworthiness. He knew Rus wanted him, but Rus was very used to denying himself. And he had—as he'd let Adares know—some impressive prohibitions and taboos to overcome. He was quite capable of shutting the whole thing down if he decided it wasn't worth it.

When Adares came back into the temple storeroom, Rus was reclining on his side on the bed, Pseuchaian-style. He had brought out the bundle of food left for him by the Luth warriors and unwrapped it on the bed in front of him. He was in the process of arranging it, much the way Adares had arranged the berries and mushrooms, though the effect was less artistic because what he had to work with were some strips of smoked meat, shrivelled dried apples, and a couple of charred pieces of bread.

He doesn't want frantic kissing in a doorway, Adares thought. *He wants it to be romantic.* And that, actually, was surprisingly endearing—and what was more, it put Adares back on more familiar ground. It was something he could deal with.

He considered reclining on the bed with Rus, which was perhaps what Rus had in mind—but the way the food was spread out, there wasn't really room. He sat down on the floor instead, setting the dish of forest gleanings on the bed with the other things. He tugged off his boots to sit cross-legged.

"This looks like a feast," he said, smiling up at Rus.

Rus smiled back. He pointed to the food. "This is preserved meat that we bring on campaigns. But the bread is fresh. They bake it on a pan over the fire." He coloured slightly, as if embarrassed not to have something more significant to say.

"We should save some for later," said Adares.

"I did. I set some aside."

"You think of everything."

The bread was surprisingly good: soft flat rounds made from some kind of nutty-tasting grain that the Luth did not grow themselves but traded for. Rus quite genuinely did not know any more about it than that—thought such information beneath him, both as a kahar and as the son of a great skar family—and was amused that Adares was interested in it and then adorably embarrassed by his own ignorance. Adares let his fingers brush against Rus's at every opportunity as they shared the food.

The meat was tough and strongly flavoured, but, as Rus pointed out, tasted good with the woodland mushrooms and greens and one kind of berry, which was mouth-puckeringly tart. Others were delicately sweet, and they ate them with the dried apples by way of dessert. By this time Adares had taken one of Rus's hands and was holding it, gently tracing his thumb over the inked swirl on the back. His tattoos were symmetrical for the most part, but there were little variations, one of which was an extra tendril on the back of his left hand, curling down onto his fourth finger.

"We can get milk now, if you want," Rus said. "I mean, not *now*, but later. If you wanted milk." He looked embarrassed again.

"Did those men bring a goat as well as the horses?"

"No, I meant milk from the horses. Well, one of them. They said there's a milk-mare among them."

"Horse milk. Hmm."

"I'll have some, then, and you can sit and watch and wish for a goat."

They finished the berries except for one spray of rust-coloured fruit which Adares had picked by mistake, and which Rus said was not fit to eat.

"If you did eat it, your mouth would be stained brown for a month. We use them for dye."

Adares waggled the sprig of berries gently between his fingers. "Pity. They looked so tasty." He dropped them back into the dish and took it off the bed to set it on the floor.

"Can I come up there with you?"

Rus gathered up the cloth with the crumbs of bread and dropped that onto the floor too. "Of course."

Adares moved to sit on the edge of the bed. He looked down at Rus. "Can I do the obvious thing?"

Rus had turned to lie on his back. He looked at Adares warily. "What is the obvious thing? No—don't tell me. But ... yes. Do it."

Adares put out his right hand and traced his middle finger over the convoluted spiral that covered most of Rus's belly. He brushed over the coarse fuzz of blond hair, felt Rus's abdominal muscles tighten.

"That ... that's obvious?"

"So obvious."

"Ah."

He continued to follow the pattern, slowly, delving a little under the upper edge of Rus's kilt. Rus shifted slightly on the bed, tense again, but he did not push Adares's hand away. Adares reached the end of the line he had been following and picked another one that travelled up over Rus's chest and down the hard, smooth muscles of one arm. Rus reached up with the other hand to loosen his hair. It spilled over the pillow beside him like a sheaf of wheat. Adares traced lightly over his collarbone and back down his chest to his stomach. Rus made a small, appreciative noise.

"You like that? I could do it another way, too."

"How? Show me."

Adares bent down and followed the spiral—more or less—with his tongue.

"Ah! What? No! Adares! You can't do that!"

"No?" Adares pushed himself up to look Rus in the eye, unsure whether that had been a genuine protest or not.

Rus was flushed, his hand hovering over the place where Adares's mouth had just been. "Did I say *no*? I didn't mean *no*. I just—I never imagined anyone doing such a thing, or that it would feel ... " His eyes widened eloquently.

"What did you imagine?"

"With you?"

"With anyone, but ... yeah, with me."

"Well ... you are naked, in my imagining."

"Not a problem."

Adares unfastened and discarded his belt, pulled his tunic casually off, and dropped it onto the floor. He was wearing nothing under it. His cock bobbed a little as if half-drunk. Rus reached up and pulled him down onto himself, skin to skin, haphazard and glorious.

"What do you want me to do now?" Adares asked, settling himself more comfortably.

"You can—do that obscene dog thing again, if you want."

"*Dog* thing?"

"*Licking*."

"Oh. Only if I want?"

Rus groaned under him, a noise of unmistakable desire. "Do it, Phemian."

Adares slid down his body, laughing. He tried licking a nipple, and that earned him an amazing reaction: Rus twisting away, tipping Adares over onto his side, and grappling him to himself at the same time, breathless with astonished laughter. Adares stroked him all down one side until he relaxed, and then they lay for a while wrapped in each other's arms, sharing long, exploratory kisses. Rus's hands drifted raptly up and down Adares's body, as if he was intent on learning its contours.

But now desire was building into urgency for both of them. Adares rolled Rus over onto his back without breaking the kiss, and in a few efficient motions unpinned his kilt and stripped off his loincloth. He sat back, straddling Rus's thighs, and for a moment just looked at him, exposed and aroused, eyes bright, lips swollen with kissing, the blue spiral around his dick stretched out. Next time, Adares found himself thinking, he wanted to watch that happen.

Next time. It was foolish to think about that now. This was what they had, and he owed it to Rus to make the most of it.

"You are not waiting for me to tell you again what to do?" Rus's voice was rough, the Luth half of his accent heavily to the fore. He shifted his hips a little, impatiently. The bandage around his thigh brushed against Adares's leg, reminding Adares that he'd put Rus on his back for a reason; he didn't want him putting weight on his injured leg.

"No, I've got this." He grinned.

He shifted forward, bringing their bodies together at the crucial point, and wrapped his hand around both cocks. Rus let out a shuddering gasp—he seemed to have a whole array of different, delightful reactions—and gripped Adares's thighs, jerking up against him. Then he was pulling Adares down and pushing himself up off the bed, even as they thrust against each other, so he could bring their lips together again.

It was like nothing Adares had ever done in bed before, the combination of power and sweet, untaught eagerness in the body under his so intoxicating, he lost all sense that he was directing the action; instead they were riding out a storm together, clinging to one another, their desire like a rough sea. Sweat-slick, muscles trembling with effort, they moved in a building rhythm, still kissing as their cocks rubbed and slid together. When Adares's climax overtook him, he was so lost in the glorious strangeness that was sex with Rus that for the first instant he didn't recognize it for what it was.

Then it rolled over him, familiar after all, but huge as a tidal wave, and he might have cried out—something he never did—and he clasped Rus to him, burying his face in Rus's shoulder and Rus's sweat-damp hair as the wave rolled slowly, gloriously down the beach.

He pushed himself up on one elbow as soon as his wits returned sufficiently. Rus looked up into his face with a rapt, fascinated delight.

"You, ah, you are very beautiful when you … "

"Yeah?" His hand was on Rus's still hard, hot dick. "Well, I'd like to see what you look like, but I have an even better idea."

He moved between Rus's legs and down, and this time there was no protest beyond a soft gasp, which hardly counted. He had technically never done this to a man before, but he'd had it done to him plenty of times by women, so he thought he understood the mechanics of it, and besides he was feeling charmed and invincible.

He took the thick, wet tip into his mouth, pushing down as far as he dared—the technique was more daunting than he had imagined, and he wasn't sure he was doing a good job, but from the noises Rus made, it didn't matter. The taste was a little like tears, and a little like soap—strange to think he had never tasted it before.

He cupped and stroked with his fingers, as he tried to figure out what to do with his mouth beyond alternately sucking and licking—but that may have been enough. He felt Rus's hands in his hair, trying to grasp a handful and slipping out because it was too short, and he thought he was going to hear about that later, and shook with silent laughter.

And just as it occurred to him that Rus might not know enough to warn him when he was about to come—which he always did, because some people were happy to swallow, some not—Rus was arching off the bed with a cry, and Adares was too busy trying not to choke to make any decision about anything, and only realized afterward that he had reflexively swallowed.

He rolled off onto his back and stretched, with a long, contented sigh. Emotions aside, that was some of the most satisfying sex he'd had in years. His body felt easy, warmed and loose and somehow restored. He flung out an arm carelessly onto Rus, who had turned on his side, facing away into the room. He drew his fingers lightly down Rus's flank, not bothering to follow the patterns.

"Even your ass is blue," he observed with a soft snort of laughter.

Rus made a strange sound which Adares realized after a moment was laughing through tears. Adares pushed himself up and slid up the bed again to look over Rus's shoulder. He was indeed crying, half-hiding it behind his hand.

"I'm sorry," Rus began, "I … "

"Don't worry about that. It's normal—lots of people feel a bit … overwhelmed, you know, after."

"After you?"

"No, no, that's not what I meant. Can I—say no if you want, but—can I hold you?"

"Please."

He put his arm around Rus and snuggled close to his back. Rus made a snuffling noise. "Not on the hair."

"Oh, sorry. There's just so much of it." He lifted his head and scooped Rus's hair out of the way, pushing it up onto the pillow above their heads. He brushed his lips briefly over Rus's shoulder and settled back down again, his arm tight around Rus's chest.

They lay for a little while in silence. Rus put his arm over Adares's, lacing their fingers together. He seemed no longer to be crying.

There was a small, circular tattoo on the back of his neck, just above the torque, where it would have been hidden most of the time by his hair.

"This one looks different from the rest," Adares remarked, kissing it. "What's it mean?"

"Ah. That's the sigil of the vahat, the … the artist who did my tattoos."

"What, like a painter's mark on a vase? That's … " *Odd*, he was going to say, but changed his mind. "I guess that makes sense, that he'd sign his work. He's obviously very good."

"She."

"A woman did your tattoos?"

"Of course. It is woman's work. Most women do it only for their own men, or you may have one in the hearth who is very good, so she does them for everyone. The vahat who does our tattoos is a specialist, she is highly respected, and she helps with the patterns for the kahar hall, and other things. Genet, the vahat now, she *is* very good, even though she is young—your age. I like her. We are friends."

"Ha. Every time I think you don't have any more barbarian stuff to surprise me with … somehow, I'm wrong."

That made Rus laugh. Adares squeezed him tighter. He didn't ask if Rus felt better; it had occurred to him that Rus's tears might not have been simply post-coital melancholy but something more complicated and more real, having to do with being an offence against the great pattern of whatever, and maybe never having the opportunity to have sex with a man again.

They would have to leave the temple complex tomorrow, at the latest. There was so little time left—and they had wasted so much of the time they'd had, it seemed, misunderstanding each other. Adares felt he was to blame for that. If he'd known more about Luth customs, as he should have, he would have understood from the beginning what Rus was, what he was permitted and forbidden.

Rus rolled over onto his back and tucked his arm around Adares, resting his hand lightly on Adares's shoulder. As if his own thoughts had been following the same track, but somehow arrived at a different place, he said, "I am glad we did not understand one another fully in the beginning, Adares. I cannot think that what we just did would have been as good if we had not come to know each other first."

"No, probably not. That's been my experience, certainly."

"*Has* it."

"Yeah, well … uh, we're a bit sticky—do you mind if I get up and get a cloth? And maybe a drink."

Rus leaned in and kissed him deeply, then made a face. "Pthh. Do get a drink."

CHAPTER IX

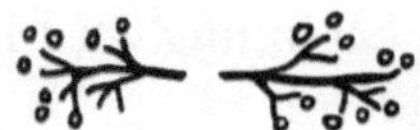

THE REST OF that day felt dreamlike. Adares said as much, as they lay together on the bed later that afternoon. Their bodies were touching all down one side, as on that first morning when they had woken together, only now deliberately, both of them openly enjoying it.

"A good dream?" Rus asked, clarifying, a little shyly.

Adares nuzzled into the curve of his shoulder. "A very good dream."

They had not spent the whole day in bed. They had explored the other buildings a little now that Rus was back on his feet in a limited way. They had gone to look at the horses, and Adares was strangely charmed to see that of course Rus had a way with horses—probably all horse-herding people did, but he hadn't thought about it. Adares had tried horse milk for the first time, and it was entirely pleasant. He had found a way to climb over the wall into the priests' garden, where the only things left in the ground were onions, and pulled up a couple.

They had played Adares's game of censer bowling, and Rus was indeed better at it than Adares, though it was a close match. They had gone into the temple of Anaxe together. They'd had an argument—a discussion, Rus called it—about whether the word "virgin" could logically be applied to a man. They had done all the same sorts of things that they had done on their first days in the temple complex, with the same easy companionship, but with something added. It was nothing much, just the touch of a hand now and then (Adares's hand, usually), a look that turned into a smile, a new honesty that had opened up between them.

Now it was late afternoon, and they lay in a pool of warm light slanting in from the open doorway.

"I thought," Rus said, "when you first saw this bed, the way you pointed at it and said, 'Look, a bed!' I thought, ah, he is a Phemian, and he wants to go to bed with me—I know what that means. I was not unhappy about that. I had already begun to like you, and of course you are … you are … " He waved a hand toward Adares, blushing.

"I'm not ugly," Adares supplied easily. "I'm aware of that."

"I—I felt sure that you were. So we sat on the floor over there and ate and talked, and I thought, we will go to bed together, and for him it will be like going to bed with a woman, because he is a Phemian. And he doesn't know that it should not be that way for me—and I won't tell him. I don't know quite what I thought would happen, since we were both very tired. Then you spoke of sleeping on the floor, and I did not know what to think again."

"And I didn't know what to think when you said there was room in the bed and I should join you after all."

"It is a great chasm that we bridged, each of us from his own side, to arrive here, isn't it?" Rus said that with a kind of mock seriousness, and Adares laughed, but it was profoundly true for all that.

Adares had been fiddling with the sprig of inedible berries as they talked, but now Rus took it away from him and rolled over to lean on his elbows. The dish that had held the rest of the berries and the mushrooms still lay on the floor, and he reached over to pick it up. He dropped the sprig into it, found the piece of broken tile that he had used to sketch the poisonous mushroom on the wall that morning, and began crushing the berries, which burst in puddles of dark brown juice.

"What are you doing that for?" Adares demanded, lying propped on one elbow, watching him.

"You'll see. Do you think there is anything here to write with?"

"I saw a dusty old tablet and stylus on the shelf with the jars. Do you want them?"

"Just the stylus."

Adares climbed over him to fetch it and climbed back to his previous spot when he returned. As he settled down, Rus dipped the nib of the stylus into the dark brown juice in the bowl.

"Give me your hand," he said with a little smile. "No, not that one—your right hand." He drew the one he wanted towards him across the pillow.

"Rus … what are you doing?"

"It's not sharp—see? It won't hurt, and it won't last, either. But this is dark enough to show up on your Phemian skin. You'll be decorated, for a little while at least."

"All right," said Adares. "If it will make you happy."

The design took some time to complete because Rus drew it meticulously, in tiny, precise dots, like his own tattoos. Unlike his tattoos, the design he drew on the back of Adares's hand was not just a pattern; it was a snake, with a fierce, crescent-shaped head, a body made of intricately spiralling lines, and a curling tail that ran down to circle Adares's wrist twice, like a pair of bracelets.

When Adares realized what it was going to be, he felt an unexpected squirm of discomfort in his gut. It was too much like the blue devices he had last seen on banners streaming from Luth spears charging towards his army. It surprised him that Rus would think to draw such a thing on him, but he said nothing. It was a beautiful snake, and the hand that drew it invested it with new meaning.

By the time the snake was finished, the light was beginning to fade. They made love again, and this time it was Adares who was reduced to tears afterward.

"What are you thinking about?" Rus asked a little while after that, when they had been quiet together for some time in the twilight.

"Oh. Well, it's not very … " Not very romantic, he thought to say, but he knew Rus would have waved that away and still wanted to know what it was. "I was thinking about the Daine camped in the hills. I was thinking they'd be much more use to us inside Tios."

"Ah. I suppose they would."

"Particularly if Gunthanaruth had no idea how they got there. Or—better still, if he thought he had reliable information that they were coming down from the north … and then they turned up in Tios, just when he was looking the other way. That seems to me like the kind of thing that might make him abandon the siege. Doesn't it?"

"It does. You are not speaking idly, are you, Adares?"

"No. Not really."

"You would take them in the fishing boats, from that village with the difficult name?"

He nodded. "When I was out in the woods today, I began to think that I *could* get to the Ikthyra road without being seen—the camp nearest to it has been moved, and the woods there are fairly thick."

"And you could get the Daine to come with you."

"Yes, I think so. I don't know how many boats we'd find,

or how many boatsmen, and I know the Daine would be no help with that—but we could make multiple trips if we needed to. It would be risky, but in the dark it might very well be possible. And it's convenient we have the horses now. A horse will give me a chance of keeping out of the way of the bull in the woods."

"That bull won't touch you."

"Well, but I thought you said he'd try to attack me out of spite."

"He'd have to get by me. And he won't."

"Rus, I couldn't possibly ask you to come with me."

"You don't have to ask. But you don't get to tell me no, either. Of course I am coming with you."

Adares frowned. "I am grateful that you want to, but … " But he couldn't think what else to say.

He got up and lit the lamp and the brazier. For their dinner, he fried the priests' onions with the rest of the mushrooms, and they ate them hot, folded up in the last pieces of bread and washed down with more milk. They ate sitting outside under the temple eaves.

"Rus," said Adares finally, having formulated what he wanted to say, "if you leave here with me, to my mind, that crosses a line into treachery—one that you haven't crossed yet."

Rus looked at him in silence for a moment. "That would be a minority opinion, I think. That I haven't crossed that line. No—" He held up a hand. "It is not what you think. I am not proposing to abandon my people and follow you to Tios and destroy your reputation or have you accused of treason yourself. I will go with you to the Daine camp to make sure you arrive safely, and I will go back to Gunthanaruth's camp and make sure he knows that the Daine are in the hills ready to descend on him. That will be a falsehood, but if it will help end the siege of Tios without another engagement, it will spare the lives of some of my people as well as many of yours. It may be treachery, but not more so than what I have already done. Even if there is further fighting, it will be the Daine defending the walls of Tios, not riding out to massacre the Luth—I trust you not to let that happen."

"Of course. As I trust you. And I don't think you're a traitor, I just … "

"You are concerned for my honour, which is … strange … but I am grateful. For what it is worth, if there is any way after this to promote a peace between the Luth and the Phemians—an equitable peace, beneficial to both sides—I will do it."

"I wish you could come back to Tios with me."

"But I can't. There's no way to disguise what I am, and no way for us to be … anything to each other, considering your position."

"My position," Adares repeated.

"Ah, you know—you are not an obscure person in Tios, you have a reputation to maintain, I think. You couldn't suddenly appear with a Luth … um … "

"Lover," Adares supplied. It struck him as a sad way for that word to be first spoken between them. "It would be … It might create difficulties, yes. But listen—you can't come with me, even still. I'm going to have to leave tomorrow morning, early, and you're not well enough to ride."

Rus laughed. "Ah, Adares, I do not know why it is, but things that I would receive as insults from anyone else, from you seem the most precious flattery. I am stronger than you think I am. I will ride with you when you leave, and if we meet the bull in the forest, I will kill it for you. Then I will ride back to my headman and lie to him for you. For Tios, but for you."

Adares sighed. "I don't … I don't know what to say to you."

"'Thank you, Rus.'"

"Well, yes. Thank you, Rus."

"Good. Now, let us go back inside and get into bed, and you can tell me another story."

"About what?"

"About you—about you in Pheme, before you came to Tios. And I will tell you about the scandal of Gunthanaruth's second wife."

"I'm scandalized already—I didn't know Luth men could have more than one wife."

"Don't be ridiculous, Phemian—his first wife was dead."

They slept early that night, comfortably curled together, both of them exhausted by the day, and they woke before the earliest glimmer of dawn. It was cold. They sat wrapped in the bedclothes and breakfasted on milk and berries. Rus stretched to warm up his muscles, and pulled back his hair and secured it in a messy knot at the nape of his neck. Adares collected the cold pieces of his armour and asked Rus if he had a use for any of it. Rus shook his head.

"It would get it my way," he said.

"I suppose it might."

There was a strange constraint between them that morning. Since rising, they had barely touched. It didn't seem appropriate, somehow. Neither of them spoke of the parting that would soon be upon them.

Rus said, "You don't mind if I keep your kilt pin—I mean your cloak pin, for my kilt—do you?"

"Of course not, but it might be better not to show it to anybody, once you get back to your camp."

"Ah yes, because they're going to find out you're not dead, so I can't claim to have taken it off your body on the battle-field."

"Well, it doesn't have my name on it."

Rus looked at him for a moment. "No, I suppose not." Adares had the impression he had intended to say something else—what, he didn't know.

Rus arranged his kilt in its proper folds and fastened it in place with the pin. The gold ship that was the emblem of Pheme stood out jauntily against the background of blue cloth. Adares put on his own black tunic again, laced his boots, fastened his breastplate and greaves, and threw his scarlet cloak around his shoulders, knotting the corners together to hold it in place. He held out his hand and looked at the snake on the back of it, as he had been doing off and on since Rus drew it.

They found Rus's spear, put out the lamp, and went out of their quiet asylum for the last time. Outside, the sky was just beginning to lighten. The temple courtyard was pale and still.

The horses watched them sleepily as they walked among them, looking for a likely pair. Adares chose a black mare; he didn't know much about horses, but she seemed friendly and looked well cared-for. Rus was not interested in any of the Phemian horses, but he had to inspect all five of the stocky, short-legged Luth animals, between which Adares could not see much difference.

Adares rummaged among the equipment that the Luth men had left in the stable, looking for a suitable saddle and bridle. He came out, with the best equipment he could find, to ask Rus what he needed. Rus had settled on a horse, already put a bridle and a curiously-shaped Luth saddle on her, and made a contemptuous face at Adares's armload of Phemian equipment. He mounted, spear in hand, as casually as if he were walking through a door rather than getting on a horse, and rode around the temple courtyard while Adares saddled his own mount.

They rode out of the temple gates, around behind the honey-coloured walls, and into the woods. Adares was slightly uncomfortable in the saddle, but less so than he had feared. They followed the trail carved by the runaway bull, since there was no other path. They rode close together, Rus leading the way, not talking. Adares didn't mind that. He enjoyed watching Rus ride, the easy, unstudied skill of it, horse and rider a fluid pair, blue and white in the darkness, like part of the Great Pattern Rus talked about.

By and by, Rus turned off of the track they had been following and led the way through the trees up to the ridge, where the grey dawn light faintly showed the Daine encampment crouched between the hills in the distance. It occurred to Adares that on his own he might well have been unable to find his way through the forested valley that lay between him and his allies. But Rus seemed to know what he was doing. They rode down the hill and back in among the trees. As the sky brightened, the forest came awake around them; the trees grew green instead of grey, more birds joined the chorus from the treetops, and the dew on the leaves glittered in the strengthening light.

They rode out into a clearing, where they could see the sky stained pink in the east. Rus rode around the edge of the open space, looking for the easiest way forward in the direction they wanted to travel. Adares let his horse graze a little in the centre of the clearing. He watched Rus and thought that he looked glad to be up and outside, in his own element again. But Adares could also see a certain, distinctive tightness in Rus's expression; it was clear that all the while he seemed to sit so easily in the saddle, he was in pain.

Something hanging off the saddle of Adares's horse had been bumping against his leg all the while he rode, and he looked down now to see what it was and whether he could get rid of it. He found a leather bag, attached by a strap to the saddle, with a stopper in it.

It must have been tied there by the officer who had ridden out of Tios in this saddle. It had survived the battle, though its owner hadn't, and it had gone unnoticed first by the Luth who had captured the officer's horse, then by Adares when he saddled this horse—it all seemed nearly miraculous. And it was probably nothing more worthy than some of the watered-down vinegar that the legions always swilled on campaign.

Adares unfastened it from the saddle, pulled the stopper, and sniffed at the contents. He took a swig.

"Rus! Feel like a drink?"

Rus turned to look. "Wine?"

"Boukossian red, and a good year. I may not know horses, but I do know wine."

"This somehow does not surprise me."

Rus turned his horse and rode back across the clearing towards Adares. He had reached out a hand for the wine, reining in his mount. Then, quite suddenly, he froze, listening. He quieted his horse and put out his hand to hush Adares's mount as well. In a moment Adares heard the noise that had caught Rus's attention: the unmistakable sound of something large moving fast through the forest, coming in their direction.

"Save some for me," said Rus, wheeling his horse around and lifting his spear. "I will drink afterwards."

The bull came out from among the trees at a loping run, the muscles of his shoulders and haunches rolling under his sleek black hide. He was a huge animal, a nightmare, half again as big as the largest specimens of Pseuchaian cattle. A mane of shaggy hair fringed his massive head, and curving horns as long as hunting bows stood above his small, mad eyes. What had Rus said? That the spirit of Nepharos, the death-dealer, the god of insanity, inhabited the bulls when they were exiled from the herd. Adares could believe it.

He held hard to the mare's reins, trying to calm her, trying to stay calm himself so that his own panic would not infect her and make her bolt or throw him. He watched Rus with a trancelike fixity.

Rus rode out to meet the bull, calling to him in his own language, in a strange, low voice that Adares had not heard him use before. The bull stopped in his tracks, pawed the earth, swinging his head around and then turning his body in a slow circle toward the blue and white pair of horse and rider.

He lowered his head, horns aimed like weapons, and gave a menacing snort. And he charged.

There was a horrible grace to it, and a malign purposefulness far from the practicality of predator and prey. Adares had time—in those frozen moments of fear-heightened perception—to notice this, and to see that Rus was no longer sitting astride his horse as the bull bore down on him. He had drawn his feet up and was crouched on the saddle. The horse, incredibly, stood her ground as the bull charged, until, almost at the same moment as Rus loosed his spear, he turned his mount aside and gave her the signal to leap out of the way.

The spear had lodged shallowly, almost harmlessly, in the bull's shoulder. Maddened, the bull thrashed his head, snorting, slewing around to follow the pair that had eluded him. But horse and rider had already separated.

As the horse took off, fleeing at the last moment so that it passed perilously close to the side of the bull, Rus had leapt from the white beast to the black. He landed on his hands, drew his legs under him, and slid down to straddle the bull's shoulders. One hand gripped a fistful of the bull's mane as the animal pitched and twisted to get him off its back; the other hand wrenched out the spear.

He raised his arm, in a flash of blue, and drove the spear down through the bull's neck once, twice, three times. Blood fountained out, and the beast sank heavily to its knees, lowered its great head, and died. Rus sprang free of the body as it subsided, and stood up, shaking out his hair, and looked across the clearing to Adares.

Their eyes met, and for a moment Adares found himself daunted, almost frightened, to be looking into the face of a man who could do what he had just seen. It passed, of course. Rus winced, and sank down onto the grass, to take the weight off his injured leg, and his expression when he looked up at Adares again was curiously wry, as if he felt he had been showing off, and was slightly ashamed. But Adares remembered that moment.

He was down off his own horse almost immediately and came to kneel in the grass beside Rus. He pulled the stopper from the wineskin and held it out. Rus looked up at him. Adares felt he could no more have touched him, in that moment, than he could have touched the goddess's cult statue in the temple of Anaxe. Rus reached out and took the wineskin.

"It's not full," said Adares irrelevantly. "You drink it all—you deserve it."

Rus held the vessel for a moment without drinking. He looked a little shaky, with spent energy and suppressed pain.

"Do you know," he said, "we do not have wine, in the Luth lands—we have no grapes, so we make mead out of honey, and drink that. We know a god that you do not, I think—Nuthar, the god of honey, who is also the god of mead, and of revelry. Even so … "

He was seeming more like himself now, with this pedantic detail that didn't seem related to anything. In another moment, Adares thought he would feel like reaching out and kissing him after all.

Rus put the wineskin to his lips and drained it in one draught. He gasped slightly afterwards. Adares wasn't surprised; he had tasted Karhan mead, and Boukossian wine was a good deal stronger.

"That's a shocking way to drink good wine," Adares said.

Rus turned the wineskin upside down and shook the last few drops out onto the grass. He said something in his own language that sounded to Adares like an invocation. He thought he recognized the word "Tios" in it.

"Are you going to tell me what that was about?" Adares asked after a moment, when Rus did not explain or translate.

Rus looked up at him. "Maybe. I am deciding."

CHAPTER X

THERE WERE PRAYERS that Rus said he needed to chant over the body of the bull. He did it in a low voice without inflection, kneeling in the grass and looking drained and exhausted now. He explained, pedantic again, how a much longer ritual would have been needed if he had killed the bull as part of one of the Luth's divining ceremonies, but this was different; only he did not feel he could omit all of the prayers, because the bull's state of madness was still the result of being captured and used by his people. It was his bull, he said, the one he'd ridden into battle. He'd know it anywhere.

Adares wanted to kneel beside him and put an arm around his shoulders, at the very least, but he felt awkward about it, unsure it would be welcome, and so he didn't.

His prayers finished, Rus wanted to get going. Adares suggested he should rest, but he shook his head. He was at least willing to wait while Adares fetched his horse for him from where she was placidly grazing by the edge of the clearing, looking as though she had already put the encounter with the bull from her mind. Rus mounted more laboriously than before, and from the look on his face, it was painful.

Adares fetched his own horse, and they rode out of the clearing, leaving the body of the bull lying in its blood in the grass. There was a spatter of blood on the edge of Rus's kilt, but he had wiped off all that had got on his bare skin, and he hardly looked like someone who had recently slaughtered a large animal.

They rode in silence again, while the day brightened around them. Eventually, because that was just the way it was between them, they fell to talking of small things again, in the same easy way that they had talked ever since they dropped to their knees laughing by the fountain that first night. Adares challenged Rus to identify varieties of trees and flowers that bordered the path, and couldn't tell whether he was bluffing when he answered. Rus made fun of Adares's horse-trappings, which he called impractical, and then apologized to Adares's horse in Luth and petted her nose. And so on. Adares thought if they couldn't find the Daine at all and had to ride through the forest like this for days, he would be happy.

"I think we must be getting close," Rus said, much later, when the sky was clear blue above the treetops, and they could see the slopes of the hills between which the Daine were camped, rising up on either side before them. He reined in his horse, and Adares did the same.

"I daresay I can find my way from here," Adares said. "I suppose you had better turn back. You don't want to meet the Daine, after all."

"Ah, no!" Rus smiled. "I would not miss this for the world, Adares. Besides, I think I will be safe with you. I am stopping because I want to tell you something."

"Yes?"

"I want to tell you what I said, back there, when I drank the wine. We say—the Luth say—that when you drink, it is an act of worship to Nuthar. Especially when you drink deep. So when you have drained the last drops of your drink, you ask the blessing of Nuthar on someone you desire to bless. Nuthar is the god of bees and honey, but I do not think he would mind being honoured with foreign grapes. What I said was: 'Nuthar give his blessing to the people of Tios, because they chose the right man to rule them.'"

There was a stretch of silence. Adares didn't know whether he felt more ashamed or relieved.

"Do you think that?" he said finally.

"I do. I thought I had better mention it, because you will want to tell the Daine who you are, and you need not think you must keep concealing it from me. How do your names go together? Phyleros Adares, is it?"

"We do it—" He had to pause to clear his throat. "We do it the other way around. I'm Adares Doriades Phyleros. Archon of Tios. I lied when I said my job was not interesting. I'm sorry I didn't tell you the truth."

Rus shook his head. "No. I understand. For yourself, you trust me—but for the safety of your city, you could not afford to take such a risk. It doesn't matter. I knew the whole time."

"Did you?"

"Not before you told me that the archon of Tios was young, and you thought he should not have been elected—but as soon as you said that, I knew that you were talking about yourself. It did not seem surprising. And I understood why you were determined to return to Tios, and when I said that I know you will prevent the Daine from attacking the Luth in open battle—I know it is in your power to do that."

And he knew that he had not been sheltering in the temple complex with some unimportant Phemian administrator; he had known when the Luth warriors arrived with the horses that he could deliver the archon of Tios into their hands if he wanted to. If all he really wanted was an end to hostilities between his people and the Phemians, that would have done the trick.

"You see," he said, looking away at the path ahead of them

instead of at Adares, "I crossed that line you spoke of some time ago."

And maybe that was true, Adares thought, but somehow he didn't believe it. He wished he hadn't mentioned it before.

"There's something else I ought to tell you," he said, "if we're going to meet the Daine together. There's no fishing village called Ikthyra."

"Is there not?" Rus looked at him, surprised.

"No. It's a, uh, naval shipyard. It's called Naukos West. It's quite new, not fully operational yet, and not at all where I said the village was."

"That I did not guess," Rus admitted. "But I am glad. You were more cautious than I realized."

"Well, I do sort of know what I'm doing. But now you really do know all my secrets."

"I will try to be worthy of the honour." He said it with that feigned gravity that he seemed to use to mask real sentiment, smiling and tossing his hair back over his shoulder.

They rode on to meet the Daine. They found them just beginning to break camp, which was a little surprising since the day was well advanced by then. The disorder was such that Rus and Adares had ridden some way out of the forest before the Daine sentries noticed them and rode out to confront them, spears at the ready. Adares glanced down at the snake on the back of his hand, and across at Rus, with the Phemian officer's pin in his kilt.

"We must be an interesting spectacle," said Rus.

The sentries, two red-haired, moustached men in striped trousers, eyed the pair of strangers warily. Adares could guess what they were thinking. The dark young man before them was clearly a Phemian, the one covered in blue swirls clearly a Luth; what could they be doing riding side by side? Both were weaponless (they had left Rus's spear behind with the dead bull), and the Phemian did not even have a helmet. One of them must be the prisoner of the other—but which was which?

Adares rode forward to meet them.

"I wish to see Baghan Kammel, your chieftain," he said, in their language, before they had a chance to ask his intention. He had not ridden right up to them to say this, but pitched his voice to carry.

The sentries exchanged a glance. Adares had, quite deliberately, used the familiar form of the chieftain's name. Whether or not the sentries knew enough about Phemians to know that a black tunic was the mark of their leaders, they seemed to get the message that the young man in black in front of them was someone to be reckoned with. They took him to the chieftain.

Derhent Baghan Arra-Kammel, as he was known to his subjects, was a big, bony man with a cloud of red hair frothing out from under a round fur cap. His victory against the Luth a summer ago had given him a right to call himself the second most powerful chieftain in the Karhan, which he certainly seemed to be doing. To greet the approaching strangers, he sat in state before his tent in a big, winged chair made of gilded wood. He started out of it, frank astonishment in his face, when he saw Adares.

"Lord archon!" He knew the correct Phemian form of address for a man of Adares's rank, and he used it—but that was as far as his knowledge of the language went. "Has the siege been lifted?" he inquired, in his own tongue. "I heard no word of it!"

"No, Kammel—you've heard no word because it has not happened." Adares swung down off his horse and handed the reins to a waiting squire. He had a sudden, pleasing sensation of being back in the world that he could understand and control; he felt like stretching, with a satisfied sigh. "With your help, I hope it will happen soon—I've come to talk over how best to go about it."

"Splendid!" said Kammel, planting his big hands on his hips and looking sincerely relieved. "Taking on the Luth is no joke—we'd just as soon know what we're up against. We've spent so much time debating the best way to approach them this morning that we've barely begun to break camp, as you see. Berhart!" he called to one of his attendants. "Don't stand around! Bring a seat, and mead—and some food, while you're at it." Turning back to Adares, but glancing at Rus, he said, "Your prisoner, I take it?"

"Not exactly—call him an indebted ally." It was a distortion of the truth, but one which preserved Rus's honour, suggesting he had not exactly defected to his enemies, not exactly been captured—something in between. Adares knew Rus could understand the exchange, since it had been the Daine language that they had spoken at first, on the battlefield. "I have a plan which involves him. I'll explain it to you. But first—how much do you know about the Luth attack?"

They talked on. Kammel had heard different reports from his scouts and wanted the details of the battle as Adares knew them; Adares asked how many troops Kammel had brought, and what kind. The chieftain's attendants hurried up with a wooden folding chair, bowls of mead, and a dish of cold meat and fruit. Adares made Rus sit in the chair, while he perched on the arm of it himself.

"He's hurt," he explained to the Daine chieftain, who had raised his bushy red eyebrows questioningly. "He needs to rest. No, don't bother with another chair—I'm fine where I am."

Kammel might not have approved of Adares's choice of ally, but giving up comforts for the sake of a wounded comrade was the sort of thing that always went over well with warrior chieftains. It was gratifying when good policy and natural inclination coincided so well.

Adares wished there were some way he could have casually put his arm around Rus's shoulders at this point. But of course that wouldn't have gone over well at all.

"Now," he said, "let me tell you my plan."

In the middle of explaining to Kammel what he wanted him to do, realizing that Rus had had nothing to drink, Adares passed him his half-finished bowl of mead. Their eyes met for a moment as Rus hesitantly accepted it, and Adares was startled by the expression that he saw there. It was almost awe; it couldn't have been very far removed from the expression that he himself had worn as he watched Rus kill the bull. Adares wanted to laugh out loud then, but he restrained himself.

By the time Rus left the Daine camp, it was buzzing with activity. Baghan Kammel was striding from one tent to another, conferring with his retainers, finding out if any of them had been on a boat before; around them, the warriors and squires were finishing their chaotic packing up of the camp, and passing worried rumours about why their headman was talking of boats. Adares had been presented by one of Kammel's elderly aides with a map of the Karhan coast, painted on a piece of horsehide, and he was trying to make sense of Daine cartography, which seemed puzzlingly abstract and decorative. He looked up when Rus appeared by the arm of his chair.

"I think I should go," Rus said.

"Already? You ... you're sure you'll be all right? You don't want to rest a while longer?"

Rus shook his head. "I'm no use here. My use now is to go back to tell Gunthanaruth that I have been riding in the

forest and seen the Daine camped in the hills. I would—”
He ran his hand through his hair, looking at the ground. “I
would rather do it soon, while it is still almost true. Either
way, it is a lie—and I don’t mind that, for your sake I don’t
mind telling it—but if I go soon, it can’t be *proved* it’s a lie.”

“I’ve told them to leave some of the tents up,” said Adares.
“The ones they haven’t taken down yet—with the banners
flying—so that if Gunthanaruth sends a scout, he’ll see *something.*”

“Ah,” said Rus. “Good. You think of everything.” His tone
was genuinely admiring.

Adares shrugged. “I can be efficient, sometimes.”

Out of the corner of his eye he saw the chieftain gesturing
in his direction as he talked to one of his men. Any moment
he would come striding over with some question.

Rus said, “I will try to make sure the towers by the harbour
are abandoned. But if I can’t—”

“If you can’t, you can’t, and we’ll have to take them by
force. If anyone seems suspicious, don’t press the issue. I
don’t—” He stopped. What he didn’t want was for Rus to
put himself in danger; but it seemed wrong to say it, and he
knew Rus wouldn’t listen anyway. “Well. Do what you can.”

“I shall.”

Rus stood for a moment, running the tips of his pale
fingers along the edge of his jaw, which bore a three days’
accumulation of scarcely perceptible blond beard.

“Well,” said Adares, “I guess … ”

He did not finish the sentence. Rus had made up his mind;
only now did Adares realize what he had been hesitating
about. He leaned down, tipped Adares’s face towards himself,
and kissed him.

It was a brief, chaste kiss—Adares was so surprised, it
could hardly have been otherwise—but it was still recog-

nizably a lover's kiss, in front of the entire Daine camp and their headman.

"May the gods bless you," Rus said, straightening up.

Adares was on his feet a moment later. "Rus, I—"

"Ah, better not, I think. Goodbye, Adares."

"Goodbye," said Adares.

He watched Rus walk to his waiting horse, mount, and ride away into the enveloping forest. He had been about to say, "I love you." He had wanted to make it clear, as he should have done long before that last moment, that this hadn't been some uncomplicated interlude for him any more than it had been for Rus. He thought—he hoped—the reason Rus had stopped him was because he already knew.

Kammel came over to ask more anxious questions about boats. Neither he nor any of his men ever said anything about the kiss. The Phemians had different ways—everyone knew that—and the Luth, well, they were of course beyond the pale. You could expect anything of a Luth.

CHAPTER XI

IT WAS THE first, and the most unorthodox, of Adares Phyleros's military successes—or the second, if you counted the fact that he had managed to survive his own heroic suicide on the battlefield four days earlier.

It all went more or less according to his plan. The Daine cleared themselves a trail through the forest, to get to the Naukos West road without detection, then followed the road down to the coast, where they found the naval yard with its skeleton crew, prepared to destroy their boats and workshops before letting them fall into enemy hands. They were pathetically grateful to find they didn't have to.

The first flotilla with its load of Daine warriors set out just after dark, before moonrise. Adares, in the prow of the foremost boat, led the way around beneath the cliffs at the harbour's mouth, and the whole string of boats passed safely through the narrows and into the harbour. Here, Adares saw with relief that the ships that had been prepared for the refugees were no longer at anchor. That meant they must have had time to get away before the Luth took the watchtowers.

They beached the boats and came cautiously ashore. While a few workers from the shipyards took the boats back, the first wave of Daine warriors approached the eastern watchtower above the narrows. They found it empty, although the signal fires had been left alight. The western tower was still garrisoned, though only sparsely, and its occupants, taken by surprise, surrendered quickly to the Daine. The second wave of boats came, with extra vessels which had not been brought the first time; they rowed straight through the narrows, without skulking by the cliffs, now that the towers were retaken.

It was now close enough to low tide for them to attempt the trip into the city. They reached the outlet of the main drain, where Adares had been waiting, and there was a tense interval during which it seemed that the locked grating on the drain's end could not be opened. Eventually they found a way of hauling it with ropes from above, so that the pins lifted free of the hinges, and the long line of warrior-laden boats rowed into the vaulted tunnel of the drain.

Adares, who had been standing on top of the stone-clad outlet, helping to haul on the ropes, swung over, hanging by his hands, and dropped down into the stern of the first boat as it went in. They rowed up the channel, in the pitch dark through murky water, until shafts of moonlight spilling down from a round sewer grate above told them that they had arrived under Tios. The men in the first boat banged on the underside of the grate with the butt ends of their spears until some frightened citizens came running to lift it up.

The scene that greeted his eyes when he clambered out of the sewer and back up into his city was not quite what Adares had anticipated. The men crowded around the drain, lit torches in hand, staring at him with disbelief, were all as unshaven as he; on these dark-bearded Phemians, it showed up clearly. Most of them wore plain, undyed tunics, although he recognized several of his high-ranking officials in the crowd. Among the tribal residents pressing close to get a look, he saw a couple of Getti men who had shaved off their moustaches.

They were all in mourning, he realized with surprise. It was almost out of his mouth: the question, "Who died?" He caught himself just in time.

"You don't seem to have been expecting me, men!" he said instead.

Dear Mother and Father, said the letter that Adares finally sent home,

In case you have heard any rumours to the contrary, be assured that I am alive and well. You have been often in my thoughts lately. I love you and miss you. If I could come home to see you now, I would; but you have probably heard enough about the situation in Tios to understand why that will be impossible for some time.

I don't know what they may be saying in Pheme about what has happened here. It is true that there has been fighting, and that for a few days Tios was under siege.

Fortunately, most of the women and children were evacuated before the siege began. We have allies among the local tribes, some of whom came to our aid and helped to frustrate the besieging force. We were able to sneak reinforcements into the city under the noses of our enemies, who were entirely disconcerted to find us fully garrisoned the following morning, and withdrew, calling off the siege, almost immediately. They have remained lurking in the hills this past week, and we are preparing for another attack; the men are busy digging trenches and building up earthworks to prevent our enemies retaking the harbour fortifications and cutting off our access to the sea.

I daresay you heard some time before I did about this proc-

lamation that makes all the people of Tios rebels for electing their own archon. The first we heard of it was two days ago, when word reached us that our refugee ships had been denied entry to the harbour at Psylos, since the people of Psylos evidently do not want to make trouble for themselves with Pheme.

You may be sure that I offered to resign my office, but the citizens' council would not let me do it. They did not say it was because they could hardly afford to change leaders at a time like this; they said it was because I singlehandedly lifted the siege, which was a gross exaggeration, but they cheered and made a big thing of it, which was very touching. There was a while when everyone thought I was dead, and they had all actually gone into mourning.

Now we are awaiting the return of our women and children, and readying ourselves for the possibility of another attack. I cannot pretend that the future looks bright. With Pheme placing us under embargo, and the most powerful tribe in Kargania still threatening us, this will be a hard winter. But at least we know the nature of our adversity now; whether we can survive it rests in the hands of the gods.

Give my love to the rest of the family. Tell Chares that I never understood geometry either, and if I were him, I shouldn't worry too much about it. Give Leta my blessing on her engagement. Menippos Xenonos is a fortunate man, and I hope he will make her happy. We have found a Kossian merchant who is willing to carry letters to and from Pheme, though he is bound by the embargo to accept no other freight. I will write as often as I can.

Your loving son,
Adares

The evening after the letter was sent, the ships bearing the refugee women and children returned to Tios. Adares had ordered a public celebration that night to welcome them back.

The autumn rain had set in now in earnest; the months of grey wet that preceded the biting cold of the Karhan winter had begun. They sacrificed in the conveniently dry interior of the Temple of Amphiaraos in the centre of the city, and hurried through the rain back to the citizens' hall and the archon's palace, where the wine flowed freely late into the night.

Tios was filled to bursting, with Phemians and Karhan locals, and since Adares had opened his doors without restriction, inviting everyone who was not on duty guarding the walls and trenches, nearly every room had to be co-opted for revelry. People were drinking in the hallways, drying their wet cloaks over the lit braziers, snatching food from the trays that slaves were carrying in to the higher-ranking revellers in the state dining room. The food was not overabundant; Adares had given the kitchen strict orders, and made sure to provide other diversions for his guests, to take their minds off eating. There were not many male dancers or flute-players in the colony, but such as there were had prepared a last-minute entertainment in honour of the women. It was very good, and well applauded. Even the Daine lords, who found the idea of men dancing and playing the flute scandalous, managed to be very polite.

Adares, reclining on his couch in the dining room, full of a warm glow of wine and goodwill, had to work to remind himself that what he had written to his parents that morning was true: it would be a hard winter, and Tios was still in danger. Someone proposed yet another toast; they had so much to drink to. When he had drunk, and set down his cup again, Adares looked for a moment at the back of his hand.

The snake was still visible, although the dye had faded in the week since it was drawn. In another day or two, there would be nothing to see.

He let himself linger for a moment on the fantasy that he had been returning to all week. He imagined showing Rus around Tios, taking him down to the harbour to see the ships, asking him how his chieftain's sod-roofed hall compared with the Tian archon's limestone palace. He didn't know how he was going to make all this possible. At the moment it was no more than a flight of fancy, not so strikingly different from the fictions he used to allow himself to create when he was a boy, about unattainable girls. But the girls had often not been as unattainable as he had thought them, and he was a powerful man now.

He looked across the dining room at a pair of friends sharing a couch, deep in conversation, and he let himself imagine Rus on his own couch—sitting upright, probably, like the Daine lords clustered at one end of the room—looking shocked by the dancers, and having to be reminded not to knock back the exquisite, aged Boukossian wine like it was watery Karhan mead. And then afterward, in private, lying in Adares's arms, neither of them caring who knew or suspected, because Archon Phyleros had single-handedly lifted the siege of Tios and could get away with anything. He could picture it all so clearly, he felt certain he would somehow make it real.

The first toast of the evening had been to Rus, although the man who proposed it, one of Adares's chief councillors, had not known his name. The whole city had heard by this time about the heroic Luth who saved their archon's life. Adares had made sure of it, telling just enough to make it a good story, but not enough for anyone to gossip about. Some of his councillors, he could tell, suspected him of making the whole thing up, for the benefit of the citizens. But then they would look at the fading snake on the back of his hand and wonder. Adares let them.

"Sir," said the man on the couch to his left, interrupting his thoughts.

Adares looked up, smiling.

"Kleisios?"

He was a grizzled military man, one of Adares's favourite councillors—deferential, but conscious of his own merits, which were substantial. Now he looked at Adares with a knowing grin.

"If I didn't know better, I'd say you look like a man in love," he said.

Adares gave a surprised laugh. "Is that so? How are you sure you *do* know better?"

"Eh? Oh, I see, sir. Very good! We shouldn't let these brutes of Luth drive all our pleasures from us."

"No—they understand love too. I mean, one assumes. Some of them, at least. Do you know, speaking of that, I heard an amusing story. Gunthanaruth, after his first wife died, married a girl young enough to be his daughter, purely for love—purely for *his* love, I should say. The tribesmen were all a bit shocked to begin with, but it got worse. She convinced him, as a way of proving the sincerity of his love, to cut his hair. Short." Adares gestured, drawing his fingers across at the level of his jaw.

"Wouldn't strike me as a very good way to prove anything, sir, but then what do I know?"

"Think of it this way, Kleisios. Suppose a woman asked you to prove your love by growing a big, bushy beard."

"Oh, I see! He must have been a laughingstock."

"Worse than that—the lords talked about deposing him for it. Luth men are very serious about their hair. They cut it short when they're in disgrace, or convicted of some crime, and that's about it."

He wondered about that woman, too. Maybe she had just wanted to make Gunthanaruth ridiculous. If she'd been fond of him, Adares thought she should have appreciated the long hair. It was such fun to run your fingers through it.

Kleisios looked up thoughtfully from his wine cup. "I wonder, do the Luth think of us as barbarians, with our short hair? The same way we think of the Sasians, who grow beards?"

"The Sasians aren't barbarians, man. They sacked Kos."

"Oh, well, those Kossians—soft bunch of … " Kleisios grinned. "You seem to have learned a lot about the Luth."

Adares nodded. "There's no substitute for talking to one of them."

Adares's secretary, a thin Boukossian freedman who had served Hesteios before him, leaned discreetly over his couch just then, and said, "Pardon me for disturbing you, lord archon."

"No trouble, Doros—what can I do for you now? More citizens carousing in my study? Or have they made it into my bedroom by this time?"

"No, lord archon," said Doros, with a wry smile. "We have made quite sure of the locks now. It's something else—one of the sentries has come in and says there is something you should know."

Adares set down his wine cup, conscious of being much more sober than he had imagined himself, and recalling why he had meant to remain so.

"Thank you, Doros," he said, sitting up and swinging his legs over the edge of the couch.

Doros gestured for a slave to bring his master's sandals.

"I don't think, sir," he said guardedly, "that it is bad news."

"Oh?" Adares looked up at him.

"He is waiting in the hall." Doros nodded towards the doorway. "I'll fetch a cloak for you, shall I? He seems to think you may want to go out to see what he's talking about."

The sentry stood at attention in the hall, spear in hand, dripping on the wave-patterned mosaic floor while a couple of nearby revellers tried to talk him into joining them for a drink.

"Lord archon," he said respectfully. "My fellows and I on the north wall have seen something. We've had our captain over for a look, and he thought I should come to you. It's the Luth, lord archon. They're leaving."

Out in the rain on the northern wall, leaning on the wet rampart and straining his eyes to look out at the dark hills, Adares could see for himself that it was true.

When they withdrew from the siege, the Luth had not gone far; they had camped within sight of Tios, in the shelter of the hills at the far end of the valley that had formed the battlefield where they achieved their short-lived victory. Now they were packing up and leaving. Even in the faint moonlight that seeped through the clouds, this was obvious. Much as he wanted to give a great shout of relief and run back into his palace to tell everyone the news, Adares felt he had to restrain himself. It seemed not only too good to be true, but also rather odd.

"Why in the world," he said, tugging at the fold of his cloak that he had thrown over his head, "are they leaving in the dead of night, in the rain?"

"I don't know, lord archon," said the watch captain. "But they were up to something earlier. The captain of the watch before mine said there was some commotion just before sunset—it was too far away to tell what, with the rain, and the light being bad. He said it looked orderly—like they were gathering to watch something." He shook back the rain-soaked crest of his helmet, scattering droplets. "Seeing this now, my guess is they were listening to their chieftain tell them it was time to go home."

"Captain!" One of the sentries came hurrying down the wall from his post. "There's a rider coming—look!"

Adares looked where the sentry pointed and dimly saw a figure on a white horse, riding toward Tios from the camp that the Luth were vacating. The effort that he needed to restrain a shout of joy suddenly doubled. Still, he made it. This might be anyone, riding from the Luth camp to bear a message to Tios—anyone at all.

"That will be a messenger, telling us that they're leaving, I expect," said the watch captain.

"Yes," said Adares. "I had better go down to meet him."

CHAPTER XII

NOT WANTING TO set off a commotion in the palace, he told the sentries to keep what they had seen to themselves for the time being, and returned to the dining room in person, depositing his wet cloak with a waiting slave, to bring away with him a handful of his men—all those who were still sober enough to ride. They did their best to contain their delight at the whispered news, and leaving the dining room, sent for cloaks and horses, and rode down to the main gate of the city, overtaking on the way the messenger coming up to the palace to report the arrival of a Luth emissary.

"I don't suppose, in all our excitement, we've remembered to bring anyone to interpret for us," someone said, as they paused in the wet street to tell the messenger not to bother going to the palace.

"I have a bit of Luth," said Doros. "Glaukos suggested I come for that reason."

"I should think they will have sent someone who speaks our language," said Kleisios.

"If they have anyone who does," said Glaukos doubtfully.

Adares said nothing. He had surrendered to the temptation to believe that the Luth really were leaving; more than that he was still trying not to allow himself to hope for.

The sentries at the gate, awaiting an escort from the palace to take up the emissary, were startled to find the archon and his councillors, dressed in their finery from the party, getting down from their horses and dripping into the lamplit interior of the gate house. The Luth emissary, who stood warming his hands over the sentries' brazier, looked up and did his haughty best not to seem surprised too.

Though he was not Rus, he was not quite a stranger to Adares either. He was one of the young men of fashion who had come with the horses to the temple complex. Adares recognized his supercilious pale face and the spiralling blue bird outlined on his forearm. He was glad he had not let himself be too sure it would be Rus. The other half of his hope he found all but confirmed by the atmosphere in the guardroom; it was clear that the emissary had come on a mission of peace.

He did not speak a word of Pseuchaian, but of course he wouldn't, not being kahar. Adares could not imagine, at first, why he had been the one sent. But he did seem to have an uncanny sense for rank.

After a year of ruling Tios, Adares was quite used to people not believing, when he was introduced to them, that he was really archon of the colony. Now he was not even dressed in black or wearing any badge of his rank, and he came into the gate house in the middle of a knot of men, several of whom were much older than he. But he had not even come out from among his councillors, and was just throwing back the wet folds of his cloak, when the Luth emissary stepped up to him and made a deep, respectful bow onto one knee. He rose and said something in his own language, looking at Adares but evidently expecting to be interpreted.

"He says," said Doros, pushing politely through the crowd of wet cloaks to arrive at Adares's side, "that Gunthanaruth sends you his greeting. Or something like that—I have only a little Luth, I'm afraid."

There were certain things Adares would have liked to say in response to this which he did not think Doros would be able to translate to his satisfaction. Instead he met the emissary's gaze, rather sternly, and simply nodded in acknowledgement of the greeting. The Luth warrior looked satisfied with this. He opened a leather satchel that he carried by his side and extracted a rolled parchment, which he held up for Adares to see and then passed to Doros.

"Oh dear," Doros murmured, fumbling with cold fingers to untie the string holding the parchment closed. "I don't know that I've ever even seen Luth writing—I shall have to get him to read it for me."

"They don't have writing," said Adares, reaching for the scroll. "It'll be in Pseuchaian." And the emissary had handed it off to an underling because he assumed the Phemian headman wouldn't be literate himself.

Adares got the string untied and unrolled the parchment. The letter was written in elegant Kossian prose in a small, rounded hand. He had never seen Rus's writing, but somehow he couldn't believe that this was it. He imagined Rus would write in a more angular scrawl, perfectly legible but somehow conveying the intensity of his personality.

Gunthanaruth Son of Durguruth, Supreme Headman of the Luth, sends greetings in peace to Archon Phyleros of Tios.

It is an honour to greet a worthy adversary, whether on the battlefield or off it. A still greater honour, in the face of defeat, is to make a worthy adversary into a powerful ally. Though our men bested yours on the field, in strategy and cunning you have proven yourself more than a match for us. We have tasted of the first honour and now desire the second.

Adares looked up from the letter.

"Don't cheer or whistle, men—we will lose face if we look like we weren't expecting this—but Gunthanaruth wants an alliance."

There was a thrilled silence, everyone trying hard to look nonchalant, and glancing at one another significantly. Adares went back to the letter.

We will return to our grazing lands in the north for the winter. Our men are preparing for departure this night. For the men of your tribe slain in battle, since they were more numerous than ours, we will offer a blood-price in tribute, as is our custom. It will be delivered once we have returned to our summer villages.

Before we depart, we desire to treat with you about the terms of our alliance, if you will agree to meet us outside your city walls, under the banner of peace. You may be assured of our good faith, and that we act in accordance with a great omen given to us by our gods, which our holy men have always told us are the same as your gods. Farewell.

Ah, thought Adares, so the truth slips out. Maybe you desire the honour of greeting a worthy adversary, and so on—or maybe you're worried that the gods don't favour your enterprise any more. And then, as that reminded him of something, a terrible dark thing loomed up in his mind.

"Doros," he said, looking up from the letter to the face of the Luth emissary, "ask him what the omen was."

"Sir?"

"The letter mentions an omen. Ask him what it was."

Doros put the question, in halting syllables. The emissary gave some answer: a sentence, expressionless, uncaring.

"I … don't quite understand, sir," said Doros. "He says there was a fight of some kind, and—"

"The bull won," said Adares.

"Yes, lord archon—that is exactly what he said. The bull won. I'm not sure what it means."

There were a few moments then in which Adares wished everything gone: all the wet-cloaked, silently triumphing councillors; all the sentries and captains and soldiers, the tired women and children who had come off the boats, the dancers and the slaves who served at the banquet; the palace of the archon and all the walls and houses and temples of Tios; the supercilious blue-eyed man in front of him, who had watched Rus die and felt nothing. If they were gone, he could have mourned. But they hemmed him in, all the stones and people of this place, heaped up around him, clamouring: *Lead us! Build us! Fight us! Make treaties with us! We don't care what has happened to your heart.*

That feeling passed, quicker than he would have thought possible. Rus had killed himself, in the rain, on the horns of a bull that shouldn't have stood a chance against him, to let Adares keep all these things. And was he going to show his gratitude by wishing them gone?

"What it means," he said, his voice sounding surprisingly normal even to his own ears, "is that we had a very narrow escape. It likely means Gunthanaruth was planning to attack tonight—but when he looked for a sign that the gods would prosper him, thinking that it would come, as it always did … it was not given. So he withdraws."

"We should make a sacrifice," Kleisios murmured.

"We already *have*," said Glaukos.

"We will make another one," said Adares. He turned to Doros. "Tell the emissary I will meet with Gunthanaruth tomorrow, at noon, outside the main gate."

"Yes, lord archon."

"Lord archon," said one of the councillors, as they left

the gate house, "do we have permission to cheer and whistle now?"

"Yes," said Adares. "Yes, by all means."

He was borne along towards the waiting horses on the wave of his companions' joy and relief. Then he made it half-way through the ride back to the palace by thinking carefully about the sacrifice. It was not a sacrifice of thanksgiving that he had in mind, but one of propitiation—in case the blood that the gods had already received should not be enough.

From the sound of it, the Luth had been profaning their own stupid bull ceremonies for years. Adares was no expert on the gods, but he couldn't imagine how they could hold what Rus had done against him. But that he had really fought to lose, which he might himself have felt to be a profanation, Adares did not doubt. He would make a sacrifice—a very proper one, the kind of thing Rus would have approved of. He made it through the rest of the journey by trying not to think at all. He threw back his cloak to get rain on his face, so that if he started to cry before he was alone, no one would be able to tell.

He managed to get inside, and through the front hall crowded with revellers, without breaking into a run. He re-membered in time that his suite would be locked, and it would take time to send a slave for the key. The sliding doors to the library were unlocked, the room beyond dark and empty. He sank down with his back to a shuttered bookcase, hiding his face in his hands.

He thought of Rus alive, remembering how he had thought of him in the warm comfort of wine at dinner, when what he imagined had already become impossible. He saw him in his mind dead, blood in his fair hair, his beautiful blue and white skin torn by the bull's horns.

He would not have thrown away his life; if he had done

it, it must have been necessary. But necessary for whom? Necessary for Tios, which Rus had only cared about because of Adares. He had said as much himself. He had died heroically, but if he had never met Adares, he would still be alive. Adares curled over his bent knees and sobbed.

It was like the plot of some insufferable tragedy. Maybe he had been fated to kill Rus on the battlefield, but because he hadn't, all this had happened, and now Rus was dead after all. The will of the gods was implacable.

Well, no. It wasn't like that. That was ridiculous. Those three days in the storeroom of the temple of Soukos had happened, and they had mattered. They mattered still, even if he was the only one left alive who knew it.

He couldn't risk telling anyone what he'd lost. He had already spread around the story that a Luth had spared his life on the battlefield, taken refuge with him in the temple complex afterward, and helped him reconnoitre with the Daine. He had let that much information out when he imagined that there might still be a way for Rus to join him in Tios, everyone would find out that they had become lovers, and it would be the romantic sensation of the decade. He thought of that now, and it felt like a knife twisting in his belly. He couldn't let anyone find out, now. The story would get back to the Luth, if there was going to be an alliance, and it would be too easy to figure out who the archon's lover had been. Rus's memory would be dishonoured. Adares owed him better than that.

He found a dry corner of his tunic and mopped his face clumsily with it. He thought of the statue of Anaxe to which he had offered Rus's kilt pin, and he remembered what he had asked of her: only that Rus should go back to his own people alive. That much had been granted, true enough. What he should do, after that, with the life that had been begged from the goddess for him—that had not been part of the prayer. At least there had been those three days.

He went back out into the party, sodden cloak draped over his arm. He met Kleisios in the hallway, coming from somewhere—possibly looking for him.

"Are you all right, sir?" the old soldier asked, concerned but not prying.

Adares drew a shaky breath and let it out somewhat more smoothly. "I think I will *be* all right," he said. He had to be; he owed it to Rus.

Kleisios smiled. "If you need anything … " He let the offer hang in the air for a moment, compassionately, and went on. "I've told the others not to start trumpeting the news around. I thought it would be best. Everyone has been drinking— we don't want riots. I figure, if we keep things quiet, try to pack them off to bed soon, we can let the good news filter in tomorrow morning, and things will stay under control."

"Good man," said Adares feelingly. "Thank you for think- ing of that."

"No trouble. If you'll listen to another thought of mine— perhaps you ought to pack yourself off to bed too. You look like you need rest."

"Yes," said Adares. "I suppose I do."

He did not sleep, that he was aware of, though he did have the sense to take off his wet clothes and lie down. Once it was light enough to rise, he got up and splashed cold water on his face. He looked at a rivulet of water running down over the back of his hand, washing away a little more of the faint, curling snake, and he dashed the whole basin to the floor with a tremendous clang, splashing water over the tiles. He dressed hastily and went out, unshaven and unattended, mumbling something incoherent at the slaves who followed him puzzledly to the door.

The old Getti woman that he found, working in a smoky little shop just inside the city gates, looked at the design on his hand in surprise.

"That's a coiled serpent. The Luth and the Hurs and some of the other tribes all use it. It's the mark of a headman."

That was how the Luth emissary had known who he was. Rus had marked him as a leader of men, without telling him what he had done. The old woman's daughter, a striking blonde girl who stood in the shadows inside the shop, looked at Adares with embarrassment.

"Mother, he's archon of the city. You ought to know that."

Adares smiled at her, though it must have looked half-hearted. She blushed. He looked away, feeling raw with grief. Afterwards he was grateful, in a strange way, that there was a certain amount of pain, and even a little blood involved. He paid the old woman and returned to the palace with barely enough time to make himself presentable to meet Gunthanaruth.

"What happened to your hand, sir?" Kleisios asked, seeing the bandage.

"Nothing. I'll tell you about it some time—later."

Gunthanaruth was a small man. Short and wiry, he moved with a restless energy, and it was hard to tell from a distance how old he was. At close quarters, Adares saw that although he dressed and carried himself like a young warrior, his face was lined, and there were streaks of dead white in his pale curls. His hair fell far down his back; the scandal of his second wife was many years in the past. Between his thick gold torque and his scarlet kilt he wore an embroidered wool jacket, open down the front to display the huge blue snake tattooed on his chest.

Following the chieftain out to meet Adares came a soft-faced man in white, with curls of blue on his round cheeks.

Adares guessed that he was a priest even before he spoke, translating Gunthanaruth's greeting with a half-Kossian, half-Luth accent that was painfully familiar. Though he met the gaze of the chieftain's fierce blue eyes as they talked incomprehensibly back and forth, Adares was more interested in the interpreter, whose soft voice filled the pauses during which he and Gunthanaruth stared warily at one another. This was a man who had known Rus, who might even be grieving his death. He would have liked to be able to talk to him.

What Gunthanaruth said amounted to little beyond a confirmation of the peace proposal made in the letter of the night before. This, of course, was monumental enough in itself. Adares found he had to work to remain as lordly and nonchalant as he thought he ought, in order for Gunthanaruth to take him seriously. It might have been partly because he had not got any sleep, but the temptation to give way to relieved laughter was greater than he had imagined it would be.

It was true, even if the Luth had attacked that night, the Tians, with the Daine reinforcements, might well have been able to drive them off, or at least keep them from retaking the harbour watchtowers. But the women and children had been back in the city, with nowhere to escape to, and if the Luth had chosen to settle down for a siege after all, that winter would have been worse than hard.

When they had finished talking, Gunthanaruth held out his hand for Adares's and gave him a stern smile as he took it. Adares smiled back, and the Luth chieftain looked frankly surprised. Releasing Adares's hand, and turning to go, he said something to his interpreter, gesturing to Adares.

Finally Adares looked the priest in the eye.

"My lord says: 'I thought before that you were lucky. Now I think that perhaps we are lucky as well.'"

They remained looking at one another for a moment. There was no way for Adares to ask about Rus—*Was it a quick death? Did he suffer? Will he be remembered for the three fights he won, or only for the one he lost?*—without disgracing his memory and jeopardizing the peace he had died to secure.

But the priest himself had more to say. "My lord," he said, "feels that he has been rebuked by the gods for waging war on your people. He takes these matters very seriously. You may be sure he will abide by his decision."

"*He* feels?" said Adares. "You don't think it's true?"

The priest looked startled, then smiled faintly. "Ah—he has been rebuked, indeed."

"Went well, then, did it?" Kleisios asked, as Adares returned to his waiting councillors by the city gate.

"Very well. We will have peace, for this winter at least." He looked up at the carved gate that arched overhead, the yellow limestone glowing in the noon sun, which had emerged from the clouds to light his meeting with Gunthanaruth. "Strange to say it," he said aloud, to all the assembled councillors, "but we are not Phemians any more." When he looked up at the walls of his city, it was as if he had known this for a long time.

"Oh, Pheme will take us back, eventually," someone said.

There were murmurs: assent and disagreement.

"I expect," said Adares, "that they will try to. Eventually. It may be that by the time that happens, we will neither need nor want to be taken back. And it may not. In the meantime, we are one tribe among many in the Karhan. It is time we started acting that way. I think we may find that we get along pretty well. We are, after all, a tribe with stone walls, a gold mine, and a defensible harbour. And an alliance with the Luth."

Who knew how many lives that would save, in the end? Certainly Rus could not have known, when he laid down his life to make it possible, how many people in Tios, aside from its young ruler, stood to benefit from his sacrifice.

Part II

Rus

CHAPTER XIII

"THIS IS WOMAN'S work," Rus said cheerfully as he put the finishing touches on the snake's tail that curled around the Phemian's wrist. "But then, I have been like a woman with you already."

Lying under him in bed, moaning and crying out. Sobbing afterward, overcome. Strangely, he found he wasn't ashamed of it, even now.

Adares held up his hand to the light, examining the snake with a trace of a frown between his perfect eyebrows.

"Not *strikingly* like a woman—not from my perspective."

"Ah. Well, you would know."

"Yes, I would." He smirked. Rus smacked him, not hard.

In Luth poetry, there was a formula used to indicate a very beautiful woman: you would fall off your horse trying to keep looking at her, as you rode past. That was what the Phemian Adares was like. He had a face like one of the gods painted on the Kossian urns that stood in the summer hall of the kahar—except that unlike them he was always breaking into a smile. And such a smile. You would fall off your horse.

His skin was dark, even for his people, an incredible colour like old bronze, all over, and smooth as bronze too. He was tall, long-limbed, almost willowy, his body only lightly muscled, his hands barely calloused. His hair was absolutely black and cut absurdly short, so that you could see the shape of his head. His eyes were narrow and very dark and fringed with beautiful long lashes.

Rus moved the bowl of ink and the stylus he had been using to draw with back off the bed, and settled against Adares's side again. He felt awkward doing it, and knew he was beginning to blush, thinking how obvious his intention must have been. Adares just smiled at him and drew him closer.

"May I kiss you?" It was charming that he asked, since surely he had not been told "no" many times in his life.

"I—I was hoping that you would."

He leaned over, and his mouth was warm and gentle on Rus's, his hand stroking through Rus's hair. They moved apart again and lay looking at one another.

"I love kissing you," Adares said. He ran a thumb over Rus's lips, parting them a little. "Your mouth is so … I don't know how to describe it." He laughed softly as Rus opened his mouth to the probing thumb, caressing it with his tongue. "Inviting. It's very inviting."

He talked like this, joking and tender at the same time, easy compliments one moment and teasing the next. It wasn't something Rus had ever imagined, that he might want it, but it was wonderful.

"So," said Adares. "What would you like me to do?"

"Ah, well … " Should he say, *Whatever you want?* But he was learning the things Adares liked, and that giving pleasure was high on the list. "Touch me."

"Somewhere in particular?"

"Yes, my … " His face was probably bright red by now. He waved a hand indicatively.

He was wearing one of the Phemian tunics again, with nothing under it. Adares pushed up the skirt of it, delicately, touching only the fabric. He was naked already himself—he tossed his clothes off without ceremony now, although he had been more circumspect in their first days together, when he had still thought Rus was a respectable Luth.

"Can you not say the word 'dick' or something?"

"Of course not." Rus squirmed, arching his back. The Phemian was just *looking* at him now, and he felt exposed and absurd. "I didn't *know* that word."

He hadn't known an appropriate Kosoth word at all. He'd seen the body part mentioned only in medical treatises, and once in a Kossian poem, where it was called "the staff of manhood," which he was certainly not going to say. But perhaps he should have, because then his beautiful Phemian would have laughed—he laughed almost as easily as he smiled—and it was one of the wonders of the world.

Later, he would find a time to mention all this. Right now, his dick—that was a good, plain word—was in Adares's hand, and he couldn't form words in any language. He let his knee drop to the side against Adares's flank, his hips making small, jerky thrusts up into Adares's hand. He was lost to everything but the feeling of Adares's fingers, too light on his hot skin, moving with a teasing gentleness.

"It's a lovely dick, by the way. The size, the shape—the decoration. Definitely one of the best I've encountered."

"Do you want me to—penetrate you with it?" There was probably a short, plain word for that, too. It was a joke, in any case. It was something you did to a woman.

Adares raised his eyebrows, one of them higher than the other. Rus fell off several horses at the same time.

"Do you want to?"

"What?"

"*Penetrate* me—as you so scientifically put it."

"No!" It had been a joke. What if it weren't a joke? "I mean—how? *Where?*"

"Oh, Rus. Immortal gods." Adares was giving him a genuinely appalled look. "Is that a real question?"

"Ah. No."

It had been, but only because he'd been momentarily out of his mind and forgotten that of course there was that way, you could do that to a man—just as a woman could do what Adares had done earlier in the day, take a man into her mouth—and he knew about a number of ways like that, because some of the kahar talked openly about things they could do with women without risk of getting children, though of course they never admitted having actually done them, but …

With a heroic effort, he stopped himself saying *any* of that. Adares was still stroking him, with a steady, leisurely rhythm.

"Doesn't it … hurt?" Rus managed.

"What, hurt you?"

"No, you!"

"Oh, well, not … not much. Not if you do it properly. And it's, uh, it's worth it."

Rus wasn't sure that made sense to him, but he realized they had landed on a thing that Adares wanted and was—a little—embarrassed about. It was an amazing discovery.

"I want to do it," Rus said fervently. "How do I do it?"

He did it lying on his back, with Adares kneeling astride him—surely not the usual way, but of course Adares was still worried about Rus's hurt leg. There was lamp-oil involved, and Adares guided Rus's hand and showed him where to slide his fingers—it was very strange, but it was clear the Phemian liked it—and Rus's own dick, unattended, felt like a tent pole.

There is no way Adares can take that inside him, he thought—he will be hurt. But he did it, though in truth it didn't look easy, and Rus felt he would prefer their positions not be reversed in the future. Adares looked down at him with a raw expression, like a boy.

"I haven't done this in a long time," he said, and however he meant that to sound, it came out like a whispered confession.

Rus held hard to his slim, bronze hips, and pushed up into him, setting the rhythm, because he'd discovered already for himself how good that felt, to be at the other man's mercy in such a small, safe way. He watched to see if the Phemian would like it too, and everyone in the world fell off all the horses that had ever been bred.

Adares had raised his arms, hands clasped behind his head, eyes closed, his whole body thrown into a pose of impossible abandon, and the evening sun from the doorway glowed on his smooth, bare skin, all down one side, golden-bronze, as if he were kindling into flame. Rus reached that moment when his body seemed to contract into one pure arc of pleasure and then release, slowly, shuddering. It was smaller than the first time, not so overwhelming, and he was glad of that, because his beautiful Phemian had not reached his own ecstasy, and Rus knew what he wanted to do, while his body was still primed for it.

He rocked Adares forward and then back, catching him and putting him down on his back without breaking their union—he had trained from childhood to jump on and off horses and ride wild animals that didn't want to be ridden, and a little bit of athleticism in bed, even when he was injured, was no kind of a challenge—and he shifted his grasp from Adares's hips to his shoulders, pressing their bodies together, thrusting faster and harder, feeling the Phemian's beautiful dick rub against his belly. Adares yelled—not words, just a sound of delight—and his seed came hot against Rus's skin.

They collapsed together in a tangle of limbs, Rus on top. He shifted after a moment to pull out of the Phemian's body. Adares made a noise, and Rus looked up and saw that there were tears on his cheeks. He pushed up onto his hands, alarmed. He forgot about his leg then, and was rewarded with a bright stab of pain, but it barely registered.

"Ah, no! What is it? I hurt you! Did I hurt you?"

Adares turned his face away, scrubbing at his eyes.

"Speak to me! If I hurt you, I will never forgive myself."

Adares groaned, covering his eyes with his hand. "Immortal gods! Rus! Did I flip out on you like this when you started crying after the first time?"

"No, you did not, but I'm not like you, Adares. You're a sophisticated man from Pheme who"—*who rules a whole colony*, he was going to say, but he was still pretending not to know that—"who's had countless women and men. Of course you do not 'flip out.'"

Adares looked at him, half-smiling now. "I don't usually cry, either. That was … You're like a force of nature, when you want to be."

"You liked it. I didn't hurt you."

"No. Only in a good way. I liked it a lot."

"Good. Good."

He lay down again beside Adares. *What a man you are,* he thought, *to be able to want that and not be ashamed. And,* he thought, *I have just taken the archon of Tios, the headman of the colonists, like a woman. Let anyone try to tell me I'm not a man.*

They were lying the wrong way around on the bed now. Rus moved to retrieve the pillows and make them more comfortable. He rearranged himself carefully, because his leg was aching again.

He said, "Now we have both been a little bit like women

to each other. I think it is good to be like women. They are mothers and brave, loyal wives and take care of the hearth. We should want to be like that if we can."

Adares was silent for a moment as if thinking about that, as if perhaps he hadn't before. "Yeah," he said finally. "You're right. When you said that before, I thought you were insulting yourself."

"Ah. No, not really."

Adares got up then—wincing slightly as he climbed off the bed—and brought water and a cloth to clean them up. Rus honestly rather liked being sticky with the Phemian's seed, if only for the bizarre novelty of it, but he would not say so and invite remarks about his dirty barbarian ways. He let Adares run the cloth over his skin, and then took it away from him to return the favour. He took his time with it. He wanted to say something about how lovely Adares was, but he had no idea how to put it, what to say.

What he found himself saying instead, as he fingered the damp black curls at Adares's groin, was, "You do not have any other hair on your body but here. You don't shave it off, do you, as with your beard?"

"Um." Adares gave him a tolerant look, as if maybe he could tell Rus had been trying to come up with something more poetic. "Not exactly. We use wax."

"Wax?"

"It's completely normal, all Phemian aristocrats do this—don't make that face." He sat up, tossed his pillow back to the head of the bed, and scooted around to lie back down the right way. "You see, this is what I was talking about, why our women don't talk about their beauty regimes—you may think you want to know, but actually you want to go on thinking it's all a gift from the gods, and they don't have to do anything."

"It—it looks nice," Rus ventured.

Adares snorted. "Yeah? I'm glad you approve."

Rus moved his pillow and lay down beside Adares again. They were silent for a little while, and it was not awkward, but Rus was somewhat annoyed with himself. It should not be difficult to speak of such obvious, extravagant beauty. It should be like talking about the weather. But it wasn't, not unless there was a kind of weather that was disgraceful for a man to notice and impossible to comment on.

By and by he looked into Adares's face and saw that he too seemed lost in thought.

"What are you thinking about?" Rus asked.

"Oh." Adares recalled himself with a start. He looked embarrassed. "Well, it's not very … I was thinking about the Daine camped in the hills."

CHAPTER XIV

IT WAS A good plan, daring and heroic, and Rus was proud of his lover (his lover!) for having come up with it. Adares cared for his people, clearly. He really was a leader of men, even if—maybe all the more because—he thought he was not worthy to be.

Rus was less happy about Adares's reluctance to let him come along and help, but truthfully, he could understand it. Adares didn't think that Rus knew who he was, and probably didn't want him to find out. He didn't realize how far Rus had compromised himself already, knowingly being here with the leader of the Phemians and making no effort to take him prisoner, as honour and loyalty to his own people demanded. And it was strange, but Rus was actually afraid that telling him would reveal the extent of his own treachery and destroy Adares's good opinion, and he didn't want to do it.

But he was going to ride with Adares into the forest. He was stronger than the Phemian, and would sleep wrapped around him tonight so that there would be no possibility of anyone waking early and sneaking away without the other's knowledge.

He was used to sharing a bed, but how strange it was to be allowed to touch the person he shared with. At first he didn't think he would fall asleep at all. Then he thought that he shouldn't sleep; he should savour this, because he would never have it again. The next moment, it seemed, he was opening his eyes in the cold pre-dawn. Adares was sitting up already, on the edge of the bed. He had slipped out of Rus's arms without waking him, after all, but Rus didn't think he had intended to sneak away. He was looking down, as if waiting for his lover to wake, and he smiled.

I want to wake like this every morning, Rus thought, *but this is the only time I ever will.* Something of his thoughts must have shown in his face, because Adares's smile faded.

Or perhaps Adares had been thinking the same thing—but no, that couldn't be it. This wasn't the first time *he* had woken beside a lover, and it wouldn't be the last; it was just that the person beside him would never again be Rus.

Adares seemed withdrawn that morning as they breakfasted and dressed and readied themselves for the journey. He was preoccupied, Rus guessed, with his plans, thinking ahead to the difficulties of the return to Tios and what would happen after. It was not the time to speak of anything else, and after all, what was there really to say?

"You don't mind if I keep your kilt pin—I mean your cloak pin, for my kilt—do you?" Rus asked.

"Of course not," Adares said warmly, "but it might be better not to show it to anybody, once you get back to your camp."

Rus was weighing the heavy gold pin in his hand. "Ah yes, because they're going to find out you're not dead, so I can't claim to have taken it off your body on the battlefield."

There was a moment's pause. "Well, it doesn't have my name on it."

Rus looked up at him. The pin might as well have had his name on it; it had a device, an intertwined letter and numeral, that was surely an indication of his rank, and must have been unique, since there was only one archon of the colony. Rus wondered if he should mention that he'd worked this out. Now might be a good moment. But the truth was, he still didn't want to bring it up.

"No," he said. "I suppose not."

They finished dressing and went out to choose horses. There were some fine animals; even the Phemian horses, which Rus made fun of, were impressive, beautiful in a lean, dark, aristocratic style that was not unlike Adares. Another time, Rus would have enjoyed finding out how they were to ride.

The horses had obviously been chosen and set aside by the hearth headman whose retainers had brought them here— probably to hide them and keep them to himself while some general distribution of spoils was going on. Rus paid little attention to such things, and didn't know how it was done, but he did know good horses when he saw them. He searched for one that looked calm and rested and had the fearless temperament he needed in a mount with whom he would face a mad bull.

He found a mare he recognized and had ridden before. She had belonged to the son of a friend of his father. He wasn't sure what her presence here meant about her old owner, whether he had been killed, or traded her, or what. Adares, meanwhile, had chosen the darkest, most aristocratic-looking horse, and came out of the stable carrying an armload of foolish-looking Phemian horse-trappings. Rus made a face at that, and Adares laughed.

Rus had time to ride several easy circuits of the courtyard while Adares was saddling his horse; probably the Phemian wasn't used to doing such things for himself. He watched Adares mount, competently enough, and saw him squirm a little in the saddle, and realized with a start why he was uncomfortable.

If I don't make a joke about that, he thought, *I am shamed forever.* But he couldn't make a joke. It had really happened; he had really done that to Adares, and it had been glorious. Yet to think that Adares was suffering for it now was not funny.

Then of course the Phemian looked at him and raised an eyebrow—and poetry was poetry, after all, and Rus did not literally fall off his horse, or even come close, but he did feel a little breathless for a moment.

"Force of nature," Adares mouthed, and grinned.

Force of unnature would be more accurate, Rus thought, but he did not say it.

And, as it seemed, Adares was not really in much discomfort, and it was Rus for whom the ride through the forest that morning was painful, because of the stupid wound in his thigh.

It annoyed him. He'd been injured more than a few times—sprained limbs, a dislocated shoulder, a broken nose, bruised ribs, and he'd been gored once, though not badly—but he was young and strong and healed quickly. And the Phemian arrow, poisonous though it may have been, had been such a small thing. He felt as though it should have been about as serious as a bug bite, but of course it wasn't, it had gone right through the muscles of his thigh, and he'd had a fever after, and Adares was right to think he should still be resting instead of riding around in the forest.

Adares would have ridden out here whether Rus came with him or not—he had to remind himself of that. If they met the bull and Rus failed to take it down because his stupid leg gave out on him, Adares would still stand a better chance of getting away than if he had been on his own. And he would get away, Rus felt sure. He wouldn't linger pointlessly trying to save Rus when it was too late; he would put his heels to his horse and take off for the Daine camp and Tios and his duty to his people. He was—there was no other way of putting it—a better man than Rus.

And then they met the bull, and Rus forgot all this. They met him in a clearing that might have been designed by the gods for this fight. Rus felt the familiar stirring of his blood as he heard the bull's approach. Adares was well back by the trees, and a good enough rider—just—to keep his horse under control. There was nothing but Rus and the bull, and the old enmity between them.

That was real: the bull remembered him from the attack on Tios, and of course Rus remembered that bull. Pain had receded in the tide of exhilaration. He and his horse, as fearless as he had known she would be, rode toward the bull.

"Come! Come, let us finish this!" he called. And the bull came for him.

When it came together the right way, it was like riding the wind, like the hawk's flight, and the hawk's brutal impact with its prey. He threw unerringly, just catching the bull's shoulder with his spear, wheeled his horse, and leapt. He landed flawlessly, retrieved his spear, and the hard part was over. He'd never had any difficulty with the actual killing, which required a calm precision as well as strength and speed.

It wasn't until he jumped clear of the bull's body and stood up, and it felt as if someone had just thrust a burning brand through his leg, that he remembered he was injured. Still for a moment he did not react, because he was looking across the clearing at Adares, and the look on the Phemian's face …

Of course it hadn't been just Rus and the bull at all; it had been Rus facing the bull with his lover watching him.

There was an anecdote in a Kossian book Rus had read

once—it was a book of philosophy, and the anecdote was meant to illustrate something, he couldn't remember what—about a boy athlete winning a race against the odds because he saw his lover in the stands at the crucial moment. Of course Rus was not a boy, he was a grown man of nineteen, and after all this had been a matter of life and death, not showing off in a sport contest like an effete Kossian. But he had shown his skill in front of the man who had traced over his tattoos with his fingers and his tongue, and he thought he had an idea how the boy in that anecdote must have felt.

So they rode on toward the Daine camp, and things became easier between them after that. Rus, no longer afraid to let Adares see that he was in pain, and more at ease now that the bull was dealt with, found a more comfortable but less secure way to ride, and agreed to stop several times to stretch and drink water and rest. They had almost reached the place where the Daine were camped when he remembered that he still had to tell Adares that he knew who he was.

He couldn't think of any other way to do it, now that the moment was upon him, so he just explained what he had said when he poured out the last drops of wine beside the bull's body.

"What I said was: 'Nuthar give his blessing to the people of Tios, because they chose the right man to rule them.'"

He watched Adares react, his expressive face going still, his gaze dropping briefly, then meeting Rus's again, apologetic.

"Do you think that?"

That is your question? Not "How long have you known?" or "How did you guess?" *OF COURSE I think that—what is this nonsense?*

"I do," he said.

He wanted to say, "I knew you were someone special the

moment I pulled you out from under that cart. You were covered in mud, but you looked like a prince." He still did, sitting there in his battered armour without a sword, his cloak knotted on his shoulder, heavy black stubble on his chin. Rus wanted to say, "I think the people of Tios probably elected you for your looks."

He didn't say that, and later it occurred to him that it was good he hadn't, because it was probably more or less what Adares seriously believed. He was lavishly good-looking, and he knew that, but he was less certain of his other merits. Of course he would go through life thinking that people only liked him for his looks. All the while Rus had been searching for a way to compliment his beauty, he would have done better to praise his kindness and courage and wit.

All that would occur to him later. First they rode into the Daine camp, and Rus watched his laughing, boyish, carefree lover unsheath his claws like a cat and become casually commanding, a young, aristocratic leader to whom even the Daine headman respectfully deferred. Rus thought of the philosopher's anecdote again. Now he felt as if he were in the other role, except that he didn't really think the Phemian needed him cheering from the sidelines at this point. What he needed was the practical help that Rus could provide, slight as it was.

While Adares was busy conferring with the Daine headman and his men, Rus considered the lie he would tell his own people. He could ride to the watch-towers first—he would have to disguise himself somehow—and tell a story that would make the men abandon the towers. Then he could ride into the camp with a different story …

It all sounded good in his head for a few minutes while he thought about it, but it was a plan for some other man, not something Rus could ever do. He doubted whether he could tell the simplest lie convincingly. So after all there was going to be very little he could do to help Adares's deception.

"I think I should go," he said.

Adares made a token protest but accepted the necessity of it. He had even thought to ask the Daine headman to leave some tents up so that Rus's lie would be harder to detect.

"You think of everything," Rus said.

Adares shrugged, the claws disappearing for a moment. "I can be efficient, sometimes."

Rus made an effort to stick to practicalities. "I will try to make sure the towers by the harbour are abandoned. But if I can't—"

"If you can't, you can't, and we'll have to take them by force. If anyone seems suspicious, don't press the issue. I don't—"

You don't want me to risk my life for you, Rus thought. He waited for Adares to say it, and he didn't. Rus realized he wasn't going to. Unexpectedly, that moment of silence lanced through him with a kind of piercing happiness. *He knows how much he means to me*, Rus thought.

"Well," Adares finished. "Do what you can."

"I shall."

He hesitated a moment.

"Well," said Adares, "I guess … "

He should probably have waited for Adares to finish his sentence, but he couldn't. He reached out a hand, touching Adares's face. He leaned down.

It was the opposite of that feeling of flying that came over him in a fight. He had to think about every motion, and at the same time he felt distant from his body, as if some part of him simply could not believe he was doing this. The Daine headman was *right there*, looking at them. At least a dozen of his retainers were close enough to see, and Adares had been the centre of attention since he walked into the camp. Rus kissed him on the mouth.

He meant it, in some confused way, as the kind of parting gesture Adares would expect; and he offered it in an abandonment of his own honour in front of the hostile tribesmen of the Daine. Of course it was obvious from Adares's expression that he *hadn't* expected anything like that.

Rus straightened up. "May the gods bless you," he said formally.

Adares spent a moment looking taken aback before he jumped up from his chair. "Rus, I—"

But he hadn't expected the kiss; he hadn't intended to say whatever he was about to say in front of the Daine headman and his retainers. Rus couldn't let him make matters worse for himself. Besides, it didn't really need to be said.

"Ah, better not, I think. Goodbye, Adares."

"Goodbye," said Adares.

Rus turned away and walked toward his horse, trying hard not to limp, not looking back. Later, he thought it might have been at that moment, when he leaned down to kiss Adares in the Daine camp, that it dawned on him. He was not just going to risk his life—he was going to die.

CHAPTER XV

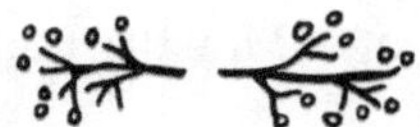

HE WAS SURPRISINGLY content as he rode back toward Tios. The day was warm, the sky clear overhead, birds singing in the trees. He rode leading the horse that Adares had brought from the temple, so that he could return it. He would explain, if he needed to, that a thief had tried to take it, and he had ridden in pursuit and recovered it. He hoped that story wouldn't be necessary, though, as he would have enough lies to tell without it.

He thought over his time with Adares, pleasurably, treasuring up his memories of things they had said and done together. His life had changed irrevocably. Even if—as seemed likely—he and the Phemian never met again, Rus was different now, he thought, because they had been there together and done what they had done.

He still didn't think you could call a man a "virgin," but if you could—apparently in Firhat Kosoth, Pseuchaian, you could—then that was what he had been, and now he was not. But it didn't feel as if he had stopped being something, rather as if he had begun to be something else. At the moment it felt like something better.

He had a friend at home, Kuth, who had trained to become kahar, but on the eve of his initiation, changed his mind and instead married one of the apprentices to the vahat, the girl who would have helped to ink his tattoos. People told the story to laugh about it, and Kuth always laughed with them, because that's the sort of man he was, but if you asked him seriously whether he thought he had made the right choice, he would say yes, and that he had never regretted it.

Of course it was not quite like that for Rus. No one would know how he had changed, and there was no new life waiting for him, side-by-side with the person he loved, the way Kuth lived. Perhaps it was just as well that such a thing was not possible. He wouldn't have known how to ask for it, even if it was, and he wasn't sure it was what Adares would have wanted.

It was early evening by the time he reached the edge of the forest and saw the yellow walls of the Phemian holy place ahead of him. He rode through the gate prepared to tell his story about the stolen horse, but it wasn't needed. There was no one there, only the remaining horses.

He returned the Phemian mare, dumping her saddle and bridle in the stable with the heap of other equipment. He went out of his way to avoid the corner of the courtyard with the door to the little back room where he had sheltered with Adares. He thought it would make him sad to see it now.

He rested for a little while, sitting outside the stable, before hauling himself back up onto the white mare and taking her at a slow walk out through the gate in the direction of the Luth camp. By this time, the sky was twilit.

The Luth had several advantages in warfare over the tribes of the Karhan. One was that they lived on campaign the same way they lived for part of each year, in the same comfortable, well-made tents with which they followed their herds down to the winter pastures and back up to the summer villages in the highlands. They were at home in their tents, and even Rus, riding toward Gunthanaruth's camp at the base of the walls of Tios, couldn't escape the feeling that he was coming home. He was bone-weary by this time, hungry, and ready to fall off his horse from sheer exhaustion, and there would be hot mead in the camp, fresh-baked bread, and spit-roasted meat, and he could already faintly hear the sound of someone singing from the nearest tent. He wondered where Adares was now and what he was doing.

The men at the tent where he arrived were strangers to Rus, but of course they could see what he was. They welcomed him respectfully.

"Come and share our fire, kahar," they said. "Hathum, fill another mead-horn!"

Rus accepted the drink, and a few bites of bread and meat, but reluctantly declined the spot by their fire.

"I must see Gunthanaruth," he said. "And if I sit now, I think I will not get up before morning."

He left them and led his horse through the alleys between tents to the headman's fire. It was crowded and lively with music and laughter. Gunthanaruth had brought his favourite bard with him, and he was singing, accompanying himself on the lyre. One of the captive Tak women whom they had taken in the summer sat by Gunthanaruth's side, working on some inscrutable Tak handicraft in the firelight. She did not look unhappy, but there was no reason why she should. The Luth treated captives well—it was one of the things they said about themselves—and of course they were better off than any of the poor forest-dwelling tribes of the Karhan.

The rest of the fire was ringed by retainers and hearth headmen enjoying their chief's hospitality. And of course Suthus. He was the current stathan, a cousin and childhood friend of Gunthanaruth. He had opposed this campaign, but in a friendly way, and when Gunthanaruth decided to pursue it in spite of him, of course Suthus had come along. His own days of riding bulls—or really of riding anything other than a placid, sturdy mare—were long past. He had been stathan for more than twenty years, since he was a young man.

Rus tethered his horse and approached the circle of firelight. One of the hearth headmen, seeing him, nudged Suthus and pointed. The stathan looked up, then started forward and half-rose, then sat down again abruptly, his eyes wide in his round face.

"Rusanarath?"

Rus made the correct obeisance to his superior, though not a very good version of it, and by that time Gunthanaruth had noticed him too.

"Rusanarath! Excellent! Come, come, join us. We heard you had fallen, and Suthus was distraught at losing you. But here you are after all!"

There were three ranks among the kahar, below the stathan and his deputy, and Rus belonged to the highest, the bull-fighters. Among them there was no official hierarchy, but the spirit of competition was strong, and everyone knew who was better than whom. Currently, it was generally acknowledged, there was no one better than Rus.

Gunthanaruth had shooed away the Tak girl and made room for Rus to sit at the fire beside him. He sank down onto the folded rug where she had been sitting, and stretched slightly to ease his injured leg, no longer troubling to hide his wince of pain.

"What happened?" Suthus asked, from the other side of the headman. Gunthanaruth was calling for a servant to bring food and drink for Rus. "Kaman told me you came to him with a poisoned arrow in you. He said he wouldn't draw it because he had no way of healing the poison. We looked for your body on the field, but … "

"But it wasn't there," Rus supplied. "I was still using it."

Suthus chortled. "And I am glad! What an unexpected blessing, to have you back. But how did you survive? And where have you been?"

Here it was: the time to lie. And not only to lie to Gunthanaruth, for whom Rus had little affection, but to Suthus, whom he liked and respected.

"It's true I took an arrow in the leg." He shifted his kilt to show the bandage. "And it was poisoned. Or made of poisonous wood, I think, actually. Kaman sent me away with the arrow still in me, and I went out onto the field to see … ah, what I could do, I suppose, in the time I had left."

Suthus made an approving noise, and Gunthanaruth grunted.

"I found a Phemian soldier who was still alive, but injured too badly to survive, and I did all I could do for him. Then I found another … He had been trapped under an overturned cart, and I dug him out, not knowing if he was a Luth or a Phemian. He was a Phemian, and he was not badly hurt—he was almost uninjured, only he had been trapped by the cart, and would have died there without my help."

"Ah!" said Suthus eagerly. "I see what must have happened. You spared his life, and in return he gave you the antidote to the Phemian poison!"

Gunthanaruth made a face as if he had eaten something rotten. "You insult him, Suthus. You think he spared the life of an enemy, on the battlefield?"

"The battle was won," Suthus offered, but he looked uncertain.

"I did spare his life. As my lord Suthus says, he offered me the antidote for the poisonous wood. It was a bargain—my life for his." The lie would have had to begin somewhere, Rus thought. So here was where it began.

He remembered that moment, his first glimpse of Adares.

He had always intended to spare the man, whoever he was—to let him go, if he could, or to give him a merciful death if he was beyond help. He wouldn't have bothered to dig under the cart or lift the heavy wood if he hadn't intended that. When he saw the face of the man he had rescued, he thought it was a final blessing from the gods, that he should have used his remaining strength to return such a person to the world.

"He said that the Phemian priests keep antidotes to many poisons in their holy place, and he told me how to find the one I needed. That is where I have been since." He pointed into the gloom in the direction of the temple complex. "I was some time recovering—maybe I didn't mix the antidote correctly—but I explored the buildings when I was well enough. There was not much to find. I think they had been evacuated before we arrived. I was about to return to camp when some of Gundurus's men came into the holy place with horses—"

"What?" Gunthanaruth cut him off. "Whose horses?"

"Gundurus's horses," Suthus supplied helpfully. "I suppose."

Rus had known this part of the story was going to prove distracting to the headman, but there was no way of accounting for why he had ridden off into the forest without it.

"They said they had orders from Gundurus to pen the horses in the Phemian holy place," he explained patiently. It was quite true. "I don't know why. But they also told me a bull had broken lose and was in the forest nearby. My bull, they said."

"Eh?" Gunthanaruth's mind was obviously still on the horses. "That's true, we did lose one of them."

"They should all have been slaughtered, as is proper," Suthus put in mildly. "We will not need them again on this campaign."

"We may need them," Gunthanaruth said. "But these horses—"

"Let him finish his story," Suthus suggested.

Gunthanaruth grunted assent, and Rus went on: "I felt it my duty to pursue the bull in the woods—"

"Ah, no!" Suthus threw up his hands. "I mean—yes, in a strict sense, and it does you credit, Rusanarath—but alone, and injured? You didn't, did you?"

"Let him finish his story," said Gunthanaruth sardonically.

"I—" Rus cleared his throat. "I did ride out into the forest. I did meet the bull, and I killed him."

"Good lad," said Gunthanaruth. "These horses of Gundurus's—how many did you say there were?"

"Perhaps two dozen, my lord. But there is one more thing. While I was riding in the forest, I saw the Daine camped in a valley."

That got Gunthanaruth's attention at last. "Ah, yes? How far off, would you say?"

"Twelve miles. Maybe less, but the terrain is rough. I rode down as close as I dared, and I came upon a pair of their outriders without being seen, and overheard their talk. I think—from what they said, I believe they intend to attack before dawn tomorrow."

"Do they indeed? Well, they will find us ready. This is fine work you've done, Rusanarath. Fine work indeed."

"They said, 'The Luth will never see us coming,' my lord. They spoke of moving before dawn, and one of them wished they had an extra day's rest, which made me sure they meant dawn tomorrow."

"Mm," said Gunthanaruth. "We'll be ready for them whenever they come, but if it's to be tomorrow, I'll summon the men back from the watchtowers and have a full force waiting for them."

"If you think it wise, my lord," said Rus doubtfully, and felt almost dizzy with his own daring.

The headman gave him an indulgent look. "You stick to your bulls, kahar, and leave the strategy to me. I'll have an answer out of Gundurus about those horses, but I suppose that will have to wait now."

Rus sat a little longer by the headman's fire, but now that his message had been delivered, his work was done, and he found all the strength ebbing out of him. The mead and food in his belly made him suddenly very sleepy, and he excused himself to stagger back to the tent of the kahar, where he flopped down on a rug and was asleep almost at once.

If the Daine had truly been attacking before dawn, there was a real possibility he might have slept through it. It was certainly well past dawn when he woke. One of the votive boys was shaking him by the shoulder and telling him to come look at something.

"It's the Daine, kahar! They're inside Tios!"

And they were. In the sunlight, the walls of the city were bristling with them, their yellow banners snapping in the wind. They were parading, showing off their numbers to the Luth, not just patrolling the defences.

"How did they get in?" Rus asked innocently.

"Who knows?" someone replied. "Witchery!"

He went and made an unnecessarily abject apology to Gunthanaruth, who accepted it with an equally unnecessary benevolence and said nothing about the abandoning of the watchtowers. Later that day, a few survivors from the tower that had not been fully abandoned returned to the camp to strengthen the rumour that the Daine had used supernatural powers to get inside the city. They had come up from the harbour, these men reported. They must have swum.

That afternoon, amid speculation about the Daine raining

poisoned arrows down on the Luth camp, Gunthanaruth ordered the tents taken down and the camp relocated into the eaves of the wooded hills. It was an awkward place to camp—the biggest of the tents couldn't be pitched, and the hearth headmen worried about losing their horses to raiders. Most people seemed to hold the opinion that the campaign was over, and the Luth force should cut their losses and turn homeward. The autumn was wearing on, and they had a long journey back to the winter pastures ahead of them.

They camped there for a week. The hearth headmen got more and more impatient. It began to rain steadily, and there was nothing for anyone to do but hunker in their tents and pick fights. Even Suthus was heard loudly quarrelling with Gunthanaruth. Rus spent as much time as he could on patrol, guarding the horses. He needn't have done it at all—as kahar he was exempt from regular patrol duty, and he could have pleaded injury, too—but he wanted to be out, even in the cold rain, rather than mewed up in the cramped travelling tents with the remaining kahar.

There had been six bull-riders when they left the summer villages, and there were three left now. Suthus's deputy, the second-in-command of the kahar, had also been killed. There were six votive boys and twice as many of the lower ranks, as well as Suthus, so the loss of three riders didn't diminish their numbers too starkly. To lose half their riders on a campaign like this was no more than might be expected. But it cast a gloom over the rest.

Suthus in particular was unhappy about it, and his mood infected the rest of the kahar. Buth, Gorus, and Sul had been experienced riders—Sul had been very nearly as good as Rus—and of those who were left, Hath was past his prime, and Dudun had yet to make a kill. Neither of them had ridden in the assault on Tios, and both of them were clearly eager to go home.

Then one morning, Suthus himself rode out through the grey rain to the pasture where Rus was riding on patrol.

"My lord?" Rus pushed back the hood of his cloak respectfully, but Suthus waved away the gesture, so he tugged it back with a grateful smile. "Is there something you need of me?"

"I don't know, Rusanarath." Suthus called all his kahar by their proper names, though among themselves they always used short forms and nicknames. The stathan was formal and old-fashioned in other ways, too. "I wish there were not, but I am afraid there is."

Rus looked at him, thinking, for some reason, of Adares and that expression he made with one eyebrow raised. But he spent a lot of time thinking of Adares these days.

"Gunthanaruth is unhappy with the outcome of this campaign," Suthus went on. That hardly needed saying, Rus thought, but he kept quiet. "He is losing face with the hearth headmen—that is, he *may*—he fears … " Suthus frowned. He was trying hard not to show disrespect, but there was really no other way of putting it.

Rus nodded. "They want to be moving. They're restless."

"Yes."

And what does this have to do with me? Rus wondered. Surely Suthus wasn't trying to recruit him to wheedle or reason with the headman. That would never work.

The stathan cleared his throat. "Gunthanaruth has it in mind to show the hearth headmen a sign, to convince them that we must press the Phemians harder. He wants to stay on through the winter, to resume the siege or find some way into the city … "

Suthus shook his head, his expression pained. Rus knew how he felt. The prospect of the campaign dragging out through the winter, with the current state of their forces and with the Daine inside Tios, was awful—even if you didn't have a lover inside the city whom you wanted to protect.

"I have tried to argue with him," Suthus said, "but it hasn't done any good. You have seen how it is."

"My lord." Rus tried to sound sympathetic and respectful. He had indeed seen how it was—he'd known how it was for a long time—but Suthus had never spoken so candidly to him before.

"He wants a bull ceremony," Suthus said.

For a moment Rus couldn't quite take it in, what that meant.

"Ah, I see," he said finally. "He wants to show the hearth headmen that the gods favour his plan to stay through the winter."

Suthus nodded. "He is determined. I think he must have had it in mind all along—it's why he didn't allow the bulls to be properly slaughtered."

"And you want me to fight," Rus said.

Suthus looked up at him, his blue eyes strangely bleak. "Of course—who else? He'd never let me send Hath or Dudun, not when you're here. And he has seen for himself that your wound is healed, or nearly healed. Of course I have to send you." He stopped and passed a hand wearily over his face. "And of course you have to do your best—which, as we all know, will be very good indeed. I fear the hearth headmen will see this for what it is—a mere spectacle, like a bard singing after dinner, not a true appeal to the will of the gods. But I cannot tell Gunthanaruth this—he prides himself on his piety, but he doesn't listen when I tell him that things like this are nothing but impious."

This was uncomfortably, even dangerously frank talk, and Rus would have been hard-pressed to think of a response, if he had been trying. He agreed with Suthus in general; the bull ceremonies proved nothing. But there would be worse impiety done here than Suthus could know, because this time the bull was going to win.

CHAPTER XVI

HE REMEMBERED THAT it had been raining. He remembered that he had expected to die. He didn't remember much else.

He stared at the leather ceiling of the tent above him. He thought he had woken and stared at it before, but perhaps that was a dream. His body hurt, all over, but with a special dull throbbing in his head. His mouth tasted foul, a familiar taste that he could not identify. When he tried to move, the spike of pain in his right arm took his breath away. He squeezed his eyes shut.

Theraka. That was the taste in his mouth. Theraka eased pain. It must have worn off. He lay as still as he could. Even the little movements of relaxing his muscles hurt. The throbbing in his head had built into a sharp pounding. But he was alive, and he had expected to die.

He couldn't remember why.

Light from the opening of the tent flap stabbed at his closed eyelids. When it dimmed again, he opened one eye a crack and saw Kaman, the healer who had accompanied the warriors on campaign.

"Awake, are you?" Kaman grunted.

Rus made a hoarse noise, then tried to moisten his lips to speak. "What happened?" he managed finally.

Kaman was pouring something from a flask into a cup by the side of Rus's pallet. "Broke your arm, but it was a clean break—I've splinted it, it'll heal up fine. Nothing else broken, just cuts and bruises. You hit your head a good wallop, knocked yourself out for a spell, but didn't crack your skull."

That hadn't been the information he was looking for, but Kaman was holding out the cup now and scooping Rus up to put it to his lips. Rus gulped down the liquid. More theraka—a strong dose, he thought, from the bitter taste. That reminded him of something he couldn't quite hold in his mind …

Kaman laid him down again, lifted the blanket briefly to check on the splinted arm, and then left. Rus stared at the ceiling of the tent, waiting for the drug to take effect.

He slept, eventually, floating in the easy numbness of the theraka. He woke before it had quite worn off, and stared at the ceiling some more. It was dark now, and he could barely see it, but this didn't bother him. He heard soft sounds of other people sleeping in the tent around him. He'd had a dream which he tried to remember but couldn't. The drug made it hard to feel bothered or even bored, made his thoughts feel comfortably slow and unfocused.

He was thirsty. That reminded him of something.

Oh Water! Divine beverage! I will never drink wine again!

The words so unexpectedly spoken in Firhat Kosoth, and that beautiful laugh. You would fall off your horse.

It was like stumbling across buried treasure, like bright gold glinting up at him suddenly from the dirt. Rus smiled up at the tent ceiling in the dark. He had remembered Adares.

He also remembered now why he had expected to die. He had been going to face a bull and had intended to lose. It had been raining. There was still a kind of hole in his memory after that. And now the pain was returning, and he felt too tired to think much. He closed his eyes again and focused on that memory of Adares at the fountain, laughing as he splashed water on his face.

Later, after he'd drunk more theraka and slept and woken again, and it seemed to be morning, with a lot of noise and voices outside the tent where he lay, Suthus came in to see him.

"How are you feeling? No, no—don't answer that. Not well, obviously." The stathan sat down cross-legged beside Rus's pallet. "You hit your head pretty hard. Do you remember—"

"Not even a little bit. What happened?"

"Ah. Well, you fought a bull … "

"Yes, yes—in the rain, to decide whether we would leave or go on with the siege. I do remember that. It's the fight that—that's gone." So utterly gone that he hadn't been sure until Suthus said so just now that it had actually taken place.

"Well, we're leaving." Suthus gestured to the open tent flap behind him and the dismantling of the camp going on outside. "You lost, rather spectacularly."

"Ah."

He tried hard not to look pleased. Suthus, he saw, was doing the same thing.

"What did I do wrong?" Rus asked finally.

"Nothing, really. That was—partly—what made it so spectacular. You threw beautifully, as always, landed with perfect form, had a good seat—I would have said—but then the animal bucked hard, and you must have lost your grip, because he just pitched you off. You went flying. You *almost* managed to turn in the air and make a clean landing—which would have been the first time I've seen that, if you'd done it—but you couldn't quite, and you hit the ground hard. Still,

I understand you're not as badly hurt as you might have been—though I doubt that's much consolation to you now."

"What happened to the bull?" Specifically, why had he not trampled Rus or tossed him on his horns and finished him off?

Suthus shifted a little where he sat, looking away from Rus for a moment. "We let him go. The fight went out of him. That was the other remarkable thing. You hit the ground, and he … shook himself and turned away, quite calmly. We felt certain that meant you were dead already—your neck broken or some such. We were astonished to find you were still alive. Gunthanaruth thinks … " He cleared his throat and looked embarrassed. "It seems to him a definite message from the gods. He gave the order to strike camp almost immediately. I think, myself, that the bull was tired, but … we cannot know the whole shape of Heva, and the gods are the gods." It was a saying, less pious than resigned. "And you remember none of this?"

"No, not even when I hear you tell it. It's as if it never happened."

"It can take you that way when you hurt your head, I believe. And it may be for the best. It would be a bad thing to remember—all the more since it was … the merest fluke, that it happened. Nothing you did wrong."

He was giving Rus an interesting look, and Rus thought, *He knows I did it on purpose.* Or he suspected, anyway. But he wouldn't speak of it. Perhaps he thought Rus didn't remember that part. Perhaps he just felt too guilty to say anything, because if he thought Rus had fought to lose, he must have thought he, Suthus, put him up to it. *I wish I could tell him the truth*, Rus thought. But he knew he could not.

"It may be for the best," he agreed.

The journey back to the summer villages took more than a month. It should not have taken so long. The distance was not so great, but they had to take a meandering route, to avoid territory held by hostile tribes—allies of the Phemians—and they travelled slowly through the wooded hills, a miles-long train of horses and men and a few light vehicles. The big siege wagons—the surviving ones, the ones Adares had not ridden his horse into—had been dismantled, the heavier pieces abandoned, the rest packed up and loaded on horses.

Rus rode for the first week in a litter that jolted uncomfortably over the rough forest tracks. He swilled down theraka like mead and spent as much time as he could asleep. He got back on a horse as soon as Kaman would let him—sooner than Suthus would have let him, if Suthus had been in charge of the matter, but he wasn't. It was more comfortable in some ways to ride, but he seemed to tire very easily, and would have to go back to the litter before the end of each day, some days while the sun was still high in the sky.

His head hurt, in a low, draining ache, almost all the time, so that he noticed as a novelty the times when it briefly stopped hurting. The broken arm didn't trouble him nearly as much; he understood what was wrong with it, and could avoid the worst pain by keeping it still. The pain in his head was more mysterious. There was nothing broken there, and no evidence that anything was healing, either.

He felt low and irritable much of the time, and couldn't quite say why. Sometimes he could lift his spirits by thinking about his lover—just picturing his face, or recalling some moment from their days together. Sometimes that didn't work and would bring him close to tears instead. One day, when he was feeling particularly low, it finally dawned on him that it was only in his own mind that Adares was still his lover. That day he actually did shed tears, and after that it became harder and harder to escape the sadness.

He knew he had meant something to the Phemian, maybe even something like what the Phemian meant to him. But Adares never expected to see him again. Adares might very well—would surely—think Rus was dead. Adares would have heard why the Luth abandoned the siege, and he would know what it meant—what Rus had done. Wouldn't he?

When Rus had known, beforehand, that he was going to do it, there had been no doubt in his mind. Adares would know what he had done. Now, turning it over endlessly on the long ride north, he was less sure. He thought Adares probably knew, and of course he had wanted that—selfishly, he had wanted that—but if Adares knew what he had done, then Adares thought he was dead.

There was a sad logic to it. Either the Phemian hadn't loved him enough to guess what Rus had done—or he had, and so he thought Rus was dead. He would mourn him, no doubt, but after all they had been together for a couple of days, and Adares was fall-off-your-horse beautiful, liked women as well as men, and ruled a city. He would find some-one else.

Even if he had known Rus was alive, he would still have found someone else. They must be lining up.

Drinking theraka helped. At first he took it strictly for the pain, and it did continue to help, somewhat, with the lingering ache in his head. But after a while he was taking it mainly for the way it made him feel as if nothing mattered. Time was just passing; nothing bothered or worried him very much. He took just enough to be able to stay awake and keep on his horse, and the days slid by more easily. He kept the sadness at bay.

He might not have been able to get away with dosing himself like this for as long as he did, but the mood of the whole horse-train was low by this time, and no one was paying much attention. The Luth warriors had ridden down to the coast in high spirits, full of confidence in their own strength, ready to besiege the Phemians in their walled city and drive them out of the Karhan. Now they were slinking back with their boast unfulfilled. Once they reached the summer villages, most of them would have to journey still further north, to the lowland pastures, or risk losing large portions of their herds to the harsh winter. It was a lot of riding, even for men accustomed to spending half the year on horseback.

To make matters worse, the weather was unrelentingly wet. Water dripped off the trees and sprayed and sprinkled out of the undergrowth even when it was not, strictly speaking, raining. Their clothes would be drenched by the end of the day and still damp when they emerged in the morning after an unsatisfactory night in a poorly-pitched tent—the best they could do in the cramped spaces of the forest. Sickness laid many men low. Fights broke out, and rumours spread quickly up and down the train. It was a miserable time. At some point during those weary, wet weeks, as Rus realized later when he reckoned up the dates, he turned twenty.

The one good thing was that nobody blamed him for losing his last fight. In fact, he was viewed as a kind of a hero, not only because everyone had wanted to go home, but also because they seemed to feel that his defeat had somehow restored the bull ritual to its ancient purity—as if there was no way it could have happened except by the hand of a god personally reaching out and flipping him off the back of that bull. And then, presumably, cushioning his fall and calming the animal so that a decisive result could be achieved without a kill. The warriors had a lot of time to talk on the long ride north, and this was what they came up with.

Rus didn't believe any of it himself, but if it left his honour intact, even enhanced his already high status a little, he would not quarrel with it. He expected that at least Gunthanaruth would be annoyed with him, but instead the headman seemed to regard him with a kind of pious awe. Rus would have been embarrassed if he could have mustered the energy to care enough.

Finally they rode out of the dripping gloom of the forest and began to ascend the grey, wind-scoured slopes that marked the edge of the Luth lands. It was the wrong time of year to be riding up to the highlands, but spirits lifted all the same. The moon was full, so they rode late into the night to make up time, and singing echoed up and down the train as they went up the trails carved by their ancestors. Rus had a splitting headache that night, and everything that suddenly spoke of home—the familiar songs, the taste of the air, the stars spread across the clear sky above them—all of it seemed to be reminding him how far he had travelled from the coast, from Tios, from Adares. He slid down from his horse, stiff and exhausted, curled up in the litter, and fell asleep as the train moved on through the night.

"Rus. Wake up. You look like shit."

He opened his eyes, blinked, and squinted against the sunlight, so much brighter up here in the highlands. A familiar, beak-nosed face, framed by faded red curls, looked down at him.

"Kuth. Good to see you too."

They were in the kahar hall, where Rus had apparently slept late after arriving late the night before. It was empty but for themselves. Kuth squatted by the side of Rus's pallet, frowning at him.

"What happened to you?"

Rus rubbed his hands over his face. He badly needed to shave. "You haven't heard? Ask anyone—they're all still talking about it."

Kuth made an impatient gesture. "Yes, yes, you flew off the back of a bull and landed on your head, and it was a miracle wrought by the hand of Kahait—I know all that. What happened *after* that?"

"After that? After that we rode for a month in the rain. What do you mean?"

"I *mean*, you look like shit. Like you were thrown off a bull yesterday, not like you've had a month to recover."

"I haven't. We were riding the whole time. In the rain. Camping in the forest. It was miserable." He levered himself up on one elbow and looked around for his clothes.

"Who looked after you? Kaman?"

"Mm." Rus pulled his shirt and kilt in under the furs with him. It was too cold to get out from under the covers to dress—too cold for the kilt, really, but his winter trousers were packed away. He would have to go looking for them as soon as he had some breakfast inside him, and some more theraka. His head was hurting already. He didn't understand why Kuth wasn't being nicer to him.

"What's he been giving you for pain? Theraka?"

"Yes, of course." Rus pulled his shirt over his head and shook out his hair. He wrapped his kilt around his waist under the covers, awkward with his still-healing arm. "What's all this about? What happened to, *Hello, Rus, old friend—it's good to have you back*?"

"How much theraka?"

"I don't know!" Rus felt around the edge of the bedclothes for his kilt pin. "He just lets me have as much as I want."

"That's what I thought!" Kuth looked triumphant. Rus glared at him. "You've all the signs of it. That *idiot*"—lowering his voice a little, since Kaman was technically his elder—"has been giving you too much for too long—and after a blow to the head? Tcha! He's lucky you didn't die on him. I mean you're lucky. You know what I mean."

Rus looked at his friend for a moment. Then he sighed. "I know what you mean."

"It is good to see you, of course. But I'm worried about you. Here, were you looking for this? Wait, what *is* this?" He held up the thing in his hand, looking at it with wide eyes.

"A Phemian officer's rank badge." Rus took it out of his hand and slipped the sharp point of the pin through the folded layers of his kilt.

"Trophy of war?" Kuth said, with a trace of distaste that he couldn't quite conceal.

"Something like that. Am I going to have to stop taking theraka altogether?"

"You are, yeah. Sorry."

Kuth was a healer, a better one than Kaman, the most knowledgeable man Rus knew on the subject of drugs. He could read Firhat Kosoth, because he had been brought up with the kahar before his marriage, so he had all that knowledge too. If he said Rus needed to stop taking theraka, it was true, and there was no use arguing with it. Rus tossed back the covers but didn't get up.

"Why were you still taking it, anyway?" Kuth asked. "You can't be in much pain by this time, surely?"

"My head still hurts," Rus admitted. "Not much, though. It's not the pain, exactly, it's just … I don't know what's wrong with me. I get tired when I shouldn't, and I don't feel like myself sometimes. I get … just *sad*." It was a surprising relief to tell someone even this much.

Kuth looked at him for a moment, and Rus thought he could tell there was more to the story that he wasn't being told, but he didn't ask.

"Well," he said finally, "you are going to have to stop taking the theraka. In the long run, you'll feel better for it, though in the meantime you'll feel worse for a bit. But as for the other, hitting your head can do strange things to you. Some men lose their memory altogether, forget their own names even. Sometimes they can't walk, or they limp, or they can't do things with their hands. Sometimes it's like they're different people. I suppose this might be something like that—only not so bad, obviously."

Rus gave him a horrified look. "They're *different people*?"

"They act differently, is all I meant. And this is right after they hit their heads. It's not going to happen to you now. You're probably going to get better."

"Ah. Probably."

"Well, no one can say for sure. But one of the Kosoth medical men made a study of it. That's where I read all this. I can find the book for you, if you want."

"No, thank you," said Rus hastily. He generally liked to learn about things, but this sounded like something he might be better off not knowing too much about. But after a moment he added, "Maybe you can read it again yourself and tell me if there's anything I can do. To get better, I mean."

"Of course. I had it in mind to do that." He clapped Rus on the shoulder. "It *is* good to have you back."

CHAPTER XVII

WINTER IN THE summer villages was hard: the weather bitter, the food monotonous when it wasn't scarce, the loneliness of the empty fields and closed-up houses depressing to the spirit. It suited Rus, in a way, that winter. He would have been unhappy wherever he was, and there was some solace in seeing his mood mirrored in the bleak, wind-scoured landscape of the highlands and the deserted silence of the headman's village.

He was lucky, too, that Kuth and his wife Genet were staying the winter—had been planning to stay, they claimed, even before he turned up—so he did not lack for sympathetic company. He slept in the kahar hall but spent most of his time in their house close by. Their eldest child, a boy, had ridden with the departing herds for the first time this year, but the two girls, Meret, who was six, and Gil, the baby, were at home with their parents.

In the kahar hall, the company was not so good: just two of the votive boys and one senior kahar, Unumus, whom Rus had never liked. There was work to be done over the winter, but not much, and the two boys were both very keen, so Rus was idle much of the time.

At first this was just as well. After the village emptied out, he spent the first weeks of the lonely winter being wretchedly sick when he stopped taking theraka. If he'd known it was going to be like this, he thought he wouldn't have started taking it in the first place; he couldn't believe that the relief it had given him could have been worth this. He had chills, ran a temperature, threw up everything he ate—he *hated* throwing up—and couldn't get a night's uninterrupted sleep for weeks. Kuth and Genet looked after him, coming over to the kahar hall every day and taking turns sitting with him at night for the first little while because they had no faith in the votive boys, keen as they were.

It was during the worst of this period that he had the dream about the Pseuchaian woman. He had odd dreams whenever he managed to sleep, but he only remembered them in bits and pieces. This one was different. He woke up with every detail still clear in his mind, with a confused feeling as though it had really happened.

He felt a little better than usual that morning, and thought he might attempt eating something. It was very early, but Unumus and the votive boys were up, sitting by the hearth, where something was steaming in a pot on the fire. Rus pulled on his trousers under the covers, wrapped himself in the warm robe he had borrowed from Kuth, and shuffled down off the sleeping platform to join the others at the hearth.

"I had a strange dream," he said, folding himself down onto a seat and tucking his feet under the edge of the robe. He felt creaky, like an old man, and stupid for having led with this remark instead of bidding them good morning like a sane person.

"Ah, yes?" Unumus looked up from the pot, which he had been stirring, looking interested. Rus remembered that he was fond of interpreting dreams, and was doubly annoyed with himself for mentioning it. But it was too late now.

He settled for trying to make the whole thing as boring

as possible. "Well, it was nothing much. I dreamt about a woman painting the pattern on the kahar hall. It seemed strange to me because she was a Pseuchaian woman."

"Interesting," said Unumus. "A Kosoth woman, he means," he added for the benefit of the boys, who were still learning Firhat Kosoth and wouldn't know the word "Pseuchaian." Rus hadn't known it himself before that fall.

"I don't know if she was Kossian," Rus said. "She wore a blue gown, and gold in her hair."

"Was she beautiful?" one of the boys asked. The other one elbowed him, and they both blushed and snickered.

"Like a goddess," Rus said solemnly. "Actually, she looked a little like the statue of Anaxe in the temple outside Tios. I saw it when I was there in the fall."

"Ah!" Unumus's eyes lit up. "That is *most* interesting. Anaxe is what the Kossians call Kahait," he reminded the boys, who nodded earnestly. "And she was painting the new pattern on our walls, you say?"

"That was what it looked like. A strange thing to dream, isn't it?"

"Perhaps. Or perhaps not. Did you know that the Kossians believe Anaxe is a chaste goddess?"

Rus didn't see what that had to do with anything. "Yes, actually. I did know that."

"Ah." Unumus looked surprised, which Rus found insulting. He knew Unumus thought the bull-fighters were all muscle and no brains—and that Rus, as the best of them, was also the worst of them, so to speak. He stuck to that opinion no matter how many examples he might see to the contrary. It was one of the reasons Rus disliked him.

"Is that porridge?" Rus asked, to change the subject.

"I'll serve you some, kahar," said one of the votive boys, bobbing up eagerly.

"I believe I know what your dream signified," said Unumus, ignoring the diversion. "You saw a vision of the goddess, the pure Anaxe, painting the great pattern of Heva on the Hall of the Heavens. It is a great blessing to have seen such a thing. We can only think that it is a message for us—and I believe I know what that message is." He turned to the two boys. "Can you tell?"

"No, kahar," said one. The other opened his mouth, closed it again, and shook his head.

Rus slurped his porridge quietly.

"Why should the goddess appear to him in that form? Why not as Kahait, as our ancestors have always known her? Surely it is because of Anaxe's reputation for chastity—this is what sets her apart to Kossian eyes. And so it should be for us as well! It is as I have always said—we, the kahar of the Luth, have been set apart not only from begetting sons to continue our line but from the corruption of bodily lust. We must shun it as we would shun rotten food. That is why, Rusanarath, you saw the chaste goddess performing our work, the painting of the shadow of Heva on our walls—work which is not properly undertaken by any mortal woman, but may be performed in the Heavens by the pure Anaxe because, being both divine and chaste, she is free from the taint of womankind."

There was more, but Rus couldn't have stayed to listen to it if he'd wanted to—which he very much didn't—because the few mouthfuls of porridge he'd swallowed were already threatening to come back up. He mumbled some excuse and crawled back onto the sleeping platform to curl up, fighting the wave of nausea that had come over him.

It was the usual thing, the after-effect of too much theraka, nothing to do with what Unumus had been saying. He'd heard Unumus say much the same thing plenty of times before, and he didn't believe it. Nobody but Unumus really believed it, much; that was why he was always boring the votive boys with it, because they were the only ones who would listen to him. Or because he hoped to convince the next generation of his way of thinking while they were still young and impressionable.

There had been a little more to the dream that Rus had not related. He had, in the dream, thought that the woman painting the hall was the Pseuchaian instance of the goddess. She had looked a little like Adares, and he remembered, in the dream, feeling glad because he knew she would take a message to his lover for him.

Now that he thought about it, if she had been Anaxe, she should have been wearing his kilt pin. He thought if it had really been a vision from the gods, he would have seen that.

He spent the rest of that day in bed, too sick to eat, too restless to sleep. Genet came to keep him company, but he did not mention the dream to her. He forgot about it, or at least forgot about Unumus's interpretation of it, until the visit of Gunthanaruth's bard more than two weeks later.

The bards earned their keep in the winter travelling from one camp to another with news, and Gunthanaruth always had his bard travel to his summer village to visit the kahar who were wintering there. Officially he came to hear about any important omens that might have been observed, or if the kahar were running short of food. But really it was a courtesy, and the visits were welcome in the dreary months of cold, so they would always try to have some news for the bard when he came, even if it was trivial. Rus might have known, if he had thought about it, what Unumus would seize on this time.

By now, the grip of the theraka on his body and mind had relaxed considerably, and day by day he felt better. He was able to eat and drink again, had started to sleep more soundly at night, and had even gone for a short ride a couple of times without needing to slide down off his horse to be sick. He followed Kuth and Genet's younger daughter around as she learned to walk, holding onto one of her tiny hands as she stumped through the dead grass in her first pair of soft leather boots. He was sitting at the hearth in the kahar hall with the other winter residents of the village, a dozen of them in all, while the bard entertained them with a new song.

When the song was finished, the bard set aside his lyre and turned to Unumus, as the highest-ranking member of the party.

"Well, kahar. And what is the news?"

"Great and propitious news," said Unumus sententiously. "One of our number has been granted a true vision of the great goddess."

For a moment Rus didn't realize what he was going to say, and by the time it struck him, it was too late—not that there had ever really been anything he could have done. But now Unumus was off and running, describing Rus's dream—or something vaguely like Rus's dream—in more detail than Rus had related it to him, and adding a long diatribe on its significance.

Gunthanaruth's bard could not hide his impatience with the diatribe, but he thanked Unumus for the news when he finally finished, and he looked across at Rus to say, "My lord will be glad to hear this, kahar, that the goddess has so favoured you." He offered a friendly smile. "He asked me for news of you in particular. And are you quite recovered from your injuries?"

Talk moved on, and no one returned to the topic of the dream while they sat around the hearth. It was a little esoteric, especially the way Unumus had framed it, not the sort of thing to discuss casually. But Rus knew he would have questions to answer when he was alone with Kuth and Genet.

That didn't happen until the following morning. Rus had been out for an early ride, and came back by way of their house, hoping to join them for breakfast. He met Kuth at the woodpile outside.

"Rus! You'd better come in. Genet wants to know about this vision that you somehow failed to mention to us."

"I'm sure she does," said Rus, sliding down from his horse and setting her loose to graze as best she could on the sparse vegetation around the house. "I assure you, it wasn't what Unumus made it sound."

Kuth rolled his eyes. "We know that, kahar. Come inside."

Genet looked up from where she sat by the hearth as they came through the door. She had bread baking on a pan, and the house was warm and fragrant with the smell.

It was a large, round, well-kept house, with hangings on the walls and rugs on the floors, the roof-posts carved and painted, bunches of dried herbs, flowers, and onions hanging from the rafters. Kuth and Genet both held positions of high status and lived comfortably. The paraphernalia of their trades—his medicines and her ink and needles—were stored in painted chests around the edges of the room, and the family's sleeping-platform on the far side was screened by more colourful hangings.

Genet herself, sitting by her hearth, looked, as usual, like the ideal Luth wife: blonde and rosy-cheeked, with a figure for child-bearing and for comfortably hefting and herding the children once they were born. Her arms, bare in the warmth of the house, were tattooed symmetrically in a style like Rus's—the work, in this case, of the last vahat, Genet's tutor. Genet and her husband were the same age, five years older than Rus. Meret, a girl as pretty as her mother, sat on the opposite side of the hearth, trying to get Gil to stay in her lap.

"Roos! Roos!" the baby announced as he came through the door. He was a favourite now.

"Ah," said Genet, "the great mystic joins us."

"Did you really have a vision, Rusanarath?" Meret asked, hauling her little sister back onto her lap.

Rus took a seat between Meret and her mother. "No," he said, "I don't think so."

"You don't *think* so?" Meret repeated indignantly. "Why do you not *know*?"

"Because," said her father, settling by the hearth himself, "it can be hard to tell what is a vision and what isn't." To Genet he added, "It's as I said—he would have told us about it if he thought it important. Isn't that right, Rus?"

Rus nodded. "I forgot about it, to be honest."

"ROOOS!" Gil threw herself back against her sister and wriggled out of her grip to lunge for Rus, who caught her and scooped her into his own lap.

He told his story as they ate breakfast, pausing to snatch mouthfuls of bread and beans past the baby's grabbing hands, and to offer her small pieces of bread which she would nibble and then push generously back into his face.

"I think it was just a dream," he concluded, "because we'd been talking about painting the hall the night before, and … and I'd been having other odd dreams around that time." And because the goddess had not been wearing his kilt pin, but he couldn't explain that. "I wish I hadn't told Unumus about it—I knew it was a mistake as soon as it was out of my mouth. And I suppose all dreams come from the gods in some way, but even if this was a vision, I don't think it means what he thinks it does."

He paused there. This was a dangerous topic for him. He didn't think the only reason he disagreed with Unumus about chastity was because he was no longer chaste himself, but he was afraid of revealing too much.

"Of course not," Kuth agreed. "It's the one string to his lyre, purity this, purity that. He thinks just because he gets it out of the Kosoth books, no one can find fault with it, but I'll tell you what. The Kosoth men don't respect their women."

"They don't," said Rus, "but what does that have to do with it?"

"It's at the back of all this talk about purity," said Genet. Obviously it was something husband and wife had talked of together. "When you scratch the surface, what it means is, stay away from women because they're dirty."

"But that's … " Ridiculous, of course. But she was right; that was where the logic took you. "And Unumus thinks because the kahar are set apart from women, we should think like this too."

"What I'd like to know," said Kuth, "is why. What's in it for him, peddling this nonsense?"

"Oh, I think he's sincere, in his way," said Genet. "A zealot."

"I think you're right," said Rus.

"Bread!" said the baby. "Bread bread! More bread!"

"What's a zealot?" asked Meret.

When breakfast was finished, Rus followed Genet out of the house to help with the morning chores, leaving Kuth with the children.

"You don't like the idea of having a vision, do you?" she said, looking at him shrewdly.

"I wouldn't say that. I don't think I'm worthy of it, but … "

"I don't know anyone worthier. I'm quite serious."

"Thank you."

"You don't believe me."

You don't know me as well as you think you do, he wanted to say. Or he thought of saying it, but he didn't really want to.

He wished he could believe she would still call him a friend if she knew the truth, but he wasn't sure.

After a moment she said, "Kuth says it's the blow on the head. That it did something to you, and that's why you seem sad. Is that it?"

"Partly, I think. I still get headaches, and I get tired doing things that should be easy. It's not … what I'm used to." *Not who I am*, he'd thought to say.

"You've been sick. You have to give yourself time."

"What if I can't fight again, Genet? What is there left for me?"

She frowned at him. "You're getting well ahead of yourself, I think."

They were interrupted by the arrival of Gunthanaruth's bard, who came striding up the hill toward them with a greeting. They exchanged some chat, and the bard came back, as Rus had suspected he might, to the subject of the vision.

"I thought I'd get the story from you," he said. "You know, without … " He gestured in the direction of the kahar hall. "Your version, I mean. To be sure I have it straight."

"I'm not sure my version is as interesting," said Rus. "It seemed to me merely a dream." And he described it again, adding, "I was ill at the time, from taking too much theraka. It can affect the dreams, I think."

The bard waved a hand dismissively. "I wouldn't worry about that. If Unumus Kahar says it was a vision, I'm sure it was. Gunthanaruth will like it, be sure of that." He flashed a smile. "He's been wanting Suthus to name a new deputy, you know. Since Duhath was killed in the fall."

"It will be a good thing for Unumus, then."

"For Unumus?" The bard looked genuinely surprised. "No, kahar. For you."

"For—what?" Rus glanced around at Genet to see if she

looked as nonplussed as he felt. She didn't. "You don't mean that Suthus would name me as his deputy."

The bard nodded earnestly. "Before the winter is over. Mark my words."

In a way, it made sense. Rus had time to think about it in the slow tail-end of winter. Of course he knew both Gunthanaruth and Suthus liked him. He had distinguished himself as a bull-fighter, but he was known to have other skills as well, and if he was to be forced to retire from fighting at twenty, he should be put to some good use. He was popular with the other kahar. And the obvious choice was Unumus—unpopular, disliked by the headman, but senior enough that he would expect to be offered it as a matter of course, probably already had plans for what he would do when he inevitably succeeded Suthus, who was an old man now. It did make sense.

It wouldn't be a terrible thing, to be Suthus's deputy. It would be an honour, and the duties would be interesting. But it seemed wrong, in a way he could not quite explain to himself. It wasn't that he believed himself unfit for it because of what had happened with Adares—or it wasn't only that, it wasn't *exactly* that.

But there was the fact that Suthus was old, and even if he lived to be very old, Rus would still be a young man when he succeeded him and became the next stathan. And the thought of *that* was like a horrible weight settling on him, threatening to crush him.

Was this what it had been like for Adares, he wondered, being made archon of Tios?

He spent a lot of time riding by himself during this period, partly to be away from the kahar hall, partly to rebuild his stamina. It was working, slowly but surely. The weather was improving, the bitterness of winter slowly subsiding, and he felt his strength gradually returning with it, as if he were a plant regaining vigour. He let it take as long as it needed, convinced that was the best way. There was nothing much he needed to be doing.

He had a lot of time to think, and he could almost feel his mind growing stronger, too. One morning, as he rode along the ridge to the south of the headman's village, with the sun warm on his back, it occurred to him that there was no particular reason why he should never see Adares again.

He turned the thought over in his mind. He had been focused for so long on the impossible, on how he would never touch Adares again, never wake up beside him, never be his lover again. All of that *was* impossible. Even if he were well enough to make the journey from the Luth lands to Tios alone, he wouldn't do it, just to show up on Adares's doorstep and make a nuisance of himself. But if all he aimed for was a chance to *see* the Phemian again, there were other ways to achieve that.

He thought about it all the rest of that day, and by evening he had a plan.

He thought he would be able to talk Suthus out of naming him his deputy. Unumus wasn't the only possible alternative; there were others who could do the job, especially if Rus recovered enough to go back to bull-fighting. But in the meantime, Rus's star was clearly on the rise, and he would make the most of it. Gunthanaruth would soon be thinking about the tribute that he owed to Tios. Rus would offer some suggestions about that.

The next time Gunthanaruth's bard returned to the summer villages, it was with the news that Suthus Stathan had formally named Lachan Rusanarath as his new deputy, second-in-command of the kahar of all the Luth. The appointment would be confirmed with a ceremony in the spring.

CHAPTER XVIII

"WE CHOSE WELL," said Gunthanaruth, wiping his moustache and holding out his mead-horn for the servant to refill. Then, seeming to realize what he'd said, he corrected himself lazily: "You chose well, I mean."

Suthus snorted tolerantly. He reached over to pat Rus's shoulder, but his hand slipped and somehow ended up on Rus's knee instead. He withdrew it quickly.

"I know," he said. "I did."

Rus laughed.

They were sitting at the upper hearth in the headman's hall following Rus's investiture as deputy and successor to the stathan. It was late, and the occasion had not merited a full-blown feast, so the hall was fairly quiet by now. It was early spring, the weather still chilly, but the hall was warmed by the throng of bodies and the flames of the hearth, and Rus was wearing a formal wool jacket. It was too warm for the jacket, but not warm enough to take it off when he had no shirt under it.

His investiture had gone well. Unumus, who had not concealed his anger when Rus was chosen, had pulled himself together enough to be gracious, and the rest of the kahar had seemed genuinely happy for Rus. His parents had been there to express their pride, stiffly but sincerely, and that had made Rus happier than he would have expected—had made him almost feel that it had not all been a terrible mistake.

Others had congratulated him warmly. Kuth and Genet, who knew how little he wanted this, had been stoutly sympathetic while at the same time giving him friendly reminders that it was something to be proud of, being made successor to the head of the kahar at twenty. Their children enjoyed the day, and Meret acted as though he was a member of the family. Hath, the old bull-fighter, had embraced him with tears in his eyes and confessed that he had hoped Suthus was going to choose him, "But he knew better. You are worthier of it than I will ever be." Rus didn't think that was true at all, but didn't say so.

"We must soon think of sending tribute to the Phemians," said Gunthanaruth some time later, speaking to Rus. Suthus had nodded off, leaning back against the cushions.

"Ah. Yes, my lord." Rus roused himself as best he could from the drowsiness brought on by the warmth, the lateness of the hour, and the mead he had sparingly drunk. "If I can be of any help—the Phemians are like the Kossians in their ways, as you know." And the kahar were the guardians of the knowledge of Kossian ways.

"So I understand. That is why I mention it. Will they take horses, do you think, or will we have to send hostages, as the southern tribes do?"

Hostages were just what Rus had at one time meant to suggest, but that was when he had hoped to make himself one of the hostages, or at the very least part of the escort for the hostages. Neither was possible now.

Earlier that evening, Suthus had been reciting a list of things he would need Rus's help with that spring. There were lessons to organize for the votive boys, whose education had been neglected during the campaign in the fall, and it would soon be time to begin arranging the competition for new votives. There were divinations for the coming year to be performed, paddocks to be blessed, repairs to be made to the kahar hall before the repainting of the walls, hunts to be organized, and some badly moth-eaten ritual costumes to be repaired or replaced altogether. Some of their library of Kosoth books needed recopying, and some reports of omens that had come in from one of the villages over the mountains would need to be investigated before long. There was no way Suthus would let his new deputy travel south any time soon.

"I don't believe the Phemians care about hostages," he said truthfully.

It was something Adares had told him: "The tribes all exchange hostages among themselves, as pledges of loyalty, and when they send them to us, we have to take them, but we don't know what to do with them. Of course they don't send us stonemasons or cooks or anyone who can earn their keep. It's all useless chieftains' younger sons and things."

"They might like horses," Rus went on, "but their tradition is jars of wine and oil of olives."

Gunthanaruth gave him an impatient look. "Where are we going to get that? Will they not accept anything else?"

"Herds of cattle or goats."

The headman's look changed to one of alarm. "*Herds*?"

"They keep tame ones on their islands—they wouldn't know what to do with wild cows or mountain goats. The wine and oil could be … approximated. For wine, mead, with some fine drinking horns, perhaps, and for the oil—I think they use it mostly for soap."

"Soap," Gunthanaruth repeated. "You are sure?"

He was not, and all of this about tribute came from the story Adares had told him about the king of the Black Isle, which had also involved men who were goats from the waist down and a woman who had sex with a goose, so it was doubtful how rooted in fact any of it was.

"It is recorded in the tales," he said, as a sop to the truth.

Gunthanaruth shrugged. "Well, if I can get away with sending them casks of mead and soap instead of men and horses, I won't complain."

"There is one other thing you must not omit to do, my lord."

"Ah?"

He glanced at Suthus, who was still sleeping peacefully. Here he ventured into the territory of pure invention. If he had been less tired, thinking more clearly, it might have been harder.

"You must invite their headman to your hearth." He gestured at it, the flames dying low in the circle of ash and charred wood under the fire-dogs with their ornamental iron bulls' heads. "They expect it of an ally. He will be waiting for your invitation."

"Ah! I am glad you told me. He won't accept, of course. It's a long journey to make for form's sake. He wouldn't come all the way up here. Would he?"

Rus shrugged. That was the question, really.

"He may," he said.

The letter began: *Gunthanaruth Son of Durguruth, Supreme Headman of the Luth, to Adares Doriades Phyleros, Archon of Tios, greetings.*

In accordance with the ancient custom of your people and ours, we send you this tribute of one hundred horses, fifty casks of mead, fifty drinking-horns, and fifty jars of soap. May they be the first of many tokens of friendship exchanged between our people.

We are at present settled in our summer village, where we hope to receive you at our hearth before the next autumn rain. There we will drink together in true friendship as is proper.

Farewell.

"Read it over to me," Gunthanaruth said.

Rus read out what he had written, translating as he went.

Suthus had delegated the handling of the whole tribute business to him, saying, "You seem to know more about the matter than I." Rus couldn't be sure there wasn't a touch of suspicion in that, but if there was, Suthus seemed content to let him play whatever game he was playing.

"Good, good," said Gunthanaruth. "I like the sound of the beginning, where you wrote out his whole title—clever of you to know it. Mine's still longer, isn't it?" He looked over Rus's shoulder at the writing-tablet, waving a finger vaguely at the words.

"It is," said Rus, and didn't explain that what he had added was the archon's full name, not a title. He hoped he had spelled it correctly.

"He wasn't what I expected at all, you know." Gunthanaruth sat back, stroking his moustache thoughtfully. "Young fellow."

"Yes. Ah. Yes?"

"Yes. Well, older than you, I suppose. Tall ... " He shrugged.

Rus looked at him for a moment, waiting. *You can't even say the word "handsome,"* he thought. *You're thinking it—you noticed, of course, because how could you not—but you won't say it because you can't.*

"Of course they were all different than I expected," Gunthanaruth went on. "More manly. When Suthus told me they were like the Kossians in their ways, I expected an easy victory over a gang of soft half-men—but they were tougher than I thought to find them. Well, you recall."

I wish Suthus had told me that, Rus thought, and then wondered if that was true. If he had known the Phemians lived and thought and even spoke like Kossians, he would have been even more reluctant to fight them—and he had never been enthusiastic—but then, if he had found a way to stay behind, the best thing that had happened in his life would not have happened.

"I rather liked their clothes," said Gunthanaruth. "Didn't think they looked womanly at all, actually."

That reminded Rus of Kuth saying the Kossians didn't respect their women. Neither did the Luth, really, when you scratched beneath the surface. You didn't use "womanly" as an insult for men if you truly esteemed women. It made him sad to think about.

The headman recalled himself to the topic at hand. "You're sure they won't be insulted by the soap?"

"Insulted, my lord? No, I'm sure not."

Puzzled, though, he hoped. Intrigued enough, he hoped, to take up the Luth headman's bizarre invitation to drink at his hearth. One of them, at least.

He wrote, *"By the hand of Lachan Rusanarath Kahar"* at the bottom of the letter. He didn't know if Phemian archons read their own correspondence, but even if they did, other people—secretaries and councillors and things—surely read it too. He didn't dare add any more personal message. He didn't think he had ever mentioned his family name to Adares, or said that "Rus" was short for anything.

It didn't matter. If Adares wanted to come to the Luth lands, as he had once told Rus he did—if, perhaps, he wanted to see the place all the more now because it was where Rus had lived, and he thought Rus was dead—then, when he found the opportunity amid the demands of his position, he would come. If he didn't, he wouldn't. And it had been six months since their three days in the temple. (It had taken some time to make all that soap.) He might be married by now.

Six weeks passed. The chill of winter was gone from the air, wildflowers were beginning to bloom in the mountain meadows, and the villages were full of life again. It was Rus's favourite time of year. They painted the new pattern on the kahar hall, and repaired the leaks in the roof, and Rus organized lessons for the votive boys. Suthus travelled with several of the omen-readers to the village that had reported strange signs, and Rus was left in charge.

One morning, when he was sitting outside the kahar hall with Hath and a couple of the votive boys, repairing spears and discussing the plans for the first hunt of the year, Kuth and Genet's son came by with a message.

"There are visitors coming to the headman's hall—an outrider just got in—and I'm to tell you they want to see a mask dance tonight at the feast."

"A mask dance?" Rus repeated. "It's not the season for that."

The boy shrugged. "That's what he said. I'm to return to say if you can do it or not."

"Of course we can do it," Rus said. "Tell him—tell him it will be our honour."

He looked across at Hath as the boy skipped away. "I didn't have a choice, did I?"

"No, I don't see that you did. But you're right, it's not the season … "

"And Unumus won't like it," Rus finished for him. He set down the spear he had been working on. "Well, let's see what he'll say."

The mask dance was a ritual in honour of Kahait, usually performed in the autumn—it could be done at other times, but there was supposed to be a reason, and that reason was not generally, "Because a guest wants to see it at dinner." Rus didn't much like the idea of putting it on as an entertainment, but he knew Unumus would like it even less. And the mask dance was Unumus's specialty.

Unumus flatly refused to do it.

"We do not perform the mask dance as an entertainment at a feast," he said, as if he thought that Rus might not know this.

"No, and I do not mean that we should—we'll go to the standing stones and do an invocation, and we'll perform the *whole thing*, and it may be that the guests will be bored, and we won't be asked to do it again."

Unumus looked at him haughtily and said nothing. *You fucker*, Rus thought. He hardly ever swore even in his head.

"It isn't unlawful for us to do the mask dance whenever we want," he went on. "It isn't impious. It's just a nuisance."

Unumus's nostrils flared. "It is more than a nuisance. It is—"

"Well, we're doing it."

"You will do it without me." Clearly he thought that was impossible.

"Yes," said Rus. "We will."

Preparations for the stupid dance took up the rest of Rus's

day. First he had to recruit six kahar who knew the dance but weren't so staunchly Unumus's men that they would refuse to participate. He probably could have ordered them to do it, but he didn't want to test allegiances so openly just yet, and not over something so silly.

Then they had to find the masks and costumes, which had been packed away, without any help from Unumus or his partisans, who had probably been the ones to pack them, and who were now making it known that they were insulted at not being asked to dance. Some of the masks had to be repaired, which Rus got Genet and one of her apprentices to do while they rehearsed outside the hall.

Hath drummed for them, and they ran through the steps of the dance. They formed up into a circle and moved in swaying, stamping steps to a slow beat, symbolically tracing out parts of the Great Pattern.

The costumes they would wear for the dance were heavy and enveloping, the masks dramatically oversized, so that their movements would be exaggerated. After a while the drum beat quickened, and the dance changed. Here they ran into difficulties, as a couple of the younger dancers forgot the transition, and they had to rehearse it several times to get it straight.

The circle broke up, and the dance became a reenactment of the battle between Kahait and Genhath, which was at the same time a kind of mock bull-fight. It was a fine spectacle, when performed well, and Rus could not really blame Gunthanaruth for wanting to show it off to his guests.

One of the votive boys, the best dancer among them, wore the gold mask of the goddess and leapt on the shoulders of a horse-masked dancer. Rus wore the bull mask of Genhath; it was the heaviest and most uncomfortable mask, and no one else particularly wanted it, but he was also a good dancer, and

Genhath was a demanding role. The others circled around, stamping and shouting, while Kahait on her horse faced down her crazed brother and felled him with a blow from a wooden spear hung with clusters of bells. Then it was time to make their way to the standing stones, located several miles outside the headman's village, to perform the invocation to the goddess.

"I wonder who the guests are," Hath remarked as they rode back up toward the village in the twilight.

"Southerners, I suppose," said Rus. "Who else would want to see a mask dance done out of season?"

They were laughing about that when they came up the slope behind the headman's hall, and in the fading light Rus saw the horses in the nearby paddock. Among the whites and greys and duns of Gunthanaruth's herd, the sleek, dark Phemian horses stood out clearly.

Rus counted six of them, an inconclusive number: more than a scouting party or a messenger, but surely not the whole entourage of the archon. Besides, it was too soon to expect him. It hadn't even crossed Rus's mind that it could be him. He would have had to leave almost the moment the train of horses and jars of soap arrived in Tios in order to be here by now.

Perhaps it was someone from the southern tribes after all, who had bought horses from the Phemians—though why you would do that and then bring them on a visit to the Luth headman, unless you intended a deliberate insult ...

In any case, it wouldn't be him.

The dancers marshalled outside the hall, adjusting their costumes, and at the signal from Rus, all ducked their heads and settled the heavy masks over their faces. The masks were attached to hoods over wicker frames, so that they rested on top of the wearers' heads, and long manes of horse-hair hung down over their shoulders. Rus pulled his own hair up and twisted it on top of his head to provide some extra padding before pulling on the Genhath mask with its curving bull horns. He signalled Hath to begin the drum beat, and they processed into the hall.

If they had really been doing this as entertainment for the headman and his guests, they should probably have waited outside and sent one of the boys in to ask for a signal to enter. But they were *not* performing an entertainment, so they didn't wait. It was a compromise, in Rus's mind. It probably didn't matter, as the effect they created by striding in to interrupt the feast was quite spectacular.

Gunthanaruth's hall was a large, long building with one rounded end, in the middle of which, raised up on a stone platform and surrounded by furs and cushions, was the headman's hearth. Below it were several smaller hearths, laid out down the length of the hall, where his retainers and lesser guests ate and drank, and between the first of the lower hearths and the steps up to the headman's dais was an open space of packed earth for dancers and other entertainment.

As Rus and the rest of the dancers entered the hall, the lower hearths were full of the usual members of the headman's household, and around the fire on the dais sat the Phemians. There were more than six of them—perhaps twice that number, though Rus didn't have time to count them—which must have meant that some of them had ridden Luth horses. They sat awkwardly around the headman's fire, looking like they didn't know what to do with their legs. Some of them held their mead-horns in both hands and peered suspiciously into them; others, more relaxed, were trying to flirt with the girls serving food.

And on Gunthanaruth's right, leaning back against the cushions propped against the wooden rail behind him, mead-horn held loosely in one hand, deep in conversation with the Luth headman, was Adares.

CHAPTER XIX

THE MASKED DANCERS formed up in a circle, stamping and swaying, and Hath took a seat on the steps of the dais with his drum. The bull mask narrowed Rus's vision so that he could only glance up at the dais when he was facing in the right direction. He saw some of the Phemians watching the dance with unease, others with polite interest. He saw Adares lean toward Gunthanaruth, pointing out at the dancers, asking for an explanation, a smile on his face.

He looked just as Rus had pictured him every day for the past seven months—he hadn't changed—and he looked like a stranger. He was not dressed in warrior gear now. He wore a short, pure white tunic with no sleeves and a border of gold thread, simple and princely, so he sat there with his beautiful bronze limbs all bare, one knee drawn up, one arm wrapped around it.

The dancers circled around, and Rus lost sight of Adares. The bull mask and the heavy, shaggy Genhath costume were intolerably hot in the warm hall, and the movements of the dance felt ponderous and silly. It no longer felt as if it meant anything, and he wished he had not insisted on doing the whole thing. It was only a spectacle, after all, put on to amuse the Phemians. No one was taking it seriously but him.

Of course that wasn't true. Hath, drumming away on the

dais steps, took it very seriously. The other dancers took it seriously too, if only, in some cases, because Rus had insisted they do, and they respected him. And he remembered sitting in the temple of the horse god with Adares, and how Adares, who seemed not to be particularly pious himself, had been charmed by Rus's serious questions—as if Rus's piety was something he found attractive.

He had to hold these things in tension: he had to live his life of service to the gods at the same time as loving Adares. The dance shifted again, and Rus caught another glimpse of the dais.

Adares still wore his hair very short, and he was clean-shaven like all his companions, who were dressed much as he was. Still, anyone in the hall could have recognized him as the Phemians' headman. There was a gold arm-band of Karhan design around his right upper arm—and on the back of his right hand, and curling twice around his wrist, a tattoo of a coiled serpent in the Luth style.

He was talking to Gunthanaruth without an interpreter.

Rus wanted to fling off the mask of Genhath there on the dance floor and shout. "Look, it's me! Did you guess? Did you know?" The drum beat began to quicken, and he brought his mind back to the dance with a huge effort.

They made the transition cleanly enough, reformed for the second part of the dance, and now Rus had to pay attention to what he was doing and had none to spare for the watchers on the dais. The boy in the gold mask somersaulted nimbly onto the shoulders of his masked steed, and Rus circled them, faster and faster, in the character of crazed Genhath.

Ordinarily, he would have found it easy to lose himself in the story of the dance, to feel a faint echo of Genhath's rage flowing through him. Not enough to be really frightening—it wasn't in his nature to lose control like that—but enough to set the experience apart, to make it feel like ritual. But up to this point, tonight, the dance had just felt like a chore.

He was hot, his costume was uncomfortable, he wanted the dance to go well but doubted whether he should have agreed to do it in the first place. He wanted the rest of the kahar to respect him, but he believed Unumus was wrong in his ideas, and wanted not to care what the man thought about anything. And beneath it all, he was queasily, paralyzingly terrified of meeting Adares again.

All of this was swept away, unexpectedly, in the second part of the dance, by the spectators' reaction. Something about the mock battle must have struck the Phemians as familiar, reminded them of some entertainments they enjoyed at home, perhaps, and they began to applaud and cheer.

It was not the done thing, of course, but how were they to know? They were at a feast, and this looked like entertainment, and they liked it, so they clapped. Hospitality was an iron-clad law of the Luth, and the Phemians were guests, so after a moment or two the men and women in the rest of the hall began to clap too. Before long there was whooping and stomping and laughter. The Luth, who knew what the dance was about, began shouting encouragement: "Ka-hait! Ka-hait! Fight, fight, fight!"

It worked on the dancers like a frenzy-fuelling drug. Hath drummed as though his life depended on it. Some of the dancers in the outer ring took up the cheers. All of them stamped and shouted. Rus and the boy representing Kahait threw themselves into their roles, their gestures becoming bigger and bolder, drawing out the fight, and the spectators loved it.

Rus didn't feel like Genhath, exactly. He felt like himself, caught up in the dance, conscious of his lover watching him, having fun. He didn't know whether it was right, but it was at least an improvement. At the climax of the dance, when the boy Kahait leapt onto Rus's shoulders and flourished his spear, someone on the dais whistled. Rus made a production of his death, staggering and reeling, to the delight of the crowd.

And then the dance was over, and the time had come to face Adares. The other dancers were forming up to process out of the hall, and Rus could have pretended not to see the headman beckoning to him from the dais with big hand gestures. But that would have been stupid.

He parted from the others, who were heading out to return their costumes to the kahar hall, and mounted the steps toward the headman's hearth, still wearing his costume and mask. The Phemians looked faintly alarmed by this, but the headman grinned and slapped his thigh, obviously delighted. Gunthanaruth's wife, sitting on his left, moved over to make room for Rus.

"This is our deputy stathan," Gunthanaruth told Adares, shouting as if at a deaf person, and waving his hand in an unhelpful gesture. "That's … hum."

"Yes, yes," said Adares eagerly. "I know it. The stathan is your high priest." He used the Pseuchaian word. "The headman of your kahar. This is his second-in-command."

"Ah, you know! Good, good." Gunthanaruth clapped him heartily on the shoulder.

Rus had seated himself, by this time, in the place vacated for him. Adares leaned forward to look at him past the headman.

"You dance well," he said, smiling into Rus's eyes.

Rus pushed the bull mask up and off, tugging it free from his sweat-damp hair. "Thank you," he said in Luth.

There was a moment's silence like the crash of a cymbal. Adares's eyes were wide, his face a frozen mask, expressionless. When he moved, leaning back and bringing his drinking-horn to his lips, he had the look of a man woken abruptly from sleep.

Gunthanaruth noticed nothing.

"Your mead is stronger more than I thought," said Adares. "I am a little … suddenly … " He touched his forehead with a rueful laugh.

"Hah?" said Gunthanaruth. "Nonsense! Have some more, have some more."

Rus realized he had not introduced himself. He tugged on the ties that held his costume closed at the neck and shrugged it off onto the cushions behind him. He was wearing only his kilt underneath, the same as when he had first met Adares. He shook out his hair.

"Lachan Rusanarath," he said, reaching out a hand past the headman.

It took Adares a moment to register what this was about, and to switch his mead-horn to his left hand to offer Rus the right. They clasped hands briefly, let go—nothing out of the ordinary.

"Say that again?" Adares said, in Pseuchaian—probably without intending the switch.

"My friends call me Rus."

"I'll bet they do. But"—switching back to Luth—"say your name again, will you please?"

"Lachh-an Rus-ana-rath." He separated the syllables with exaggerated care.

"He is learning our language, you see," said Gunthanaruth.

"Yes," said Rus, "I noticed."

"He said I speak very well already," Adares added.

"Did he? And I have never known him to flatter anyone."

At that both Gunthanaruth and Adares shouted with

laughter. Rus felt as if he were in a dream, and he wasn't sure whether it was a good dream or not. From somewhere, a mead-horn had got into his hand, and it was full. He took a gulp.

In truth, Gunthanaruth hadn't really spoken flattery. The Luth language was complex, and Adares's grasp of it was still basic, his Pseuchaian accent so thick it could have withstood axe blows—but it didn't matter. He *did* "speak very well." He was unselfconscious, obviously eager to learn. He talked with his hands more than he did in his native language.

"If he is assistant to your high priest," he said, indicating Rus, his expression giving nothing away, "the … the dance, the play of the bull fight, is it … religion?"

"Ritual," Rus supplied. "Yes."

"It is! I thought that. And we should not have … " He mimed clapping. "Yes?"

"Ach!" Gunthanaruth waved a hand. "Doesn't matter. He'll tell you it does, but it doesn't."

"I won't," said Rus mildly. "It isn't usual, but I liked it."

"Ah! You see! I knew I was right to want him as our next stathan."

"If you are sure," said Adares. "I do not like to defend your custom. Defend? Is that the word?"

"Offend," Rus suggested.

"Eh?" said Gunthanaruth. "Doesn't matter, doesn't matter."

"It does if I want to learn," said Adares in a deadpan tone which Rus recognized as an imitation of himself. Gunthanaruth, of course, did not.

"Rus," said Gunthanaruth's wife, on his left, "you are not eating."

"Ah, am I not?"

"No." She pushed a dish of meat toward him. "Eat."

He murmured his thanks and made himself eat. He realized he was hungry. The food tasted better than he had expected. The rest of the kahar and the votive boys returned to the hall, costumes discarded, and found seats around the lower hearths.

Gunthanaruth was telling Adares the story of how the Luth came to leave Tios, with special attention to the role Rus had played in it. He was, in fact, telling Adares what had happened to Rus after the siege of Tios. Stealing Rus's opportunity to tell the story himself.

"He doesn't remember any of this, mind you," Gunthanaruth went on. "He struck his head, and that takes away the memory sometimes."

"I have heard that," said Adares.

Rus looked up and realized that Adares had been watching him, unnoticed by Gunthanaruth, who was busily eating while he talked.

"But you see," said the headman, licking his fingers, "how you owe much to that bull and to Rus here. Eh?"

"I do," said Adares. He was still looking at Rus, his dark eyes unreadable.

"And then, you see, as if that weren't enough, in the winter he had a vision of the goddess—nothing I understand myself, being a man of war, though I am no disrespecter of the gods, but they tell me it's all very mystical—and Suthus, our stathan, and I thought he was just the man to replace Suthus's old deputy, who was killed in the autumn."

Gunthanaruth turned away to call for more mead. Adares leaned forward to look past him at Rus.

"Rusanarath," he said, and Rus thought he should have told the Phemian his full name last autumn, because it sounded so beautiful, the way he said it. "Do you remember me at all?"

He said it in Pseuchaian, of course. It took Rus a moment to understand what he meant.

"Ah, my love!" That just slipped out, so naturally. It was incredibly indiscreet, with other Phemians present, but none of them seemed to have heard. Rus collected himself. "Of course," he said. "This is what's known as 'pretending.'"

Adares stared at him for a moment, and then he put his hand up to cover his mouth, and Rus thought he looked as though he was going to be sick. It occurred to Rus suddenly that this was all much harder on Adares than it was on him. And Rus wasn't finding it very easy himself.

"I am sorry," he said, still in Pseuchaian. "I have made it difficult for you. I should have … "

"No," said Adares, pulling himself together. "Immortal gods. No. Don't think that."

"What are you two talking about?" Gunthanaruth inquired jovially. "He speaks your language beautifully, does he not, Headman Filerus?"

"It's like he's trying to set us up together," said Adares. While Rus was wondering if that could really mean what he thought it meant, he answered Gunthanaruth, in the Luth tongue: "We talk about you, of course."

Gunthanaruth grunted as if this seemed entirely natural and didn't worry him. He began telling Adares the history of the Luth, with a heavy emphasis on the greatness of his own family. Adares seemed genuinely interested, or did a good job of looking genuinely interested, though in unguarded moments his gaze would always come back to Rus. Gunthanaruth's wife pushed a stack of savoury pancakes under Rus's nose, followed by a baked apple, followed by a bowl of milk pudding, followed by a dish of nuts. It was a lavish feast.

Gunthanaruth's bard joined them on the dais, and sang about the history of Gunthanaruth's family. One of the Phemians had a musical instrument, a kind of big Phemian lyre, and he played it for them and sang a Phemian song.

"The soap," said Adares, looking at Rus, while they were listening to the Phemian song and Gunthanaruth's attention was distracted. "Was that you?"

"Yes."

Adare shook his head, smiling. "I should have suspected something then, shouldn't I?"

"Talking about me again?" said Gunthanaruth, chuckling.

The Phemian sitting next to Adares, a young man with curly hair and a snub nose, had been glancing between Rus and Adares, and now he leaned over to the archon and said in a loud whisper, looking at Rus, "Sir, is he the one?"

"Shh-shh," said Adares.

"Lord archon, I mean the Luth who—"

"Thank you, Kagieros."

"Oh." He grimaced. "Sorry, sir."

Kagieros looked across at Rus and smiled tentatively. "Really terrific dance, earlier. Enjoyed it immensely."

"Thanks," said Rus. To be polite he added, "Do you have anything like it where you're from?"

"Oh!" Kagieros looked surprised. "Well, yes, as a matter of fact. Back home in Pheme, at the dramatic festivals, you know, they have all kinds of plays, and some of the really ancient ones are done in masks, with dancing and so on. They're great fun. We don't have a regular dramatic festival in Tios yet—we haven't yet built a theatre, which is—"

"The building where you go to watch plays," Rus supplied, and enjoyed Kagieros's surprised look. "I have not seen one, but I have read about them in the works of Lisophiles."

"Gosh. Well, you're one up on me there. I haven't read any Lisophiles—except, you know, the one about the talking animals."

"And what are they talking about *now*?" Gunthanaruth wanted to know.

"Kosoth books for children," said Adares.

Gunthanaruth looked at him as though he assumed that must have lost something in translation.

The Phemian song ended, and Gunthanaruth's bard began a tale about the hero Gunrana and his horse. The headman had closed his eyes and might have been asleep. Some of the retainers at the lower hearths were beginning to leave. Adares seemed to be trying to follow the bard's words and finding them puzzling. Rus remembered him joking about epics where horses talked, and wondered if he was thinking of that now. Gunrana's horse had a lot to say.

Rus felt an urgent need to make something happen, even something as unsatisfactory as himself leaving the hall. He turned to Gunthanaruth's wife.

"You want to go to your bed," she guessed.

"Would you excuse me?"

"Of course. Leave all that," she added, waving at his mask and discarded costume. "I'll have a girl take it back for you in the morning."

"Thank you, my lady."

He got to his feet, stiff and awkward from sitting for so long after the exertion of the dance. Adares looked up at him, glanced down at the oblivious headman, and then at Gunthanaruth's wife.

"My lady, I am about to become like him"—pointing at Gunthanaruth—"in a moment, if I do not have some new air. Would you excuse *me* also?"

"Of course, Headman Filerus, of course."

"I will wait for you, and we can walk together," said Rus, hoping that sounded innocent to other ears—it certainly didn't to his own.

"Oh, are we leaving?" said Kagieros, seeing Adares move to get up.

"No. I'm going out for a breath of fresh air."

"We'll come with you, sir," said another of the Phemians, an older, warrior-looking man.

"Yes, please!" said Kagieros fervently. "We're dying of boredom here."

Adares shushed them irritably. The bard was still singing. "We can't all leave. And I'm coming back."

Rus stood uncertainly at the dais steps, where he had gone to put on his shoes and the shirt that one of the votive boys had brought for him earlier.

"You should have attendance, lord archon," said the older Phemian. "For the look of it. Kagieros and Doros and I will come, and the rest will stay."

Adares sighed. "Thank you, Kleisios. It's a good thought. Come." He caught Rus's eye and gave the minutest possible shrug.

Rus waited while the Phemians tied their sandals and fastened their cloaks. He gave instructions for a couple of the kahar who were still in the hall to go sit at the headman's hearth and make conversation with the remaining Phemians. He should have done it before, he thought guiltily. He led the way out into the night, Adares and his men following.

"Would you like to walk along the ridge out beyond the paddock?" Rus asked when they were all outside. "The air is cool, and you can see the mountains."

"Can I take a piss there?" asked Kagieros. "Because—" The older man hushed him fiercely.

"I would like it, if it is not too far," said the third Phemian, Doros, in stilted Luth, but with a better accent than Adares's.

"Blessed Orante!" Kagieros groaned. "Can we not all talk Pseuchaian now, *please*?"

Adares turned and strode ahead of the group, and Rus caught up to him. The others took the hint and lagged behind. They walked around behind the hall and followed the fence at the edge of the paddock. The night air was soft and pleasant, the moonlight blue on the mountain peaks that rose up around them.

Adares looked at Rus. "Do all your feasts last *fifteen years*, or was this one special?"

Rus laughed. "This was special, just for the two of us."

"The two of us," Adares repeated after a moment, softly. They had reached the end of the paddock, and they stopped. Adares looked at Rus. "I thought you were dead."

"I know." He remembered that hadn't been true until that evening. "I mean … "

"You mean you hoped."

"I—I didn't hope you thought I was dead, I … " It had seemed complicated even at the time, and now it was hard to remember how it had been.

"You hoped I knew what you did. I know. And I did. As soon as I heard why the Luth were leaving, I knew it was you. I knew what you'd done. I wished I could have stopped you— but I wished that for myself. For the city … you saved us, Rus. We wouldn't have lasted, if Gunthanaruth had pressed the siege. We've been declared rebels and placed under embargo by Pheme—we're on our own. It happened at the worst possible moment, and it hasn't been lifted. At this point I don't think it will be. Obviously I don't want Gunthanaruth to know that yet, by the way. We're working up to declaring ourselves an independent republic, when we've got enough support among the tribes, but we're not quite there yet."

"That's why you came up here so quickly after getting our tribute."

"No, I came up here so quickly because I wanted to see

where you lived—because my heart has been broken since last autumn, and I've never felt like this before, so bereft for so long, and I haven't been able to *tell* anyone for fear it would get back to your people and dishonour your name." He paused, drew a breath. "I wanted to come up here and remember you. If I'd known you were alive, I'd have come quicker."

"I'm not sure that's actually possible—given the terrain."

Adares frowned at him. "Do you have no poetry in your soul at all?"

"I do. I do. It is all about honour and horses."

"And none of them have—I don't know—wings made of love?"

"No, they don't."

"Tch."

It was such a Luth noise to make. Rus flashed him a delighted look. Adares stood there on the edge of the mountain meadow, his cloak thrown back from one shoulder, moonlight silvering the planes of his face. He had said, "I've never felt like this before," and "wings made of love," and though Rus had known, of course he had known, still it meant something to hear it. It meant so much. Rus moved toward him, caught himself, raked his eyes over the dark landscape.

"No one sees us here but the horses and your men. Do you … " He couldn't finish the sentence, felt himself rather breathless.

Adares reached for him, one hand tangling in his hair, the other catching his waist, and drew him in and kissed him, not gently as that first time in the temple doorway, but with a hunger that told its own story about how the last seven months had been for him. It must have been quite a sight for the watching Phemians.

Rus had thought he was tired, but at the touch of Adares's

hands and lips he went up like a lightning-struck tree, body and soul, and it was Adares who broke the kiss, turned it into a tight, possessive embrace. And after all, there were watchers.

"You're alive. You're *alive.*"

"Yes, I have been the whole time. Ah, Adares. I am sorry I made you suffer."

"You've done nothing that you need be sorry for, Rus. Well, not as far as I know. You were willing to die, but you didn't have to. Were you badly hurt?"

"No, but I was a long time recovering. I was very … unhappy."

"Yeah."

They stood a moment longer in each other's arms, then Adares stepped back a little, keeping one arm around Rus, and beckoned to the other Phemians. They had been pretending they weren't watching, so it took them a moment to shuffle sheepishly forward. Their eyes were wide.

"I believe you can guess who this is," Adares said.

"I *did* guess!" Kagieros was indignant. "He's the Luth who saved your life after the battle! I *knew* it!"

"Yes, but you were going to talk about it in Gunthanaruth's hall, where there were men who understand Pseuchaian perfectly well. And you *must not breathe a word of it.* We are allies of the Luth now, but we were their enemies at the time, and the siege would have gone very differently if Rus had taken me prisoner when he had the chance. I mean"—he shifted his arm around Rus, drawing him a little closer—"other than metaphorically, of course."

It was like being in another world. The Phemians laughed and groaned and grinned at Rus, and then the older, warrior-looking man turned grave again and shook Rus's hand—

and all of this while Adares had his arm around him, and after they had seen Adares kiss him.

Then Adares said, "I don't think I'm going to come back to the hall with you lot," and the Phemians all laughed again and said no, of course he wasn't.

"We'll make your excuses for you, lord archon," said Kagieros.

"Thank you, Kagieros," said Adares, "and I hope you won't have to, but if you do, you'll remember, won't you, that these people have a fantastically strict taboo against this sort of thing?" He gestured between himself and Rus. "This is strictly illicit?"

"Oh," said Kagieros, eyes widening again. "Right. Of course. Gosh." And he gave Rus a parting up-and-down look of surprised respect.

CHAPTER XX

THEY STOOD FOR a few moments watching the other Phemians return up the hill and around the side of the paddock. Then they turned together, without speaking, and began to walk further down into the valley. Adares's hand found Rus's, and their fingers slid together.

The hillside was steep here, and it was slow going; they picked their way carefully in the moonlight. Adares lost his footing a couple of times, and Rus caught him, and they both laughed.

Finally they stopped, close to the floor of the narrow valley, the fences and buildings of the village lost to sight above them, hidden by the incline of the hill, though they were not really so far away. A stream filled the bottom of the valley, noisy with winter run-off, and the opposite slope was bare and rocky. Adares looked up. Rus followed his gaze. Only a few stars were visible above them in a patch of dark sky. Gaunt, grey, snow-streaked peaks blocked all the rest.

"Now these are real mountains," said Adares. "The mountains of Pheme are just big hills, compared to this."

Rus leaned back against Adares, and Adares drew him close, still looking up at the mountains. His right hand gripped Rus's shoulder. Rus traced his fingertips over the barely-visible lines of ink on the back of it.

"You kept the snake," Rus said.

"The what? Oh. The snake. Yes, I did. On impulse, the day after I heard that you'd … when I thought you had died. I found a Getti woman in town who did the work for me. I knew the Getti use brown ink, almost the same colour as those berries." He held his hand out to look at it. "I wouldn't expect you to understand, but that was quite possibly the craziest thing I've ever done in my life."

Rus gave him a sceptical look over his shoulder.

He shrugged. "I'm a Phemian. We don't tattoo ourselves. It's not even on the list of things Phemians never do, like wear long sleeves or grow beards—it's just too bizarre. Of course, as it turns out, I'm setting myself up as an independent chief in the Karhan, so it's entirely appropriate—but I didn't know that at the time. You didn't tell me the snake was the mark of a headman."

"No, I couldn't have. I was still pretending not to know who you were."

Adares put his arm back around Rus, and they stood like that for a little longer.

"Did you write that letter, about the tribute?" Adares asked.

"Gunthanaruth told me what to write, but yes, I did write it. I even signed my name to it."

Adares considered that for a moment. "Your full name. Was I supposed to be able to decipher that?"

"No, I didn't think you would. It didn't occur to me just to write 'Rus' at the bottom of an official letter, though. It would have looked odd."

"No one would have seen it but me."

"No?"

"No! It was addressed to me—no one else reads my correspondence unless I show it to them."

"I didn't think of that."

"And I suppose even if you had, I'd have just thought Rus was a common name."

"It isn't."

Adares nuzzled his face into Rus's hair, laughing softly. He was standing behind Rus, and the sloping ground beneath their feet added extra inches to the difference in their heights. He moved his hand from Rus's shoulder, stroking slowly down over Rus's chest to his belly, warm through the thin fabric of his shirt.

"Part of me," he said, his breath warm on Rus's neck, "wants to just sit and talk with you all night."

Rus pressed back against him, eyes shut. "What part of you is that? The inhuman part that … that delights in the suffering of others?"

He felt Adares's tongue trace the curve of his ear, and he made a noise low in his throat. Adares's hands travelled lower, one gathering up Rus's kilt, the other moving over the inside of his thigh, smooth fingertips tracing over sensitive skin.

"You've changed," Adares whispered. "You're not so skittish. I like it."

"You should. It is all your doing."

Adares's left hand was under his shirt now. It was so strange for this to happen here, in the heart of the Luth territory, almost within sight of the headman's hall. It didn't seem real.

"Rus? Say something to me in Firhat Luth."

"What?"

"Anything."

He turned in Adares's arms, looping his hands behind Adares's neck.

"You are so beautiful," he said, lingering on each word because it was such an astonishing thing to say in the Luth language, the word for a desirable woman but with the masculine ending. Something no one ever said. He wanted to explain this in case Adares's understanding of Luth grammar was not advanced enough to grasp it, but Adares was looking at him with a little smile.

"Thanks. I wasn't expecting that."

"I assumed you knew." He went back to Firhat Kosoth for that; it felt more natural.

"Yeah, well." Adares gave a small shrug. "It doesn't hurt to be reminded."

Rus laughed out loud. The sound echoed faintly in the steep valley, and he put his hand over his mouth. Adares's hands had found their way under his kilt again, this time at the back.

"I'd like—" Rus switched back to Firhat Luth, though he had to force the words out: "I'd like to see you naked again."

"Would you? There aren't any of those poisonous white mushrooms around here, are there?"

"Of course not. They don't grow out in the open like this."

"Out in the open," Adares repeated, raising one eyebrow the way he did. But he reached up and unpinned his cloak.

He took his time shedding his clothes, and he made Rus help, sliding Rus's hands under the thin fabric to glide over his skin. They ended up with Rus sitting on the steep hillside, all his clothes still on except his loincloth, and Adares naked on his knees in front of him. Rus dropped onto his back in the grass, and Adares pushed up his kilt.

"I keep promising myself I'm going to see what it looks like when you get hard, the way this business transforms." He was trailing a finger around Rus's dick as he spoke, tracing the tattooing. Then he seemed to realize what he had said. "I mean, it was something I'd thought. Before."

He leaned down, and his mouth was as warm and soft as

Rus remembered, lips and tongue and even just a suggestion of teeth, but so gentle and careful. Rus remembered Adares saying that when he had done this before, it had been his first time, and he wondered now if this was the second. But that was a fleeting thought, soon buried in the flood of sensation as Adares got to work on him.

Not that the Phemian made it seem like work. He so clearly enjoyed Rus's reactions, holding him down with a teasing lightness that just encouraged Rus to push back, and making little noises of satisfaction when Rus moaned. And he was doing something else that he hadn't done that first time. He was making it take longer, drawing it out. It was exquisite, and Rus didn't know how long he could stand it.

Adares drew off altogether and pushed up on his hands to look at Rus. His lips glistened wet in the moonlight. His hair was very, very slightly mussed. Rus nudged him with one knee, flipping him over onto his back in the grass, and swung his other leg over him, gathering up the front of his kilt with one hand.

The position was shocking, and he was fiercely amazed at himself for daring this. Adares slid his hands over Rus's hips and took him eagerly in again.

Rus moved gingerly, afraid of choking him, but he had guessed right that Adares would like this. He could feel Adares make a sound almost like purring, his beautiful hands roving under Rus's kilt. He thrust in tiny, careful motions, the tension in him building and building to the moment of release, like an ache in his thighs and a warmth in his belly, and the heat suddenly and slowly flooding his whole body, like the slowing of time in the exhilaration of a fight, and like the opposite of that, as far from it as the distance between ha-tred and love. He cried out, and it echoed off the mountains.

He knelt there catching his breath, one hand braced in the

cool grass, the other holding onto his bunched-up kilt. He felt so good, he was afraid to move or speak and break the spell.

Then Adares half-slid, half-wriggled up under him, and tipped his head back to look Rus in the eye, and the expression on his face—open, easy, obviously pleased with himself—made Rus want to cry out again, with simple joy. Made him feel there was no spell here that could be broken, just the two of them back together, the way they were meant to be.

He dropped his kilt and backed down the hill over Adares, putting one knee between Adares's thighs, which were already sprawled apart, his dark bronze dick looking like something fresh from the forge, hard as a weapon.

Adares was watching him with a look that was hard to interpret in the dark. He slid a hand down his own flank and over his thigh, fingers and thumb framing his genitals as if offering them to Rus.

"That's the most beautiful thing I've ever seen," Rus whispered.

And a small dog barked—*yap-yap-yap!*—somewhere quite close by.

Rus started and froze. The dog barked again, even closer, and then a woman's voice—Genet's voice—called from above: "Kaily!" Rus had thought he recognized the bark. It was a puppy beloved of Kuth and Genet's children, especially Meret. Adares had rolled half over beneath him, pushing up onto one elbow. Rus scrambled to his feet, scanning the hillside. He couldn't see Genet yet, but he could see the puppy, and now the puppy had seen him. She came barrelling down the hill, yapping excitedly. Rus reached down and put a hand on Adares's bare shoulder.

"Go." Adares touched his hand, his voice barely above a breath. "I'll be fine."

He felt strangely unworried as he strode up the hill to meet the bounding dog. Maybe it was the afterglow of love-making still warming him—it was certainly partly that—but it was also joy in that easy understanding they had between them still, so that they hardly needed words for each to know what the other wanted to say.

He caught the puppy just as he heard Genet call for it again, sounding mercifully far away still. He tucked the furry bundle under one arm and went loping at a diagonal up the hill, using his free hand for balance, moving as far away from Adares as quickly as he could. The night air felt cool under his kilt, because he was still missing his loincloth. At least that was all the clothing he had shed.

"Kaily!"

The dog yapped and wriggled under Rus's arm. "Over here!" he called back, because at this point it would seem strange if he didn't. "I've got her!"

"Rus?"

Genet emerged on the ridge above him. He didn't dare look back to see whether Adares was still visible below.

"Ah, there you are! Thank you, Rus. I knew she wouldn't have gone far. She's been missing since supper. Meret was worried about her, so I said I would come look."

She plucked the puppy out of his hands and tucked it under her own arm. But she didn't move to climb back up toward the paddock.

"What did you think of the Phemians?" she asked. "You stayed at the feast, didn't you? I left early with the children. Did you talk with their headman?"

"Yes. A little." He was out of breath, his heart pounding. He couldn't quite believe she didn't notice.

"He's *handsome*," she said, as if she were telling him something he couldn't be expected to have noticed. "What's he like?"

"Ah, well. Very charming. I didn't really … " He trailed off, unsure how to end that sentence without a colossal lie.

"You should have stayed and talked to him more. Do you think he will be a good ally for the tribe?"

"Yes," said Rus, with feeling. "I am sure of it. Yes."

"Well! You feel strongly about it. I didn't know. I thought perhaps after you fought his people … " She shrugged.

"That was not my idea."

"Ah, no. I suppose it wasn't."

He opened his mouth to say that they should go back up to the village, but before he could, Genet gasped and pointed behind him.

"Look! Is that not one of the Phemians?"

"Is it?" Rus turned reluctantly.

Adares was coming up the hill toward them. There was something odd about the way he held his cloak wrapped around himself.

"It is," said Genet after a moment. "It is their headman. What is the matter with him?"

"Hello!" Adares called in Luth. "Excuse me!"

He scrambled up the last stretch of hillside to where they stood.

"I am very glad to see you," he said. By this time Rus could see that he was dripping wet and shivering with cold.

"Lord archon," said Rus, barely resisting the urge to reach out and put his arms around Adares. What had he been *doing*? "We didn't know you were there. This is Genet, our vahat." Was he talking too loudly?

"Oh, yes! The one who does the tattoos!"

"Did you meet with an accident, lord archon?"

"Not an accident." Adares hitched his cloak higher around his shoulders. It was rather carelessly wrapped, and he was wearing nothing else. "I was trying to … in the stream … "

He gestured vaguely. He was looking for the Luth word for *swim*, Rus realized. There wasn't one.

"Bathe?" Genet's voice rose with astonishment. "In a mountain stream, my lord? In the dead of night in spring?"

"I'm used to much warmer water where I'm from. I was … surprised."

"You might have been drowned," Genet said severely. "Come. You may warm up at my house. It is not far."

"You are very kind," said Adares meekly. "I hope I may also borrow some clothes? I have lost the rest of mine."

"Of course. Come." She beckoned to Rus to come too, which he'd had every intention of doing whether she liked it or not.

"We were talking about you," Genet said, looking back over her shoulder as she led the way up to her house.

"I thought so," said Adares. "I do not know so much of your language, but I thought I heard 'very fine fellow'—did I not?"

"I think it was 'very *vain* fellow,'" Genet sent back without blinking. "They do sound alike."

Adares laughed his beautiful laugh. Rus wondered if it affected Genet anything like the way it affected him. It might.

"Genet speaks Firhat Kosoth too," said Rus, before Adares tried to say anything private.

"Clearly, then, we will not be able to discuss her beauty behind her back."

Genet looked back in order to roll her eyes. But she looked a little pleased, all the same.

"You would not get Rus to do that, in any language," she said. "Do you not know the kahar are set apart from women? This one takes it more seriously than some. The chastest man I know, he is."

"Mm?" said Adares. He licked his lips, a tiny noise in the darkness. "Is he?"

Rus was suddenly very conscious that he was wearing nothing under his kilt.

They arrived at Kuth and Genet's house. The hearth fire was banked for the night, but a Kossian-style clay lamp—filled with grease instead of olive oil, of course—lit the front part of the house. The baby and the elder son were already asleep behind the curtain, but Meret sat up with her father, anxiously waiting for news of the puppy. Kaily ran to her, tail wagging, and Meret scooped her up and hugged her, but the dog's return was overshadowed by the appearance of the Phemian. Meret stared at him with wide eyes. Kuth looked almost as amazed himself. There was no real reason for that; he and Genet were from good skar families and on friendly terms with their own tribe's headman and need not be shy to invite anyone to their fire.

Adares sat by the hearth and accepted a towel to dry his hair—which either had not got wet at all or had dried already, being so short—and a cup of milk, and smiled at Meret and said that when he was a boy he'd had a dog that used to run away too. She stared at him as though the fact that he spoke Luth—after a fashion, with lots of hand-waving—only made him more alarming. Kuth fetched a sleeping-robe for him to wear, and he managed to get into it without flinging off the cloak first, though perhaps even he would not have done that in front of a woman and a little girl. Rus wasn't sure.

"You'll stay with us tonight?" said Kuth, and winced as he realized the words sounded insufficiently hospitable. "Stay with us, my lord," he amended. "We would be honoured."

"I would be most happy," said Adares.

Rus sat on the opposite side of the hearth, tugging on his kilt to make absolutely sure no one could get a glimpse under it, and said nothing. He was tired, and this felt dreamlike again: his friends and his lover sitting together, talking, in a mixture of Firhat Kosoth and Luth, as if it were normal, as if it might happen every day.

"Who did your tattoo?" Genet asked, pointing to Adares's snake.

"A Getti woman who lives in Tios."

She frowned. "No, no. It's not a Getti tattoo. That's a Luth snake. If she told you she was Getti, she lied."

"I … don't think so. But she didn't draw the design. It was drawn by a Luth." The word should have had a masculine or feminine ending when it was used of a person, but evidently Adares didn't know that, and he used the form you would use for a house or a horse whose sex you didn't know.

"Ah," said Genet. "Yes. I knew it was. Why didn't she ink it for you, too, this Luth? Why didn't she ink it properly in blue?"

"Well, we lost touch, after she drew it for me. I didn't know where to find her."

"Hm." Genet gave him a look as if she thought she knew what *that* meant. "You left her for the Getti woman. And then you had the Getti girl ink the Luth girl's drawing? Tcha!"

"It wasn't *quite* like that," Adares said, in a way that managed to suggest that yes, it had been pretty much like that. "I thought it was a good snake, and I wanted to keep it, that's all."

"It is a good snake," Genet agreed. "If I didn't know any better, I'd think it was done by one of my apprentices. But none of them have gone south and had their hearts broken recently. Do you have any other tattoos?"

Adares looked at her for a moment from under his lashes before he said, "No."

It was long enough for Genet to have started to blush.

They talked a little longer before retiring to the sleeping-platform behind the curtain. By this time everyone was yawning hugely, and it was the most natural thing in the world for Rus to make a pile of rugs against the wall and stretch out there, not alongside Adares exactly, but close enough that he could have reached out in the dark and stroked the Phemian's hair if he had dared. He didn't, but he fell asleep thinking about it.

CHAPTER XXI

RUS WOKE BEFORE Adares, when it was only the two of them and the baby still on the sleeping platform. He lay looking at his lover for a while, watching him sleep, a little luxury. His lover? He wondered about that.

Meret came through the curtain to summon them to breakfast, and Rus shook Adares by the shoulder to wake him. Adares blinked confusedly, taking in his surroundings. He managed to collect himself enough to smile winningly at Meret, who hid her face and ducked back through the curtain.

"Shy, is she?"

"Not normally," said Rus.

They ate a leisurely breakfast with the family. Adares flirted in a very harmless style with everyone except Rus. It was a marvel to watch. It didn't take long for Meret to stop being afraid of him and begin peppering him with questions about Tios and its people and animals and their ways. When Genet sent Rus out to the valley to retrieve the Phemian's clothes, Adares was playing with the baby.

Adares's white tunic was easy to spot in the grass. Fortunately, it lay on the sunny slope of the valley, so it was quite dry. Rus found his own loincloth, hiked up his kilt to put it back on, then found Adares's belt and sandals, and Adares's loincloth, a filmy scrap of fabric, which had blown much further away. He climbed back up the hill. On his way around the headman's paddock, he ran into Kagieros, who gave him a ridiculously conspiratorial look, glanced pointedly around to be sure no one else was nearby, and said in a loud whisper, "Where's the lord archon?"

"He is at a house in the village, with a family who invited him to stay the night. I am on my way there and can take a message if you wish." He held the bundle of Adares's clothes discreetly behind his back.

"Oh, would you?" said Kagieros. "I've been sent to look for him, which is really rather awkward, don't you think? Guntha-whatisname wants us all to go hunting mountain goats with him this morning. That's the message."

"I will tell him."

"Splendid! Well, that's my duty done, then."

He turned and fell into step beside Rus, and they walked up toward the headman's hall together.

"I have to ask," Kagieros said after a moment.

"Yes?"

"Well, you know." He looked at Rus with a little grin and made a gesture with his elbow in the direction of Rus's ribs. "How is he?"

Rus gave him a puzzled look in return. "Much as you left him."

"No, no—you know. How *is* he? Is he a good lay? Because, I mean, he's not my type at all, but he seems like he would be."

"I don't—I couldn't—" Rus put a hand to his throat and tugged on his torque, which suddenly seemed as though it was going to choke him. "I have no idea. No basis for com-parison."

"Oh," said Kagieros. "Gosh."

It occurred to Rus that if they really talked so openly about these things, then he was in danger of tarnishing Adares's reputation, so he added, "But I would say so. Very."

And he hurried off.

***

He had calmed down enough by the time he got back to Kuth and Genet's house to be able to deliver the clothes and the message almost casually. Adares accepted them with a nonchalance that was probably not even feigned, went behind the curtain the change, and set off for the headman's hall. Rus did not see him for the rest of the day.

He barely saw him the following day, this time because Rus himself was busy preparing for a ceremony that evening at the standing stones. That evening, Adares and the other Phemians arrived along with Kuth and Genet to watch the ceremony. Rus wondered whose idea that had been. Afterward, not really knowing how it happened, he found himself climbing a nearby peak with Adares, "to show him the view." Somehow none of the other Phemians seemed interested in seeing it.

"Do they all know about us?" Rus asked.

"All of my men? Oh, yes, by this time. They're all trustworthy—even Kagieros, once you spell things out for him. It's quite sweet how helpful they're trying to be. Though 'going up a hill to admire the view' isn't the *best* pretext for a tryst, is it? We can't very well get out of their sight."

"I'm sorry. After last night—I'm afraid that was very unsatisfactory for you."

"Eh?"

"I mean because you weren't able to … to … you didn't climax."

"Oh, well. That would have been nice. But I'm not the one who'd gone six—seven? seven!—months without sex."

"Ah."

Adares looked at him. "I should probably have put that more … I shouldn't have sprung that on you. I'm sorry. I wish I'd been faithful to you, but … "

"You thought I was dead. It's not really 'being faithful' when you think the other person's dead." He thought he should leave it at that. It wasn't any of his business. Adares was here, now, and it was like this between them, and that was all that mattered. But after a moment, he said it anyway: "Are you married?"

Adares gave him a look like a blank wall. "Am I married. No. Rus, I would have told you if I was married. And I, uh. I wouldn't have sucked your dick out behind the horse paddock last night, if I was married."

"I'm—I'm sorry. I didn't mean … I wasn't thinking."

"Oh, you were *thinking*. You were just thinking some nonsense."

"Yes, I suppose so."

"You'd have been angry with me if I cheated on my wife—my *hypothetical* wife—with you. Try to tell me you wouldn't."

"I'd have been sad … "

"Disappointed in me."

"Yes, I suppose so. Yes. Actually, you're right."

"There you go. I wouldn't have done it."

"You wouldn't have done it because *I* wouldn't have liked it?"

Adares shrugged. "That, and it's not the kind of husband I'd want to be. Not the kind of lover I *am*—when I don't think the other person's dead."

"I know. I do know. I've insulted you. I will give you twenty horses in recompense."

Adares looked interested. "Do you have twenty horses?"

"No. Kahar don't own horses. It was a joke."

"Oh, a *joke.*"

"How many people did you sleep with, while you thought I was dead?"

"One. The ex-wife of the First Spear of the colonial legion. He's dead—killed in the Luth assault—but they were divorced before that. So she was mourning too, but in a complicated way. We had an affair. It lasted a month. She ended it—she said we weren't right for each other, and it was true. I couldn't give her what she needed—I don't even know what it was— and she couldn't give me what I needed. Partly because she doesn't have a blue-striped dick. But mostly because she doesn't have your sense of humour."

So there it was. He had found someone else, and they had been lovers for a month. That wasn't long, Rus thought, in the realm of love affairs, but it was more than three days. And yet here Adares was.

"Did you tell her about me?" Rus asked after a moment.

Adares drew a breath and let it out slowly. "No," he said finally. "I wasn't sure she would understand."

"I'm sorry."

Adares gave him a look, eyebrows raised.

"Because you suffered," Rus explained. "Because you suffered, and it was on account of me. And yes, of course, I am glad for my own sake, that you didn't talk to her about me, because perhaps if you had, the understanding between you and her would have grown, and you would have ceased to think of me, and you would not be here now."

Now Adares was giving him a different kind of look. "That's the sort of speech that makes me want to grab you and give you a kiss, Rus. But we're silhouetted against the sunset here, and your acolytes or whatever are down below. Can you just imagine it for me instead?”

“I always do.”

They stood a little longer in silence, and the light faded as the sun disappeared into the crook of the mountains. Rus was aware that something had changed, shifted, because of all that Adares had just said, but he couldn't pin down exactly how or what. Finally he said, “We should make a plan.”

“Oh. Yes, sure. What sort of a plan?”

Rus thought for a moment. “Perhaps I could invite you to go for a ride tomorrow morning, to see one of our other stone circles—perhaps you have taken an interest in them, and I have offered to show them to you. But your men will stay behind, because the other kahar are going to teach them to play hargan.”

“They'll like that. But is it proper for me to ride out with you without any attendants?”

“It is how things are done in Tios. If anyone asks, that is what we'll tell them.”

“It's true, as it happens.”

“There you are. Will it do?”

“Yes, of course. I have a feeling they're *fascinating* standing stones, and I'm going to want to spend a long time admiring them.”

“They have many significant carvings. I will explain them all to you.”

It was getting too dark to properly appreciate the look Adares gave him at that. He had to use his imagination again.

“The thing is,” Adares said, “with you I'm never sure. That could be true.”

Adares linked his hands behind his head as he lay on his back in the grass. "This Great Pattern," he said. "Are the gods part of it, or are they outside it?"

"Both."

"Right … "

"No, do not pretend that makes sense to you."

"It doesn't."

"It is a paradox. We say they dance the pattern—that's a metaphor."

"No kidding. So they create it?"

"Maybe. Some people say so. Or they see it, and follow it in their dance."

"I see. No, I do. They're outside of the pattern, but in it at the same time." He closed his eyes. He sounded drowsy. "I don't know what made me think of that. Maybe just … Making love to you makes me feel connected to it, whatever it is. As if it flows through us all the time, but when you're in my arms I can feel it. That probably strikes you as blasphemous."

"Mm," said Rus noncommittally, because it didn't really, but he supposed that it should.

They were lying in the shadow of one of the outer ring stones at the south circle. It was the least sacred part of the site—the outer ring stones were more or less decorative—which was why Rus had picked it when he wanted shade, but the location still made him slightly nervous.

They had ridden out here early, while the dew was still on the grass. They had lain down together in the sunlight, stripped to the skin, and taken their time together. It had been the best time yet, in a way: unhurried, place and time both ideal for it, neither of them in pain. Adares had climaxed twice: once with Rus's hand stroking him, once with Rus inside of his body. That meant that the scales were balanced between them again, and Rus had pretended to take this very seriously as a point of honour, because Adares seemed to find that sort of thing funny.

Now they were lying in the shade because the sun had grown hot. Rus had made good on his threat to explain the carvings on the stones.

"So this job you have now," Adares began, opening his eyes and turning on his side to look at Rus. "It's second-in-command of all the priests of the whole tribe, isn't it?"

"Yes, and successor to the stathan when he dies."

"And you're only nineteen?"

"Twenty, now."

Adares reached out and trailed a finger down Rus's side. "We must have been born at the same time of year. I'm twenty-five this past winter. Did you want the job?"

"No."

"But it's an honour."

"It is."

"But you don't want it."

"No. Is that like you, being archon of Tios?"

"No! No, not at all. At least not any more. It's grown on me—or I've grown into it, or something. I'm … I don't know." He settled on his side, head propped on his hand, and after a moment accepted the change of topic. "In some ways, these last six months … seven months … have been the worst of my life, but in some ways, oddly enough, I'm enjoying myself. It's almost like starting a new colony, figuring out how we'll cope without Pheme. And you remember what I was most afraid of in the fall—that the Phemian army would be sent over to clean up our mess?"

"That's not a threat any more."

"Doesn't seem like it. I'm honestly glad of that. Even if it comes with a sentence of permanent exile for me—it hasn't come to that yet, but it may. Especially after the business with the publicly-owned slaves."

"The what?"

"Slaves owned by the state … You wouldn't really have anything like that here, because you don't have a concept of 'the state,' but we have a lot of them in Pheme, and had a few hundred in Tios, until this spring. But there was some suggestion that they were actually the property of Pheme, and as such should be sent back. It would have been a crisis for Tios, if we'd had to do that, because, frankly, we need their labour—we don't have a surplus of workers, and some of them are skilled.

"So we came up with the idea, my advisors and I, of offering them a choice between being sent back to Pheme as slaves or staying in Tios as freedmen—I don't think you have those here, either, but it means what it sounds like—and they all chose to stay, so we freed them. We may or may not have been legally within our rights—it's a grey area—but it doesn't matter, so long as they don't try to go back to Pheme. We minted our own coins to pay them for their work, and we offered grants of money to any private slave-owners in the city who wanted to do the same—free their slaves and rehire them as freedmen. I thought—we thought—that kind of thing might raise morale in the midst of a hard winter, and I think it did.

"But now I'm not just the rebel archon of a breakaway colony—I'm the radical who freed all the slaves. There are philosophers in Pheme who are saying we should all do that, that no one should keep slaves. It's a hot topic." He gave a one-shouldered shrug. "I didn't do it because of the philosophers, I honestly didn't even know about that. I just did it because it seemed like a good idea at the time. But if I come out on the right side of history for it—and I think I may—I won't complain."

He paused, and Rus moved to lie closer against him in the grass, wanting to make it clear he enjoyed listening to all this. "Go on," he said.

"Well, then there are ways that Tios is changing, already. Becoming less an outpost of Pheme and more its own city. I guess it had been happening in small ways for a while, as more locals moved into the city and we traded more with the tribes, but it's out in the open now, and people are talking about it. It's become deliberate. More Phemians—Tians—are starting to wear local dress, cook the local specialities, marry local women. My councillors have started looking to me to make some sort of gesture—grow a moustache, maybe, or start wearing a kilt. They thought the tattoo was the beginning of something, a transformation of some kind." He smiled. "Actually, it was a poor substitute for the gesture I really wanted to make."

"Which was?"

"You."

"You mean … " What did he mean? Rus felt as if he couldn't breathe.

Adares put out a hand and touched Rus's hair. "I mean I imagined bringing you to Tios and flaunting you in front of the council and the people. It would never fly in Pheme, an archon having an acknowledged lover—much too radical. But in Tios, why not? They would all have loved you, when they met you—you're surprisingly full of old-fashioned Phemian virtues—and the story of how you rescued me on the battlefield would make everyone think of the heroic lovers of legend. The romantic types would have lost their minds. I'd have been re-elected on the strength of it." He grinned.

"Of course, I may be re-elected anyway, if only because no one else wants the job."

Rus held his breath, aware of every place Adares's body touched his. The Phemian had spoken so easily of it—"bringing you to Tios"—as if he had imagined riding through the city gates with Rus behind him on his horse. Perhaps he had. But it was a fantasy, or a dream whose time had passed. He hadn't suggested that it might really be like that now.

Adares's fingers tunnelled in under Rus's hair and curled around the back of his neck. "Meanwhile here you are, set to be the youngest of your people ever to be made high priest—right? Tell me more about that."

Rus sighed. "If I have to."

"You do."

So he told Adares the whole story about his dream and Unumus's interpretation and Suthus making him his deputy.

"But I don't think the dream can have been a vision from the gods, because wouldn't Kahait have been wearing my kilt pin if it had?"

Adares had turned to lie on his back again, and he looked thoughtfully up at the sky for a moment. "Yes, that does seem obvious, doesn't it? I don't know. If I'm honest, Rus, if it were my dream, I don't think I'd believe in it even if she had the kilt pin. I mean, that is the sort of thing you might dream, too, isn't it?"

"I suppose it is. What are you saying, then?"

"I don't know. I guess that I'm not the type to have visions from the gods. But … " He looked down at Rus. "I wouldn't have thought you were, either."

"No." It was what he'd thought, but it was strange to hear someone else say it. Strange and a little painful. Somehow he'd thought Adares had a higher opinion of him than that.

"I don't mean it the way you're probably thinking. I think

you're the most … the most *religious* man I know. I think the gods might very well have things to say to you, personally. I just don't think they'd necessarily do it in your sleep."

Rus considered that for a moment. "You think I'm not mystical."

"Exactly. You're really not. You're lots of other things—you're pedantic, you're passionate, you're literalistic, and funny, and full of life, and so completely at home in your own body. I love you. I know that's not what we were talking about, but I missed my chance to say it once, and I'm going to take every chance I have from now on."

"I love you too," Rus said fervently. "I love you too."

Adares reached for him, and rolled on top of him to kiss him long and deeply. His hands moved firmly, expertly over Rus's body. "Mm. What would you like me to do about *this*? It's beginning to resemble one of these standing stones. I've been waiting a while to make that joke," he admitted.

"Please don't ever make it again. I'm quite serious."

Adares laughed. "You are, aren't you? Is this all right?" He was moving unhurriedly on top of Rus, rubbing against him the same way he had done that first time in the fall.

"Of course."

"It's just that I've noticed you like being on top."

"Perhaps I'll tumble you over into the grass when you least expect it."

"Mmm. Will you?"

But he didn't. He let Adares stay on top, lazily pushing them to a climax that arrived at the same time for both of them. Afterward he pulled Adares over into the crook of his arm, and they lay exhausted together.

After they had been silent for a long time, Adares said, "I suppose this is what some men make do with—living separate lives, pursuing their own careers, and meeting every few months for a day or two."

"Ah yes? Do they?"

"Well, some men in Pheme, certainly. Men in public life, who couldn't afford to have a lover openly. Like I was talking about earlier. Could you be content with that, do you think?"

"Of course." It was the only possible answer. A future in which he could still see Adares occasionally, still lie down with him like this, no matter how long they might have to wait in between times? Of course he could be content with that. He looked at Adares and realized it suddenly. "You couldn't."

"No, I … If you are happy, then … " He pushed himself up, away from Rus, and rubbed a hand over his face. "I'm sorry. It's not the time to talk about the future, and I didn't really mean … I didn't expect you to say yes."

He managed to salvage the mood, after that, by asking some ridiculous question about the stone circle, and they were soon laughing and teasing each other again. But Rus had not missed the effort it had taken Adares to turn back to a lighter topic.

CHAPTER XXII

THE PHEMIANS WERE to spend a week in Gunthanaruth's village. The day after that morning at the stone circle was entirely taken up with a game of hargan. Rus played in the morning, and in the afternoon he swapped positions with Kuth so he could sit among the spectators with Adares and explain the game to him. Adares said that by the end of the day he thought he understood what was going on.

The day after that, Gunthanaruth took the Phemians out hunting again, and Suthus returned from the village with the omen. A herd of cattle had been seen in White-Water Valley, a couple of hours' ride from the headman's village, and the kahar hall was full of talk about the first bull-hunt of the year. Rus saw Adares in the evening at the headman's hearth, where they were able to talk, almost without pretence, in Luth and in Firhat Kosoth, with Gunthanaruth beaming on them with obvious satisfaction at having caused them to become such good friends.

The rest of the Phemians were enjoying themselves. Some of them were surprisingly good at hargan, and others seemed to be keen hunters. They were all enthusiastic about the food and drink in the headman's hall, and the scenery—they raved about the mountains. A couple of them had made friends among the village women, and the women reported that as suitors they behaved themselves very well.

Rus had not been able to find another opportunity to ride out alone with Adares. He had his own duties, and Adares was busy being entertained by the headman and the rest of the tribe, being shown horses, and touring forges, and meeting all the important members of the skar who had been able to come to the headman's village on short notice. Of course he was also shown around the kahar hall, and expressed an interest in their duties and ceremonies which was probably not even feigned, and one night he dined with Kuth and Genet and their family, and of course Rus was there too. They served hashvash made with raw meat, and Adares loved it. All in all, it was a wonderful week.

There was one evening of it left—the Phemians were set to leave the following morning—and Rus and Adares had sat at dinner in the headman's hall as usual. By now it seemed natural for Rus to say, "Come for a walk with me," as he rose from his seat, and for Adares to excuse himself casually to Gunthanaruth and rise to follow him. Everyone knew the headman of Tios strolled about without attendants when it suited him, and besides, when he was with the deputy stathan of the kahar, there was nothing undignified about it.

They walked down beside the horse paddock as they had the first night, stopping at the top of the hill at the back.

"I'm afraid we don't have time to do anything," Rus said, and then felt crass, as if he had accused Adares of caring only about one thing. "I mean … "

"I know what you mean," said Adares. He slung an arm around Rus's shoulders and pulled him gently against his side. "We have time to do this."

"Yes. And I wanted to give you something."

He slipped his hand under the overlapping edge of his

kilt, where he had concealed a small gold pin. He unpinned it and drew it out, fastening the clasp again before holding it out in his palm. It was a pin he'd had for years, beautifully enamelled with the figure of a bird. He held his hand out so that it caught the warm rays of the setting sun.

"It's lovely," said Adares, looking but not reaching for it.

"It's for you."

"Yes." Still he didn't reach for it. His arm was still warm around Rus's shoulders. "I remember. It's a love token. You give it to a girl when you're courting."

"I couldn't buy a new one to give you—it would seem too odd a thing for a kahar to do—but this is one I've had for a long time. I thought … you might like that better."

Adares drew a breath and let it out. "I am sorry, Rus. I can't take it."

But you love me! Rus almost blurted out. He felt cold in spite of the warmth of the evening, in spite of Adares's arm around him.

"You can't?"

"I can't promise to be faithful to you if we go six months at a time without seeing one another, Rus. Not if that's how it would be for the rest of our lives. I wish I could. I believe *you* could—it's one of the amazing things about you."

"I wouldn't ask it of you," Rus said quickly. "I don't have any other options, but I wouldn't expect you to wait for me."

Adares withdrew his arm and clasped his own shoulder with his hand. "You'd just like to pick up where we left off whenever we can manage to meet?"

"Isn't that the best we could do?"

"It is. But … I can't promise I could do that for very long."

"Ah. No." He remembered things Adares had said earlier in the week and realized he should have known this. But he hadn't, and it felt as if there was a crack in the bottom of the world and everything was draining out. "I understand. You want to be faithful to someone."

"I wish it could be you. I love you so much. Right now I can't imagine finding anyone I'd care about half as much. And maybe I never will. But … you know … if I did, I'd want to be faithful to her. Or him—but honestly, probably her. I think there might really not be another man in the world I'd be willing to take publicly as a lover."

"But you would do that for me."

"That's what I was talking about the other day."

"I didn't think you meant that seriously."

"I did. And I didn't, because I didn't think—don't think—you want to give up your home and your whole way of life and the respect of your people to be with me. And I'm not offering to make a sacrifice like that for you, so I can't ask it of you."

Unexpectedly, Rus felt a little anger kindling at that. "My home … my home is a place where I can never tell anyone who I really am or who I love, and my way of life is a lie, and the respect of my people is another lie, and *I'm not asking you to make any sacrifice for me*. I expected you to go back to Tios and live your life and marry and rule your people, and all I wanted was to see you from time to time, but you won't even give me that."

"Because it wouldn't make either of us happy."

"Ah, yes? And if we part forever? The only one who stands a chance of happiness in that case is you."

"Rus, honestly … That isn't true. And you're not asking to be allowed to *see* me—that's not what that pin means—you're asking me to be your lover. Three or four days out of every year. Maybe."

"I don't know what you want from me! I can't go to Tios

with you. What would I do there? What would I *be*? I belong
here. This is the only place where I belong—I can't leave."

"That's what I said. You don't want to give up your way of
life. That's what I goddamn said, you nitpicking blue fuck."

Rus gave a surprised snort of laughter. He looked down
at the kilt pin that he still held. He turned and drew back his
hand and flung it as hard as he could down into the valley,
where the sun had already set and it was dark.

"We should go back," he said, looking up the hill rather
than at Adares. "You should go back into the hall. We can
say goodbye tomorrow."

They walked back up the hill in silence.

Rus didn't go back into the headman's hall. He went to
Kuth and Genet's house. Their children were sleeping inside
while their parents worked on the doorstep in the fading
light. Kuth was crushing seeds in a mortar, and Genet was
spinning. Rus sat down in the grass beside them. He thought
he would just sit there and not talk. He didn't want to talk.

"So the Phemians leave tomorrow," said Kuth.

"Kuth … " said Genet, a warning note in her voice.

Rus looked up at them, puzzled. "What?"

"She doesn't want me to talk about it," said Kuth, "but I
think we should. I think you and the Phemian archon are … "

"Friends," Genet supplied.

"Yes," said Kuth doggedly, "that, certainly. But I think
there's another word for it, too."

There was a moment of silence like a hole in the world.
This, he had not anticipated.

But it was surprisingly easy to know what to say next.

"He was the Phemian who saved my life after the battle in the autumn. We have been lovers since then. Or—we became lovers then, and we are again now. I knew who he was at the time—he didn't tell me, at first, but I guessed. I helped him get back into his city with reinforcements to lift the siege. When Gunthanaruth wanted a bull fight to decide whether we should leave or stay, I fought to lose. I let go on purpose. I don't remember doing it, but I know that's what I did. Adares thought that I'd died. I told Gunthanaruth to invite him here so that I could see him again."

Genet had fumbled her spindle, and it bounced across the packed earth in front of the doorway. She stood and bent to pick it up with a swift gesture that was oddly like a man grasping a weapon. She turned to look at Rus.

"I thought you were holy," she said.

"I'm not."

"You betrayed your people for the sake of an unnatural lust for a foreigner. You profaned the bull-fight, and you carried on as if nothing had happened and let Suthus make you his deputy."

Kuth made an impatient noise. "Genet … He chose loyalty to someone he loved. It's exactly what you or I would have done."

"It's what? He profaned the bull-fight!"

"Everyone but Gunthanaruth wanted that bull to win, and even he decided afterward that it had been for the best. And what was Rus supposed to do when Suthus named him his deputy? It seems to me that what he did was his duty."

"I don't think he knows his duty," Genet snapped. She turned and stalked into the house.

Kuth sighed. "I've known for years that the reason you never looked at girls was because you like men. I've told her before now, but she wouldn't hear it. She thought I was making it up because I was jealous, that I didn't like her having such a high opinion of you. There may have been a bit of truth to that. Still, I was right."

"Yes," said Rus hollowly. He put his hands over his face. "I didn't know."

"I could never think of a way to talk to you about it. I always sort of hoped you might find someone else like you. In fact, I used to wonder about you and … I won't tell you who, because you'd think it was ridiculous. Anyway, when I saw you with the Phemian archon, I knew I'd been wrong, because *this* was what you looked like in love. And, uh. He's very … "

"'You would fall off your horse,'" Rus supplied from behind his hands.

"That, yeah. You must have … Over the winter, you must have missed him."

"Yes."

"And now he's going back to Tios. Do you think you can find a way to go there and see him?"

"No. He doesn't want us to go on being lovers if we can't be together permanently."

Kuth was silent for a while. Finally he said, "I can understand that." He looked down at the mortar in his hands. "It's getting too dark to work. Come in the house with me."

"I don't think Genet wants me in there."

"You can't leave things like this. You two have always been friends."

He followed Kuth into the house. He felt numb, as if he was moving in a dream—definitely not a good dream, this time. Genet was sitting by the hearth, in the lamplight. She gave them both a hard look as they came in.

"What now?" she asked, her voice low because of the sleeping children. "Are you taking your leave, or … "

"We thought—I thought—perhaps you were going to leave with the Phemians," said Kuth, in explanation. "That's why I brought it up."

"I can't." He felt as though he would choke on the words. "How could I?"

"I don't know how you can stay," Genet retorted. "It seems to me you left this tribe a long time ago."

"I did not," Rus snapped back. "Kuth was right. I have done my duty. I didn't ask to be made Suthus's deputy—I didn't want it, you know that very well. I've said again and again I wasn't worthy of it, that I didn't really have a vision, that the gods wouldn't have chosen me for that. Did you need me to spell out exactly why?"

She stared into the ashes in the hearth instead of looking at him. "That night … after the Phemians first arrived, when I came looking for the dog. He wasn't—Phyleros, he wasn't really bathing in the stream, was he?"

"He went into the water because he couldn't think of any other way to account for having lost his clothes." It was really very funny, and he felt suddenly angry that they could not laugh about it together now.

"I thought you were holy," she said again. "I feel a fool."

"I'm sorry," he said, but it didn't sound sincere.

He was still standing inside the door, while she sat by her hearth. Kuth had gone to put away his medicine in one of the chests by the wall. Rus wondered if he should excuse himself, or just turn and leave, but nothing seemed to have been resolved. He'd come in feeling miserable, and now he was angry with it. He didn't see why she needed to take this as some sort of insult to herself.

"He complimented me, you know. On your tattoos." She looked up at him. "He's seen them *all*, hasn't he?"

That just seemed petty, and it made him even angrier. "Yeah. He's particularly fond of what you did with my dick."

"That—that—that is a sacred marking that signifies the— that your—that—"

"That my seed is set apart and must not be used procreate—and I promise you, *it hasn't*."

"That's not—"

"It *is* what it means!" He struggled to keep his voice down. "If you were going to say it means something else, something about purity, you've been listening to Unumus too much."

"Unumus! Unumus is a crank."

"Exactly."

"But that doesn't mean that your—"

"Will you both stop talking about his penis in my house, right now," Kuth cut in, in an urgent whisper. "Rus, sit down."

Rus hesitated a moment, then dropped down to sit by the hearth. He and Genet glared at one another across the ashes.

"Was it a seduction?" she said finally. "I think it would be, with one such as him."

Rus said nothing, just sighed angrily.

"Not that it would excuse you," she added. "You are a grown man, not a young girl, to be seduced by a ... " She gestured contemptuously, words failing her. "By such a thing."

"Don't call him a thing," said Rus through clenched teeth.

There was a knock at the door. Kuth got to his feet to answer it. Rus stared into the remains of the fire.

"Hello," said Kuth at the door, sounding surprised.

"I'm sorry to bother you so late," said the caller.

It was Adares. Rus put his head in his hands.

"Do not be sorry," said Kuth, automatically. "Please come in."

Adares came in. Rus looked over his shoulder, and their

eyes met for a moment. A wry expression passed over the Phemian's face.

"Will you sit?" said Kuth.

"Thank you, no. I'm here to ask for your help. A couple of my men just came back from the woods with a strange complaint. The, ah, the girl involved says they may have touched something called goatweed? I think the words she used were 'rolled around in it.' She says that she warned Kagieros—the man she was out there with, ostensibly—but he doesn't speak a word of your language and mistook her warning for an invitation, and then when he was stung by the stuff, his cries of pain brought Glaukos, who had been standing watch for them, or … well, watching was involved somehow, anyway, and he tried to come to Kagieros's aid, or show off in front of the girl, or something, and waded in the goatweed himself. The girl, happily, stayed clear until they'd got themselves out, and I had most of this story from her. She was talking rather fast, that's why I'm not quite sure of the details. Well, that and I don't really care or want to know. She said you would be able to do something for them. They seem to be in quite a lot of pain."

"Yes," said Kuth, obviously trying not to laugh. "They would be. But it isn't dangerous—only uncomfortable. I'll mix up some salve and come with you. If you'll wait. It will only take a few minutes."

He lit another lamp and went to the chest where he kept his medicines. There was a pause just long enough to transgress against the Luth laws of hospitality before Genet looked up at Adares and said, "Please. Sit. Lord archon."

Adares had already told Kuth and Genet to call him Adares, and they had been doing so. He looked as if he were about to remind Genet of that, but thought better of it. He sat. The three of them were at equidistant points around the hearth. None of them spoke. Genet was looking at Adares as though she was trying to see if she could set him on fire with her eyes. Rus watched her warily, waiting for her to show any sign that she was going to say something, so he could stop her. Then he glanced across at Adares, who was looking at him with a frown. The question in Adares's eyes was clear: *Are you all right?* And *If there's anything I can do, here I am.*

And this, after all, was what he was being offered, Rus thought. This was what he was refusing in favour of a duty he didn't believe in and a status he didn't want in a place where he didn't belong. He could have Adares by his side, knowing what he was thinking, caring whether he was happy or not, wanting to do something about it.

He managed a small smile and a shake of his head. *It's nothing.*

What was keeping him from going with Adares? He could pile up small answers to the question—his duty, the shame of bringing scandal on his family, uncertainty about whether it was really what Adares wanted—but maybe the real answer was that he could not imagine himself doing it. Maybe the reason he couldn't go with Adares was because he was scared to.

Kuth finished preparing his salve, and he and Adares went out to return to the suffering Phemians. Rus got to his feet as soon as they had left.

"I should go," he told Genet. "I'm tired. You must be too."

"Good night," she said stiffly.

He walked out into the night. The moon was up; it was waning, but still bright, silvering the mountain slopes in the distance and the thatched roofs of the village houses. He started across the green between Kuth and Genet's house and the kahar hall, his mind in turmoil.

Could he just leave with Adares? Even Adares seemed not

to be sure that was really possible. Adares had not actually asked him to do it. He had talked about it as a fantasy, but never proposed it as a serious option. Back at the temple in the autumn he had talked as if it wasn't possible. Now he seemed to have changed his mind, but still he wouldn't ask. Adares himself had lost his home and been made more or less an outlaw by his people, but he wouldn't ask the same of Rus. Wisely, because—apparently—Rus wasn't prepared to say yes.

Everyone had a place within the Great Pattern, and other pieces of the pattern fit in and around each person, holding them in place. Surely all of the things that held Rus here, in the Luth lands, in his role as kahar, bull-fighter, future stathan of the Luth—they must all be part of Heva.

It seems to me you left this tribe a long time ago, Genet had said.

"There you are," said an irritable voice from behind him. He turned to see Unumus approaching from the direction of the headman's hall. "No one has seen you since dinner, since you disappeared with the Phemian. One of the boys has been sent looking for you because Suthus wants to speak to you. I see he has wasted his errand."

Rus drew a breath and let it out before trusting himself to reply. "I am sorry he didn't find me."

"Tch," said Unumus. For a moment he looked as if he would walk on past Rus, but then he stopped, arms folded over his chest. "Gunthanaruth may like your friendship with the Phemian headman," he said, "but I don't."

Had the whole village guessed what was between him and Adares? This time he needed several breaths to remain calm.

"Do you not?" he said. What he wanted to say was, *Why do you imagine I would care?*

"It makes you neglect your duty as kahar. It was for his

sake that you performed the mask dance out of season, was it not?"

"It was not!" Rus almost laughed. *This* was what Unumus was worked up about? "I didn't even know he was here when I agreed to do that."

Unumus sneered at him for a moment, but couldn't come up with a reply. He had overreached himself in his anger, and apparently forgotten that Rus had—as far as he knew—not met Adares yet when he agreed to do the mask dance. But he was in the right, Rus thought. He *had* neglected his duty because of Adares. Oh, how he had. He stood waiting for Unumus to say something that he would have to admit was true.

"Can you deny," Unumus said finally, "that the Phemian has been a bad influence?"

Rus waited a moment to see if there would be more. Then he did laugh. "Yes, Unumus. Yes, I can deny that."

Unumus opened his mouth and closed it again, frowning ferociously. He looked as if he could sense that something had slipped past him there, but he couldn't tell what. He must have decided to cut his losses then, because he turned, tossing his head so that his long hair bounced behind him, and walked rapidly on toward the kahar hall, leaving Rus alone on the green. Rus stood and watched him go until he disappeared around the curve of the hall. He felt tired, as if he had no strength left even to feel anything—anger or alarm or even contempt—for Unumus and his accusations.

The kahar hall was white and silver in the moonlight ahead of him, the lines of the freshly-painted decoration around its outer wall dark and indistinct under the shadowing eaves. It was the first time since the repainting that Rus had walked up from this direction in the dark, and he saw the year's pattern as if for the first time. The painting was unplanned, laid down according to certain rules about how the lines should flow into and around one another, like his own tattoos. There was no picture, only the pattern, a representation of Heva, like a metaphor. And yet as Rus walked up across the green, he saw very clearly the form of a face under the eaves of the kahar hall.

He stopped and stood staring at it. It took up most of the space between the roof and the grass at the base of the wall. It was neither a man's nor a woman's face, but it was piercingly realistic in the darkness, like a Pseuchaian painting, although it was formed from the swirls and lines of Luth decoration. It was staring back at him, eyes wide and knowing, smiling a little, a secretive smile of invitation.

He stood still. He knew that when he moved, when he took another step, the face would be gone. It was not really there. They had not painted a face on the kahar hall. It was a trick of the shadows and moonlight in the particular place where he was standing, on this particular night. He could probably have made it dissolve into its constituent lines before his eyes if he concentrated.

He remembered Adares saying that he thought the gods would not speak to him in dreams.

He had always felt his connection to the Great Pattern to be the thing that made the most sense in his life. He remembered how he used to feel about it as a boy. He had imagined Heva as a thing that was aware of him, that desired his happiness, because someone had once said to him that to be happy was to fulfil your place in the Great Pattern. When he grew older, of course, he understood that people meant such things in an abstract way, not that the force that ordered the world, that made flowers blossom and snow melt and horses gallop also cared for his happiness.

As he stood there looking at the kahar hall in the moonlight, he was certain that it did.

To be happy is to fulfil your place in the Great Pattern. It didn't mean that you kept the world moving properly just by doing whatever gave you the greatest pleasure. It meant that you should do what was right, that happiness lay in being just and in knowing yourself—that was how the Kossians would have put it.

It meant that you defied that knowledge at your peril.

He stood a few moments longer looking into the face of Heva and feeling it looking back at him. A movement by the door of the kahar hall caught his eye, and he moved himself, and when he looked back at the wall, as he had expected, the face was gone—nothing had changed, the lines were still there, but the illusion was broken.

When he walked back to the kahar hall, he found Suthus sitting outside, on a log by the hall door, looking at the stars, as he often did.

"I heard that you were looking for me, my lord?"

"Ah, Rusanarath. Yes—it's nothing urgent." He patted the log beside him, and Rus sat. "You'll have heard that the Phemians are staying an extra day?"

"No, I hadn't." How long had he been standing out there on the green?

"A couple of them got stung with goatweed and will be too sore to ride. Gunthanaruth wants us to take the rest to see the herd of cattle that were reported in White-Water Valley. Not on the hunt—I've talked him out of that lunacy. Just to look at them."

"Do they want to do that?" said Rus doubtfully.

"Well, they haven't seen the cattle before."

"Yes, they have."

Suthus took a moment to realize what he meant. "Ah! Yes, I don't suppose Gunthanaruth thought … In any case, they agreed. I don't think they were insulted. But you'll ride with us, I hope?"

"Of course. If that is what you want. If you don't need me to stay here."

"Well, Archon Phyleros likes you, and I'm sure he'd rather you were along than have to spend a whole day listening to me talk about … I don't even know what I would talk about!" He laughed, and Rus got the impression that the real reason Suthus wanted him along was because he was somehow nervous about having to entertain Adares all day.

CHAPTER XXIII

RUS DIDN'T IMAGINE he would sleep at all that night, and he was genuinely surprised to find himself waking up with the first light of dawn, feeling refreshed and alert. The rest of the kahar hall, and indeed the rest of the village, seemed sleepy and slow by contrast. He rose and went out to the village well, and the only person he encountered there was Genet.

For a moment she looked as though she was going to greet him, but then her expression hardened, as if she had just remembered what he had told her the night before.

"Good morning, Genet," he said.

She nodded. "Good morning."

He leaned against the stone wall of the well while she lowered the bucket.

"I understand," he said after a moment, "why you would be disgusted with me. But you seem *angry* as well, and that I am not sure I understand."

The bucket rattled in the well, and she said nothing.

He went on: "Is it that you feel responsible—you think you should have known, somehow, and not done my tattoos?"

"No. I just feel a fool. I didn't know you."

"You didn't know me as well as you thought—and that's my fault, not yours."

She gave him a sour look. "I know it's your fault. That's why I'm angry with you."

"Right."

"*You* made me feel a fool. You ate at my hearth and slept under my roof and kept secrets when you should have trusted me and Kuth with them."

"I know," he said, although he wasn't quite sure that was true. "I'm sorry." That at least he could say honestly.

She nodded and began to haul up the bucket.

"*Do* you think you shouldn't have done my tattoos?" he said. "Do you think I shouldn't have been initiated into the kahar?"

She seemed to consider that as she pulled the bucket up over the edge of the well and emptied it into her pitcher. "No. No, there's no reason. Not at all. I don't even see what's so terrible about two men … I mean, it is a little odd to think about, but … "

"Ah, you know." He took the rope to lower the bucket in his turn. "Makes me less of a man."

"Tcha! Less of a man—could anything be worse?" She hefted her pitcher. "Less of a man is more of a woman, and there isn't anything wrong with *that*."

The bucket rattled down into the well again. "Exactly."

She rested her pitcher on the edge of the well and looked at him for a moment. "You don't think you've done anything wrong," she said, and he thought there was a note of admiration in her voice.

"Ah, no! I wouldn't go that far. I am ashamed that I acted as a traitor and lied to my headman. But … at the same time, I am not sorry, and I would do it again. And the rest?" He shrugged. "I'm not even ashamed."

And he realized that was something new. He hadn't felt

overwhelmed with shame before, but it had been there, lurking in the back of his mind, for a long time. Now it was gone.

Genet gasped suddenly. She looked at Rus. "That story about the Luth girl who drew the snake for him!"

Rus laughed. "He never said it was a Luth girl. I drew it. He had it inked after he thought I'd died."

"Ah." Genet nodded as though she'd personally approved of the whole thing at the time. "It is a good snake. Less of a man, *indeed*."

They rode out to White-Water Valley later that morning. Only five of the Phemians were in the party: Adares, the old soldier Kleisios, the secretary Doros, and two others whose names Rus could not remember. The hapless Kagieros and Glaukos were still in bed, and the others, Rus guessed, were not interested in coming out to see a whole herd of the animals that they had last encountered charging at their troops during the Luth attack on Tios.

Adares looked as though he hadn't much wanted to come himself, although he was putting on a good face. In fact, he looked to Rus as though he hadn't slept. Suthus, in spite of his anxiety about talking to Adares, rode beside him most of the way down to the valley, chatting easily.

Rus rode with the other kahar, the bull-fighters Hath, Dudun, and Kam, three of the omen-readers, and a couple of the votive boys. Except for the boys, they were all tattooed alike, swirls of blue from head to foot, and in their summer kilts with their sleeves rolled up, you could see it clearly. He had become used to being among men who looked like him, who wore this uniform in their skin, where everyone else knew what it meant. He wondered what it would be like to live somewhere where he was the only one, where his tattoos were a pattern that no one knew how to read.

Adares was riding a Luth horse, and he looked good on it.

They reached the valley, with the series of little waterfalls and rapids that gave it its name, but there was no sign of the herd. Suthus proposed that they stop by the river to eat, so they all dismounted, and the votive boys unpacked the food. Rus volunteered to keep a lookout for the herd on a ridge of higher ground above the picnic site. He had settled down there with his bread and cheese and fruit, and was looking down the valley away from the party when Adares dropped down onto the grass beside him.

"Hey," said Adares. Rus noticed again how tired he looked and felt obscurely guilty.

"Hey."

"I'm sorry we haven't had a chance to talk again," Adares said.

"It's not your fault. I'm sorry I got angry with you last night."

"What? No, you were right to be angry. I was being a dick."

"A what?" Of course he knew the word now, but he wasn't sure how it applied.

"A scoundrel. A blackguard. A … "

"You weren't!"

"A knave?"

"No."

"Well, if you say so. You're all right? I was worried when I saw how tense everyone was in your friends' house last night. I guess you'd just told them about us."

Rus nodded. "About me. Genet was angry that I'd kept it a secret. Kuth had guessed a long time ago. He guessed about us, even. He didn't seem to mind."

"People surprise you sometimes, don't they?"

"They do. Even Genet came around. We spoke again this morning. And she was right, I should probably not have been so secretive."

Adares shrugged. "You were just trying to protect yourself."

"I suppose so. How are Kagieros and Glaukos?"

"Idiots. They're idiots. I don't know which of them is more of an idiot. But apparently they will be all right. Kuth says it won't do them any harm to ride tomorrow, though of course they'll be uncomfortable."

"That's good."

Adares gave him a doubtful look. "I guess."

"If you stay much longer, I'm certain Gunthanaruth is going to propose that we stage a bull-fight for your entertainment, and then Unumus will have a fit, and a riot will break out in the kahar hall, and it will all be very tiresome."

"Yeah … I can see how it would be." He took a bite of bread and cheese, chewed deliberately, and swallowed as if he wasn't enjoying it. "Rus, I wanted to say something—you probably don't want to hear it. I truly don't believe that I'm your one shot at happiness. I realize it might not be easy, but I think you could find someone to share your life with. Not just someone who visits occasionally, but a real … I mean, if you wanted that. I can't imagine you don't. And I was thinking about it. You can't be the only man who chose the life of the kahar because he couldn't see himself marrying and fathering children even if he didn't. Can you at least admit that I might be right?"

"Yes. You are probably right."

"Come to Tios with me anyway."

"What?"

"I don't know. I wasn't planning on saying that. Come to

Tios with me. It's a beautiful city, and I live in a palace—a very modest palace, very homey, actually—I know you'd like it. The whole city is at such an interesting crossroads right now. I think you'd feel at home there, the way I do. I don't know exactly what you'd do, besides be with me, but you needn't worry about being idle—there's so much work to do, and you're educated and capable and … you asked what you could *be* in Tios, but wouldn't you still be yourself? You're a priest. You carry that with you. Don't you?"

"Of course."

"Look, if this wasn't what you wanted to hear, forget I said any of it. I'll come back here whenever I can. I'll be your lover. Of course I will."

He sounded so defeated, and it was so obviously not what he wanted, but he said it, and Rus believed he would have kept his word.

"It was," Rus said.

"What?"

"It was what I wanted to hear. You hadn't asked me. You had talked about how it might be, but you had not actually asked me."

"No, I hadn't, had I? I think I was afraid to—I thought you would say no."

"I might have," Rus admitted. "But now I'm saying yes."

"Are you? I thought maybe you were." He smiled as if he couldn't quite believe it. "I meant it when I said you'll like Tios."

"I know."

"And I'll—I'll look after you. Anything you need … You know what I mean."

He did, and he knew distantly that it should have felt shameful—the Phemian was saying that Rus would want for nothing, that he could be kept like a woman if he felt like it—but it just sounded like those three days in the temple storeroom in the fall. It sounded good.

They sat looking at one another, holding the moment between them, because that was all they could do just then. Just then, it was enough.

There was a low drumming vibrating in the earth under them—it had been going on for a minute or two, but only now did Rus look down the valley to see the source. The herd was there, closer than he had expected, moving in their direction. He sprang to his feet.

"Mount up! Mount up! They're coming this way!"

Everyone ran for the horses. Rus caught up his spear, carrying it loosely under his arm, at the ready. They were all safely mounted by the time the herd came through. The cattle slowed as they reached the river bank, passing by at an easy amble, a sea of gleaming black backs and swishing tails. There were thirty or forty of them, all cows with one bull, no calves yet, as it was still early in the year. The Phemians watched them pass with wide eyes—all except Adares, who barely paid them any attention. He was too busy smiling at Rus.

Rus couldn't ignore the herd entirely; too many years spent training to fight the wild cattle of the north had given him an instinctive wariness, a kind of alertness whenever he was around them. But he had never cared less about them than he did just then.

They rode following the movement of the herd, Suthus and Hath leading the party. Doros, who was on a Phemian horse, was having trouble keeping it calm in the presence of the huge, unfamiliar beasts, and Adares must have been paying more attention to his surroundings than Rus had imagined, because he rode ahead to come up beside Doros and speak to him. Suggesting that he ride away from the herd to ease the horse's anxiety, Rus thought, though he couldn't hear what was said. He smiled. He liked the way Adares took care of his men.

Suddenly there was a shout. Rus looked and saw Kleisios, just ahead of Doros and Adares, trying to cling to the back of his horse, another Phemian animal, which had been frightened by the cattle too and was bucking. In another moment, she had shaken Kleisios from her back and bolted, leaving him on the ground, dangerously close to the herd.

Several people tried to come to his aid at once. The kahar all knew better than to make noise or sudden movements that would startle the herd, but the Phemians didn't. Rus's path was blocked by Doros, whose horse was now rearing and neighing in terror. He saw Hath taking off after the fleeing mare and Adares sliding down from his mount beside Kleisios. Rus nearly shouted in horror at that. He slapped Doros's horse on the rump to urge her out of the way and kicked his own horse forward. It wasn't safe to be on foot this close to the herd.

Adares had helped Kleisios up and was giving him a hand onto his own horse while Suthus and the other Luth urged him in low voices to mount back up himself. But it was too late. The herd was agitated, moving faster now, and their party had caught the attention of the bull.

A bull defending his herd was different from a bull maddened for the divination or for battle, but it was a subtle difference. The essentials were the same—the massive body, the hooves thundering, the horns lowered—and at that moment it was all rushing toward Adares. The horse bearing Kleisios had wheeled and was galloping to safety. Adares half-turned, looking over his shoulder at Rus. As if Rus was his best hope—his only hope—for rescue.

Terrifyingly, that was true. Rus's horse wasn't an experienced bull-fighter, and he had to kick her hard to make her gallop, to cover the distance that was still much too great. He yelled to catch the bull's attention, and the big head with its heavy horns swung toward him. He lifted his spear and threw with all his strength, the follow-through carrying him half over the horse's neck. He recovered and readied himself to jump when the moment came—

And the moment didn't come. The bull's head jerked back, his body shuddered, and his legs folded beneath him. He fell to one side, landing with the thud of a dead weight. Rus's spear had gone into his right eye socket, straight through to his brain.

Rus hauled on the reins and slid back down into the saddle. He looked around for Adares, wheeling his horse to meet him and reaching out a hand. Adares grasped it and let himself be hauled awkwardly up onto the horse behind Rus. She needed no urging now to take off, galloping, even with the weight of two riders on her back, away from the dead bull and the startled, milling cows.

The rest of the party was reassembling further up the north slope of the valley, at a safe distance from the herd. Before they reached the others, Rus turned to look back at Adares.

"You're all right?"

He was looking more than a little dazed. "I'm fine. Thanks to you. That was exciting."

"You could say that."

"I suppose it often takes only one spear-thrust to kill a bull, like that?"

"Hah! Not very often, no. I've never heard of it happening."

Adares's arms tightened around him for a moment. "You don't say."

They rode up to join the others, and Adares slid down

first. Rus joined him on the ground. He was surprised to find himself a little shaky, unsteady on his feet. It had all happened so quickly and been over so suddenly. It was only now, when he was able to think back on it, that he realized he hadn't felt the exhilaration of an impending fight; all he had felt was the responsibility of protecting Adares.

"I won't miss it," he said to Adares. "The bull fight. I think … I'm done with that."

He had put a hand on Adares's shoulder to steady himself, and now he turned and looked into Adares's eyes and thought, *I'm done with a lot of other things, too.*

He had said *yes* to going to Tios, which meant the end of the life he had known, exile from his people, disgrace. He didn't know how it would feel, exactly. He believed it would be worth it, but that didn't mean it would be easy.

"Will you let me handle this part?" said Adares.

"What part?"

"Just—don't go dramatically kissing me in front of everyone or anything, will you?"

"Is that the sort of thing I would do?" It was just what he had been contemplating, actually, but he still wasn't sure what Adares was talking about.

The rest of their party was dismounting and crowding around, and Rus could already hear Suthus saying, "Once, only once before have I seen a throw like that—it was twenty years ago … "

He felt beneath his fingers the pin that fastened Adares's cloak, which had been hidden by the fold of the fabric before. He looked down at it. It was the kilt pin with the enamelled bird that he had offered Adares the night before.

"I went down into that valley and searched for it early this morning," Adares said, seeing where Rus was looking. "Trust me?"

“Of course,” said Rus.

EPILOGUE

THE BATTLEFIELD WAS covered in wildflowers. They had not yet been blooming when Adares rode north, so this was his first time seeing them. They carpeted the valley where the Luth and the Phemians had fought last fall, red and white and purple and yellow against the green of the grass, tossing and winking in the breeze.

"How beautiful," said Rus. "Was it like that before?"

"No," said Adares. "Some women from the city scattered seeds over the whole area, as a memorial."

"Ah," said Rus. "They did well."

He rode beside Adares, ahead of the rest of their party, as they came out of the forest eaves in the late afternoon. His hair was loose, stirred by the breeze that swept through the valley. He sat with one leg bent casually over the front of his saddle, in that way that he did, barefoot and relaxed.

They would reach Tios before dark; they could see its yellow walls in the distance now, standing high on its hill over the still-hidden sea. It had taken them a little more than two weeks to ride down from the Luth lands, their progress slow at first out of consideration for Kagieros and Glaukos, still recovering from their encounter with the goatweed.

They paused on the edge of the valley, waiting for the others to catch up. Adares looked at Rus. He was still feeling his way in his new role, Adares could tell, still trying to work out how to act, even how to think of himself, as Adares's acknowledged lover. His instinct for caution and denial seemed to be warring with a new desire to be openly affectionate, sometimes boldly, sometimes with an almost girlish submissiveness that was totally different from the way he was in bed. Perhaps he was trying out different things to see what suited him best, but Adares rather hoped that the duality would be permanent. It didn't matter, though; he had got Rus, and felt it was within his power to keep him, and that was the main thing.

In the end, it had not be difficult. He had spoken to Suthus when they arrived back at the headman's village after their eventful trip to view the wild cattle. The mood of the party had been slightly tense on the way back, the Phemians shaken by the close call, the Luth wanting to make light of it and congratulate Rus on his spectacular kill, but dampened by fierce looks from Suthus, who was obviously worried about the incident affecting the new alliance. They were a smaller party on the return journey because some of the kahar had stayed behind to retrieve and butcher the body of the bull. They said it would be impious to let the meat go to waste.

Standing outside the kahar hall with Rus and Suthus, Adares explained, "We have been discussing how I can repay Rusanarath for saving my life today. Of course he refuses to accept that any reward is necessary—and of course I refuse to accept *that.*"

"Naturally." Suthus smiled.

"Would you consider letting him leave your service and come to Tios? He would be very welcome, and we could put his skills to good use."

Suthus was taken aback. "Is that something that he—" He looked at Rus, as if only just remembering that he was there and could speak for himself. "Is that something that you want?"

"It is." Rus sounded hesitant and sure of himself at the same time—a nicely judged effect that was probably just the way he really felt. "I have heard so many things about the city and its inhabitants, and I think … that I would like it there. But only if you can spare me."

"I imagine I could spare you for a month or more, to make a visit. But … that is not what you are speaking of, is it?" He glanced between Rus and Adares, searchingly. "You have something in mind, I think, lord archon. Perhaps I do not need to know what it is, but I would like to."

"I do have something in mind," said Adares quietly. He slipped his hand into Rus's, lacing their fingers together, a small, discreet gesture.

Suthus did not miss it. His eyes widened.

Adares could feel Rus bracing himself for disgust and horror, for Suthus to say something like, *If that is what he is, of course I can spare him.*

But what Suthus said was, "Go with my blessing, Rusanarath."

It was more or less what Adares had expected him to say.

"I thought you were going to lie," Rus said afterward, when they were alone together.

"I thought so too, at first," Adares admitted.

"What made you change your mind?"

"Suthus … you know he's like you? Or, well, I guess you didn't know that. I mean, he might be more like me—but I don't think so."

"How did you … how can you tell?"

"You mean apart from the fact that he was flirting with me all the way out to that valley?"

"He wasn't *flirting* with you!"

Adares shrugged. "There are different ways of flirting—and I'm not saying he necessarily thought that's what he was doing. But you're going to have to trust that I'm more of an expert than you are."

Rus snorted. "I do not dispute that."

So they had left together, and Rus was not an exile or an outcast from his people, and the alliance between Tios and the Luth held firm. Adares thought that by the time the rumour of their relationship reached the Luth lands, it would not do much harm. "Adopting Phemian ways," they would say, and laugh, or shudder, but the Phemians—Tians, whatever they were calling themselves now—were all right in their way, and their archon, who'd been here in the spring, was actually a charming fellow, did you know? Apparently it had been something like a decade since anyone was outlawed from the Luth for "unmanly affection," and Adares had to wonder how soon the time would come when they would officially stop doing that altogether.

Because they hadn't snuck away or left under a cloud of disapproval, Rus had been able to say goodbye to his friends and speak to the man who would take over his job, a fellow named Hath. Conveniently, the role of deputy stathan had not carried any specific tattoos with it, so he could walk away from it without complications and without (much) guilt. When Adares remarked on that, he got a long explanation about how it was merely a job and a worldly rank, not a state of being like the kahar, so *of course* there were no specific tattoos. He listened to the whole thing, because this was what he had signed up for.

They rode out across the meadow, side by side, the other Phemians straggling behind them. They passed the temple complex, its gates open now, citizens coming and going on the well-worn path between them and the city. Adares saw

Rus smiling as he looked at it. He thought about the welcome that would await them in Tios, the people who might come out into the streets to greet him.

"We will get some attention, you know," he remarked to Rus. "When we ride into the city. Nothing spectacular, but people will be curious. I wondered … would you care to get on behind me?" He patted his horse's loin behind the saddle indicatively.

Rus threw back his head in laughter. "I thought you'd never ask."

They reined in their mounts, and Rus swung over without touching the ground and settled himself behind Adares. He wrapped his arms comfortably around Adares's waist, and they rode on toward the gates of Tios.

ABOUT THE AUTHOR

A.J. Demas writes about love and imaginary politics in a fictional world based on the ancient Mediterranean. She has been making up stories since she was a little girl but only recently discovered the romance genre. She lives in Toronto, Canada, with her husband and cute daughter. In case you were wondering, she has no tattoos.

Find out about upcoming books and more here:
www.ajdemas.com

A.J. also publishes fantasy and historical fiction with a meta-physical twist under a different name (her real one). You can find those here: www.alicedegan.com

On a night when the whole city is looking for love, two foreigners find it in the last place they expected.

The riotous Psobion festival is about to begin in the city of Boukos, and the ambassador from the straightlaced kingdom of Zash has gone missing. Ex-soldier Marzana, captain of the embassy guard, and the ambassador's secretary, the shrewd and urbane eunuch Bedar, are the only two who know.

Marzana still nurses the pain of an old heartbreak, and Bedar has too much on his plate to think of romance. Neither of them could imagine finding love in this strange, foreign city. But as they search desperately for their employer through the streets and taverns and brothels of Boukos, they find unexpected help from two of the locals: a beautiful widowed shopkeeper and a teenage prostitute.

Before the Zashians learn what became of their ambassador, they will have to deal with foreign bureaucracy, strange food, stranger local customs, and murderers. And they may lose their hearts in the process.

One Night in Boukos is a standalone romance set in the same world as Something Human, featuring two couples, one m/f and one m/m.